Adam Jerzy Czartoryski

# Memoirs of Prince Adam Czartoryski

And His Correspondence with Alexander I: Vol. I

Adam Jerzy Czartoryski

**Memoirs of Prince Adam Czartoryski**
*And His Correspondence with Alexander I: Vol. I*

ISBN/EAN: 9783337141417

Printed in Europe, USA, Canada, Australia, Japan

Cover: Foto ©Raphael Reischuk / pixelio.de

More available books at **www.hansebooks.com**

PRINCE ADAM CZARTORYSKI.

# MEMOIRS

OF

## PRINCE ADAM

# CZARTORYSKI

AND HIS

Correspondence with Alexander I.

WITH

DOCUMENTS RELATIVE TO THE PRINCE'S NEGOTIATIONS WITH PITT,
FOX, AND BROUGHAM, AND AN ACCOUNT OF HIS CONVERSA-
TIONS WITH LORD PALMERSTON AND OTHER ENGLISH
STATESMEN IN LONDON IN 1832

EDITED BY

## ADAM GIELGUD

*TWO VOLUMES*
WITH PORTRAITS

VOL. I

*SECOND EDITION*

London
REMINGTON & CO., PUBLISHERS
HENRIETTA STREET, COVENT GARDEN

1888

# ERRATA

In pages 18 and 19, *for* Woloczyn, *read* Wolczyn.

In the footnote to page 73, *for* 1795, *read* 1794.

In the footnote to page 74, *for* 1434, *read* 1595.

In page 151, line 11, *for* Wiszniowiec, *read* Wisniowiec : and in line 13, *for* Wiszniowiecki, *read* Wisniowiecki.

In page 152, line 5, and the footnote, *for* Wiszniowiecki, *read* Wisniowiecki.

In the footnote to page 152, *for* 1675, *read* 1673.

In page 170, line 27, *for* 1793, *read* 1798.

In the footnote to page 183, *introduce the words* and at Narva *after* where.

[*An Alphabetical Index to this work will be found at end of Second Volume.*]

# Contents

## CHAPTER IV

### 1784-1787



## CHAPTER V

### 1786



## CHAPTER VI

### 1794-1795



## CHAPTER VII

### 1796



## CHAPTER VIII

### 1796

## CHAPTER IX

### 1796-1798



## CHAPTER X

### 1798-9



## CHAPTER XI

### 1801



## CHAPTER XII

### 1801-2

## CHAPTER XIII

### 1803-4

# PREFACE

PRINCE ADAM CZARTORYSKI has long been known, and is perhaps still remembered, in England as the friend of Earl Grey, Lord Brougham, and other leading English statesmen of the time of the first Reform Bill, and as the representative and champion of his unhappy country during the thirty years which he passed in exile.   His Memoirs,* the greater part of which were written from his dictation in occasional hours of leisure in Paris, end at the battle of Austerlitz; they give vivid pictures of the life of the Polish aristocracy during the latter part of the eighteenth century, of the Court of the Empress Catherine, of the assassination of the Emperor Paul, and of the character of Alexander I,

* A French edition, with a preface by M. Charles de Mazade, of the French Academy, was published in Paris in May, 1887 by M. M. Plon, Nourrit, & Co.

who had made Prince Adam his Minister and confidential friend. Of the remainder of his busy and eventful life no detailed history has yet appeared. It is not attempted in the present work to furnish such a history, but only to supplement the Memoirs by diplomatic papers, and other matter hitherto unpublished, which are of especial interest to an English reader. The documents and extracts from private letters and diaries have been copied or translated from the originals in the archives of the Czartoryski family, the introductory chapter is based on facts taken from the late M. B. Zaleski's excellent biography of the Prince, unfortunately unfinished, and the account of his stay in England after the collapse of the Polish Revolution of 1830-1 is derived from a manuscript work now in preparation, which has been kindly placed at my disposal by M. L. de Gadon, secretary to Prince Ladislas Czartoryski, the son of Prince Adam and the present head of the family. In order to elucidate the text, the Memoirs and other papers have been arranged in order of date, and are connected by a brief narrative of the incidents to which they refer, thus presenting, it is hoped, a clear, if incomplete, survey of the career of a statesman whose distinguished abilities, lofty virtue, and ever-fervent patriotism mark him out as one of the noblest and most striking figures of the century.

A. G.

# Memoirs of Prince Adam Czartoryski

## CHAPTER I



THE Czartoryskis come of an old Lithuanian family, related to the royal dynasty of the Jagiellons. In 1569, John and Alexander Czartoryski took a prominent part in bringing about the union of Poland with Lithuania, and during the seventeenth century various other members of the family distinguished themselves by their valour in battle and their ability as politicians and churchmen, but it did not attain the height of its celebrity until the middle of the eighteenth century, when, in the words of Mickiewicz, it became the only private family in Europe that had a political history. The heads of the house were at that time the Princes Michael and Augustus. Michael, the eldest, a man of remarkable talents and energy, received an excellent training in statesmanship under his friend Count Fleming, the Minister of King Augustus II, and rapidly rose to a position of almost unexampled influence among his countrymen. Augustus, his brother, proud and reserved in character, but ambitious and passionate, chose the military career. He became a Knight of Malta, and took part in the capture of Belgrade under Prince Eugene, who presented him with a sword of honour in recognition of his bravery on the occasion. In 1729, he became a Major-General in the Polish army, and in 1731, after a duel with one of his rivals for the hand of Madame Denhoff, a lady of rare intelligence and immense wealth, she selected him out of a crowd of suitors, among whom were various foreign princes, such as the Duke of Braganza, the Prince of Charolais, and the Duke of Holstein. Prince Augustus thus became one of the wealthiest men in Europe, and by good management he not only paid the debts on his wife's estates, but doubled her income. At the end of the first year after their marriage, he sent to her a number of boxes full of gold pieces, representing the revenue from her estates, which she at once ordered to be returned to him; and this ceremony was repeated annually during the forty years of their married life.

When Augustus III was called to the Polish throne in 1741, Poland was enjoying the blessings of peace, while the surrounding countries were desolated with the conflicts of hostile armies; and her people presented all the outward signs of prosperity. But as a State she was powerless. In some countries it is a frequent subject of complaint that the people do not take sufficient interest or part in politics, and that the Government consequently falls into the hands of professional politicians.   In Poland, not to take part in public life was regarded almost as a crime.   Nearly every voter* was an active politician; but this produced an exaggerated sense of the importance of individuals in the State.   Each man had his own opinions, and refused to be bound by those of others; the *liberum veto*, originating in times when the principle of government by majority had not yet been discovered, was regarded as a palladium of liberty. Under such circumstances government was impossible.†   The Diets had repeatedly to be dissolved without passing the measures necessary for administration, and a wide field was opened for the intrigues of foreign powers and ambitious magnates, especially as the old principle of elective monarchy was still retained.   The two Czartoryski princes set themselves to the task of restoring order in this chaos, of combining and directing the national forces which were dissipating themselves in futile individual effort, and of enabling Poland to resume her position among the independent States of Europe.   But the difficulty of the task was greatly increased by the fact that the Poles did not see their

* It is a common mistake among Englishmen to talk of Poland as 'an aristocratic republic.'  The so-called nobles did not form an aristocracy in our sense of the term, but consisted of all those who had political privileges.  In the eighteenth century they numbered one-fifth of the population—a proportion considerably greater than that of the electorate to the population in England, even after the first Reform Bill.

† Another cause of the weakness of Poland as a State is thus indicated by Mr Lecky (History of England in the Eighteenth Century, vol. vi. chap. xxii. p. 104):— 'The objects of Governments are not only various, but in some measure incompatible, and the Dutch constitution, like the old constitutions of Poland, being mainly constructed with the object of opposing obstacles to the encroachments of the central power, had left the country wholly incapable of prompt and energetic action in times of public danger.  No augmentation of the military or naval forces, no serious measure of defence, could be effected without the separate assent of all the provinces, and the forms that were required by law were so numerous and so cumbrous that it was probably chiefly its more favourable geographical position that saved the United Provinces from the fate of Poland.'

danger and did nothing to second the efforts which were made to save them.

The princes began by associating with them in the execution of their plan some of the younger and more active members of the great Polish families—the Oginskis, the Poniatowskis, and the Zamoyskis. They thus formed a strong party in the country, which by its wealth and influence was able to give effective support to the Government and to check the flood of anarchy which was rapidly undermining the State. In the midst of the general indolence and disorganisation, people looked up with respectful awe to these self-denying patriots who, in the midst of wealth and luxury, devoted their days and nights to the improvement of the administration and the strengthening of the position of their country with regard to foreign powers. Not content with being themselves hard workers in the cause, the two princes selected a number of intelligent and able young men whom they trained at their own expense, both at home and abroad, for the various branches of the public service. Their object was, above all things, to establish a strong and orderly government in Poland, and their own conduct of affairs was a model on a small scale of such a government. With their immense wealth and extensive social relations all over the country, they constantly stepped in to remedy the defects of the existing system, protecting the poor and weak against the rich, coming forward as the champions of order in the midst of the incessant conflict of opinion in the Diets, and setting an example of steady work and high political aims. This naturally excited the jealousy and alarm of other great Polish families, such as the Potockis and the Radziwills; but they persistently carried out their scheme of action in the face of all obstacles.

Foreign alliances at that time took a very different shape from what they do at present. In 1746 England, Austria and Russia were combined against Frederick the Great, who was supported by France and Turkey. The Czartoryskis sided with the former powers, the Potockis with the latter. Poland had sunk into such a state of anarchy that no Polish statesman could gain any great influence among his countrymen unless he had the support of some foreign ambassador, and it was therefore necessary for the Czartoryskis to declare themselves openly as the partisans of one of the great powers which struggled with each other for leadership in the moribund Polish State, especially as the King himself, alarmed at their steadfast and uncompromising honesty, had gone over to the side of Prussia and France. This was the beginning of the alliance of the Czartoryskis with Russia—an alliance into which they entered with the best of motives, but which had the most disastrous consequences. The first fruit of the alliance was the mission of Stanislas Augustus Poniatowski, the nephew of the Czartoryski princes, to the Russian Court in the capacity of secretary to Sir Hanbury Williams, the British Ambassador. Poniatowski, young, handsome, and with all the accomplishments of a courtier, speedily gained the favour of the Grand-Duchess, afterwards Empress, Catherine, and this greatly strengthened the position of the Czartoryskis at the Russian Court.   Finding themselves abandoned by the King, they looked more and more to St Petersburg for support, and the accession to the Russian throne of the Empress Catherine in 1762 seemed at length to hold out a prospect of the realisation of their hopes.   In a long letter announcing the event to Poniatowski, she informed him that she would at once send Count Keyserling to Warsaw to make Poniatowski King after the death of the reigning sovereign ; or, if this should not be possible, to endeavour to obtain the election to the throne of Prince Adam Casimir Czartoryski, the son of Prince Augustus and the father of the writer of the following Memoirs.*

Catherine was thought at that time to be a sovereign of liberal ideas, who would give her people a constitution, and would introduce a new era of freedom and universal justice.   These illusions were so general that even such experienced and sagacious politicians as the Czartoryski princes were deceived by them ; they thought that the regeneration of Poland, for which they had worked thirty years, was at hand. But King Augustus's favourite Minister, Brühl, did his utmost to foil their plans.   The chief dignities in the country were taken from the Czartoryskis and their adherents and given to their adversaries, and scandalous scenes were got up in the Diets with the object of decrying them in the eyes of the public.†

* 'J'envoie incessamment le Comte Keyserling ambassadeur en Pologne pour vous faire roi, après le décès de celui-ci, et en cas qu'il ne puisse réussir pour vous, que ce soit le Prince Adam.'   Mémoires de Stanislas Auguste Poniatowski et sa correspondance avec Catherine II.   Posen, 1862.

† The following letter, of which there is a copy in the Czartoryski archives, was addressed on this subject by the Empress Catherine to her ambassador Count Keyserling: 'M. le Comte de Keyserling:   Je viens d'apprendre que la diète en Pologne est rompue et que vos amis ont pensé être massacrés.   Je vous recommande

This brought matters to a crisis. The two heads of the Czartoryski family were growing old, and Catherine was showing an inclination to conclude an alliance with Frederick the Great; it seemed to them that if they did not at once take decisive action, all the fruit of their life-labour might be lost. The occasion was afforded by the candidature of Prince Charles of Saxony, the favourite son of the King of Poland, for the dukedom of Courland. The Russian candidate, Biron, was supported by the Czartoryskis, but the majority of the senate declared itself in favour of Prince Charles, and a note asserting his claims and intimating doubts as to the legitimacy of Catherine was addressed by the Ministry to the Russian ambassador. This was equivalent to a rupture with Russia, and the Czartoryskis proposed to Catherine that they should form an armed confederacy, not against the King of Poland, but against his Minister Brühl, recalling the words of the Duc de Gramont to Louis XIV : ' We make war against Cardinal Mazarin, but we serve your Majesty.' The confederacy was to take the government of the country into its own hands, restore order and reform abuses, and after the death of Augustus III give up the throne to a prince whose election should be agreeable to Russia. In order to avoid a civil war, the Czartoryskis asked that Russia should send an overwhelming force into the country to support them, and in return they promised to recognise Catherine as Empress of Russia,

d'offrir tout mon appui aux princes Czartoryski et à leurs amis et de ne rien négliger en tout ce qui leur peut procurer sûreté, appui, et profit. Je vous fais cette lettre à ce sujet, vous assurant d'ailleurs de mon affection. Moscou, ce 13 Octob. 1762. Catherine.'

and Biron as Duke of Courland; to regulate the frontier between Poland and Russia; and to give the Empress satisfaction for the insult which had been inflicted upon her. That the Czartoryskis, mistaken and disastrous as their policy has proved, were sincere in their professions of disinterestedness and wished only for the good of their country, was universally acknowledged at the time, and even Herr Benoit, the Prussian Ambassador, wrote to Frederick the Great that 'they were too patriotic to seek the throne for themselves so long as Augustus III was alive, and only thought of the regeneration of their country.' Their only object was to establish a strong and orderly system of government in Poland; and finding that they could not obtain sufficient support for carrying out this object among their own countrymen, they unhappily trusted in the apparent liberalism and justice of the young Empress of Russia.

The hesitation of Catherine, and the death of Augustus III in 1763, necessarily postponed the execution of their projects. The Empress, who had been gradually entering into friendly relations with Frederick the Great, wrote to him that she agreed in his opinion that the crown of Poland should not be retained by the House of Saxony, and that it should be given to a Pole; and she suggested that Poniatowski should be elected king, as having the least right to the crown, he would be most under obligation to the two powers that helped him to it. Frederick readily consented, and a treaty was accordingly concluded between the two sovereigns binding them to joint action with regard to Poland. This alliance opened the eyes of the Czartoryskis to the danger which threatened their country : their nephew Poniatowski was fully aware of their plans and had so far supported them, but he was totally unfitted to occupy the throne of Poland at so critical a period of her fortunes, and it seemed only too evident that Russia and Prussia intended to use him merely as a tool for establishing their influence in Poland and perhaps destroying her independence. What they most dreaded, however, was a civil war, which they were convinced could only precipitate the dangers by which Poland was threatened; and they accordingly persisted in the course of policy on which they had started. When the Diet was convoked they came supported by a large Russian force ; their opponents protested, and left the House ; and the Czartoryskis at once took the opportunity of introducing the reforms for which they had laboured so long. The system under which the high State dignitaries were independent of each other and of the King, which was one of the chief causes of the anarchy into which Poland had fallen, was abolished, and replaced by an organisation of Ministers appointed by the sovereign and responsible to the Diet; all classes of the population were made equal before the law ; and a multitude of smaller reforms, all in the same spirit of liberty and order, became part of the Polish constitution. Rulhière, the historian of the Saxon party, could not restrain his admiration at the Czartoryskis having 'in six weeks carried out reforms which the French kings had only executed in six centuries.'*

* Histoire de l'Anarchie de Pologne, vol. ii. p. 229.

The triumph of the Czartoryskis now seemed assured. Even their adversaries, seeing the wise measures of which they were the authors, and the benefits which these measures were already conferring on the country, abandoned their attitude of passive resistance, and Poniatowski was elected king without opposition (1764), after which the Diet passed a resolution directing that statues of the Princes Michael and Augustus should be erected at Warsaw and Wilna ' in memory of the national gratitude.'  The princes did not, however, possess the qualities which ensure popularity : their strict, almost harsh, sense of justice, their aversion to compromise and conciliation, revived the dormant hostility of their adversaries and alienated many of their supporters.  Yet the Poles had never enjoyed such security at home, or greater respect abroad than in the first years of the reign of their new king, when the Czartoryskis were the virtual rulers of the country.  ' Every citizen,' it was said, ' at length felt that his life, his honour, and his property were safe,' and for the first time for many years Russia and the other neighbouring powers abstained from interference in Polish affairs.  Unfortunately the influence of the Czartoryskis did not last long enough to produce a permanent improvement in the administration. Both the King and the people grew restive at the dictation of these two rigid old men, who were so much their superiors in wisdom and self-control, who despised popularity, and sought no approval but that of their own consciences.  Moreover, the reforms which were gradually and quietly being introduced by them began to inspire anxiety in the neighbouring States.

Frederick the Great, with his usual sagacity, saw that the effect of these reforms must ultimately be to make Poland entirely independent of her neighbours, and his correspondence with the Empress Catherine and the Prussian Ambassadors at Warsaw shows how eager he was to throw every possible impediment in the way of the Czartoryskis, and especially to prevent the abolition in the Great Diet or Parliament of the *liberum veto*, to which the Poles still blindly clung as one of the pillars of their freedom. At length the Russian and Prussian Ambassadors openly declared themselves against the Czartoryskis, and taking advantage of their unpopularity, secured a majority against them in the first Parliament convoked under the new reign (1766). The Czartoryskis accepted this defeat with characteristic stoicism: the project for the abolition of the *liberum veto* was deferred for a more favourable opportunity, but they remained in office and silently but steadily pursued their work of reform. This, however, did not at all suit the views of the Russian Government, which, now thoroughly alarmed, determined to come forward in active opposition to the Czartoryskis and the King, whom it regarded as their tool. A pretext was ready to hand in the position of the dissenters, who were under the same disabilities as the Catholics then were in England, and whom Catherine had always affected to protect, thereby gaining the applause of her friends the encyclopædists, and making a display of liberalism which cost her nothing and was very convenient for her policy. The Russian Ambassador, Repnin, who had been one of the warmest of the supporters of the Czartoryskis, was instructed to demand that the disabilities of the dissenters should be removed. The princes replied that in the then existing state of public opinion it would be impossible to carry such a measure in the Polish Parliament, upon which Catherine sent her troops into the country to ravage the estates of the Czartoryskis and the King, and issued a proclamation condemning the new policy of reform and promising that the Empress would take all those who had grievances under her special protection. The Czartoryskis, in no way cowed by these barbarous reprisals, undauntedly stood their ground, and when Repnin called upon them to resign office, replied that they did not hold their posts from the Empress of Russia, but from the King of Poland.* Their steadfastness and the abuses committed by the Russian soldiery produced such a reaction in their favour that Repnin, hoping thereby to paralyse the growing opposition to his plans, caused some of the principal senators to be arrested and sent into the interior of Russia. Those who remained, threatened with a similar fate, passed all the measures that Repnin proposed to them. The disabilities of the dissenters were abolished, and a treaty was concluded with Russia assigning to that Power the right of protecting and controlling the Polish administration. But the great majority of the Polish nation indignantly refused to ratify the decisions of its intimidated representatives. On the 29th

---

* 'Je n'ai pas reçu mon emploi de S. M. Impériale, ainsi elle me pardonnera si je ne veux pas m'en défaire à sa requête. Je suis vieux, très-vieux ; elle me fera très-peu de mal en m'ôtant le peu de jours qui me restent. Mais j'ai trop soin de ma gloire pour ternir la fin d'une vie qui, j'ose le dire, a été passée sans tache au service de ma patrie, par un acte que le monde avec raison condamnerait comme lâche et interessé.'

of February, 1768, an armed confederation was formed at Bar to rid the country of its Russian aggressors. Russia, hampered by her war with Turkey, strove in vain to induce the King to declare himself against the confederates, and the Czartoryskis entered into communication with them in order to extend the movement over the whole country, and enable Poland to present a united front against her northern neighbour. These efforts failed through the unpopularity of the King and the jealousy of the other great aristocratic families. Yet the confederation stood its ground ; its principal founder, Joseph Pulaski, was an old retainer of the Czartoryski family ; and Repnin's successor in the embassy, Prince Wolkonski, reported to Catherine that 'nothing could be done so long as the Czartoryskis remained in Warsaw.' The Russian Government then confiscated their property. They persisted, however, in their patriotic attitude, declaring that whatever happened they would remain faithful to their country ; and the King, feeling that they were his only support and that he had neither the ability nor the character which alone could in such a crisis enable him to maintain himself, refused to abandon them.

Even Catherine was impressed by this noble courage and perseverance. She restored to the Czartoryskis their confiscated estates, and appointed a new ambassador to Warsaw, Count Saldern, who treated the King and his Ministers in a conciliatory spirit very different from that of his predecessors. But Prussia, alarmed at the apparent reconciliation between Russia and the King, now sent her troops into Poland. The confederation of Bar was crushed, and the first partition was arranged with Russia and Austria by Frederick the Great.

Michael and Augustus Czartoryski did not long survive the fall of their country, for which they had laboured so much and so well. The former died on the 13th of August 1775 ; the latter, on the 4th of April 1782, leaving an only son, Adam Casimir, to whom Catherine had assigned the throne of Poland in the event of its not being accepted by Poniatowski. Like the rest of his family, Prince Adam Casimir maintained frequent relations with England, and he studied English institutions when a young man in the house of his father's friend, Lord Mansfield, then Lord Chief Justice. His amiable character, wit, and accomplishments made him universally popular, and he would certainly have been elected King, and perhaps have averted some of the misfortunes of his country, if Catherine had not supported the candidature of his cousin Poniatowski. The Prince de Ligne, a man well acquainted with the various European courts, calls him in his Memoirs 'the most distinguished man of the four quarters of the world.' Joseph II of Austria frequently corresponded with him, and Frederick the Great was the first promoter of the negotiations which resulted in the marriage of his relative, Prince Louis of Würtemberg, with Prince Adam Casimir's second daughter Marie. As Commandant of the Lithuanian Guard and of the Corps of Cadets, the Prince showed remarkable ability and zeal, and some of the most eminent Polish patriots, including Kosciuszko, were trained under his immediate superintendence. His services in the promotion of national education were equally valuable and untiring. As a judge, his impartiality was such that he sentenced some of the most powerful dignitaries in the country, including his own father, for acts of oppression committed by their stewards on their poorer tenants.

Prince Adam Casimir married on the 19th September 1761, the Countess Elizabeth Fleming, daughter of the celebrated minister of Augustus II; they had five children, two boys and three girls. The eldest son, Adam George, the author of the following Memoirs, was born at Warsaw on the 14th of January 1770, and it will be seen that he describes his impressions from a very early age. His mother, who in later years was looked up to with attachment and respect by the whole Polish nation, is frequently referred to by him in terms of warm affection, and before proceeding to the perusal of his Memoirs the reader may be interested in the following description of her appearance and character taken from her 'portrait,' written by herself in her thirty-seventh year :—

'I was never handsome, but I have often been pretty; I have beautiful eyes, and as all my feelings are reflected in them, the expression on my face is often interesting. My complexion is white enough to be almost brilliant when I blush; a smooth forehead does not make my face ugly, and my nose completes the symmetry of my features. My mouth is large, my teeth white, my smile amiable, and the shape of my face a graceful oval. I have enough hair to make an easy and becoming head-dress; it is dark, like my eyebrows. I am rather tall than short: my figure is elegant, my bust perhaps too thin, my hands ugly, but my feet charming; and there is much grace in my movements. I have an extreme desire to please, and am skilful in showing both my physical and my mental qualities to the best advantage. Though vain and ill-tempered, I am endowed with such tact that I very seldom do anything which does not either give pleasure or inspire lively interest. I am most warm and constant in my friendships; nothing can abate my confidence in those I love, and I always look up to them as superior to myself. My predominent passion is the love of my country. This is a sort of religion with which all my future is bound up, and which my husband and children and my own disposition have made the dearest and most indispensable sentiment of my life.'

*(The Memoirs of Prince Adam Czartoryski, with some notes and other supplementary matter illustrative of the text which have been added by the Editor, begin in the next Chapter.)*

# CHAPTER II

## 1776-1782



MY recollections of the days of my childhood pass before my eyes like a landscape in which some objects stand out here and there in clear and definite forms, while others disappear in a mist or in the distance.

The first place of which I have any precise remembrance is Rozanka, on the river Bug, where there was an old stone mansion, with numerous underground cellars containing excellent old wines.

This was in the year 1776. My father, then commander of a regiment of the Lithuanian Guard, had taken his detachment to Rozanka during the summer in order to train his troops in some military manœuvres which he wished to introduce into Poland. He obtained some good soldiers from Prussia, and sent young Poles there to learn the Prussian system of drill.

I well remember the tents which were pitched on the green meadow, and the officers of the Guard who used to assemble there for dinner, with a monk of St

Bernard, who was the almoner of the regiment—a tall, stout man, very popular with the officers on account of his merry conversation.

I also recollect the hetman Branicki, who was for many years my father's intimate friend, coming to Rozanka. At that time the hetmans had entirely recovered their former authority, and M. Branicki was accordingly received with all the official honours as well as with the hospitality always accorded to a guest. The whole regiment was in parade uniform, and seemed to me a large army, though it was only composed of two battalions. My father's man-servant was at that time in attendance upon me. He was a Frenchman named Boissy, a native of Pontoise, near Paris; a worthy and intelligent man, who by his democratic spirit had preserved me from the influence of the habits of grandeur which at that time were pretty generally prevalent in Poland. His example induced me to develop from my earliest youth a spirit of activity and independence.

At this time my parents were in the habit of passing the summer at Woloczyn, some miles from Rozanka, and my later recollections are connected with the vast palace of Woloczyn, which was then occupied by the Chancellor Michael Prince Czartoryski, my father's uncle. It was there that my mother was educated under the supervision of the Chancellor's wife, and she was also married there to her maternal uncle, the son of my grandfather Augustus.

The two old princes were very favourable to the match, but it was vehemently opposed by the Princess

Lubomirska, my father's sister. The chief reason of her opposition was this. Shortly before her marriage, my mother went to see one of the peasants on the estate, and found in the cottage a child suffering from a very severe attack of smallpox. This gave her a great shock, as she had lost several of her sisters from the same illness; and she caught the infection so dangerously that her life was despaired of. Directly she recovered, her parents hastened the marriage, and she came to the altar with her face covered with marks of the disease and a wig on her head, as she had lost all her hair. The Princess Lubomirska was much grieved to see so ugly a woman given in marriage to her brother; but though she used all her influence with her father against the match, she could not prevent it, as it was considered a very advantageous one. Some time after, my mother entirely recovered her health, and soon became celebrated for her beauty.

The main building at Woloczyn was of wood, and the outbuildings of stone. I remember the portraits of Charles XII, Augustus II, and Poniatowski, the King's father; there was a large garden crossed by a long and wide canal, at the end of which was a statue of Neptune and his attendants, in the French style then in fashion, imitated from the statues in the gardens of Versailles.

There were some brilliant fêtes at Woloczyn, at which the guests were amused by music and theatricals. Once there was a swimming race, in which the swimmers were dressed as tritons, and among them the one who was most remarked was General Count Brühl.

My mother taught me French.   One day she told me to learn by heart some verses of Racine which we had read together, and in which Mithridates discloses to his children his plans against the Romans.   I have never forgotten these verses, as I was punished for not having learnt them by being obliged to stop at home, while the other people at the palace went on an excursion to a neighbouring village with a spring, in a very picturesque spot, which my mother had decorated with flowers.   These expeditions were very merry and noisy, and I was bitterly disappointed at not being allowed to go.

My first recollections of Warsaw are very vague. One of the incidents which struck me the most was the general mourning which followed the death of my father's uncle, Prince Michael ; * all the inhabitants of the ' blue palace 't were dressed in black.

I also recollect the shame and grief which I felt one day when I cast the blame of some fault I had committed upon one of the running footmen employed in the palace.   This man's name was Anthony, and he was so stout that his place was practically a sinecure. He came dressed as for a journey, with a sheepskin coat on, and reproached me with having been the cause of his dismissal, upon which I at once admitted that I was the culprit.   I learnt afterwards that the story of his dismissal was an invention ; but it produced a salutary effect.

Shortly after, I became seriously ill.   There were several physicians at my grandfather's, including one

* On the 13th of August, 1775, when the author of the Memoirs was five years old.   (See preceding Chapter).

† The residence of the Czartoryskis at Warsaw.

named Bart; they all arrived at the conclusion that my recovery was hopeless. My mother begged them to remain in attendance upon me, but none of them would take the responsibility. A friend of my parents then brought Dr Bekler, physician to King Stanislas Augustus, and he restored me to health.

From this date I began a new life. Colonel Ciesielski was appointed my tutor; great care was taken of my health, and I resided sometimes at Powonzki,* sometimes at Warsaw. Impromptu fêtes, in which I and my two sisters took part, used at that time to be given in the 'blue palace,' and there were several Frenchmen who contributed in a material degree to these entertainments. M. Dorigny, a very efficient dancing master, formerly attached to the opera in Paris, and ballet-master at Stuttgart, where the Duke of Würtemberg ruined himself in theatrical performances, presided over the dancing; M. Patonar directed the music, and M. Norblin designed the costumes and the scenery.

One day a fire broke out after one of these fêtes, just as the last guest had gone. It began in the wing of the building where my sisters lived. The actors, who still had their costumes on, were the first to help. One of them had red silk stockings, and while he was occupied in extinguishing the flames, a servant threw a large pailful of water on his legs, thinking they were on fire. My sisters and their governess, Made-, moiselle Petit, had to escape to the other side of the building with their friends, the Miss Narbutts.

Meanwhile the flames continued to spread, and

---

* A villa near Warsaw.

had covered the whole of the wing.   The fire did not, however, penetrate the main body of the building, and my sisters established themselves there.   A third sister, Sophia, was born at this time.   My health was still delicate, and it was thought necessary to teach me riding, which gave me great pleasure.

My rides were usually taken in the direction of Powonzki; and the time I passed there was the happiest in my life.   The estate was a sort of green oasis, whose verdure was the more attractive as it was surrounded by a sea of sand.   Each of the children had a cottage and a garden, and in the centre, on a hillock, was a larger house inhabited by my mother, with a wood on each side of it, and looking down on a little lake, whose waters flowed into a stream that bathed all the plantations of the estate.   My mother also had some artificial ruins erected, after the fashion of the time, to complete the attractions of the place. There were an island in the lake, a mill, a grotto on the island, stables in the shape of a classical amphitheatre, and a large courtyard with a great many hens and pigeons which we used to feed.

We seldom received strangers ; but living as we did for each other—our mother for her children and we for her—our life was a very happy one.   It was like an eclogue—a true picture of rustic poetry.

Each of the cottages in our colony had its particular emblem.   My sister Marie had a chaffinch with the motto, 'Gaieté.'   My device was a branch of oak with the word ' Fermeté ' inscribed upon it.   At the top of my mother's house was a hen with her chickens ; on that of my sister Teresa, a basket of white roses, with the inscription 'Bonté;' on that of the steward, a swarm of bees, and below the word 'Activité.' The Miss Narbutts also had their cottages at Powonzki; and the whole organisation of the place had been devised and carried out by my mother.

We got up early, breakfasted either at my mother's or with the steward's wife, who gave us some excellent coffee, and then went to work in the gardens. At dinner-time one of our servants named Martin used to come from Warsaw, leading a donkey which carried our food in two panniers, and which was always received with joy and expected with impatience. Dinner was laid sometimes in one place, sometimes in another, and was announced by a gong.

We often went out on donkeys, and on Sundays we used to go to Mass, some riding and others on foot.

Occasionally there were grand fêtes, at which the King was sometimes present. One day the signing of the peace of Chocim* was represented in the middle of a little wood of elder trees, in a grove generally used for theatrical performances. Lubomirski, who had succeeded Chodkiewicz in the command of the army, and a Turkish Pasha, advanced towards each other with their respective escorts. These grand ceremonies were the things that gave me the least pleasure.

Meanwhile the question of my education was being seriously considered at the 'blue palace,' and my tutor sometimes objected to my going so often to Powonzki; but the attractions of the place were so irresistible

* In 1621, when Sigismund III was King of Poland.

that, yielding to the wish of my mother, he pitched his tent next to my cottage.

Those happy times lasted for a few years and were interrupted by a great misfortune. We lost my eldest sister through a terrible accident. We looked upon her as a second mother, and were very fond of her, for she was devoted to her younger brothers and sisters. One day, as she was standing before the chimney-piece, her dress took fire. She fled in terror ; Mademoiselle Constance Narbutt tried to hold her back and extinguish the flames, but could not stop her. In the next room was the governess, Mademoiselle Petit, who as usual was playing piquet with M. Norblin. The latter, hearing the screams of the children, ran out and wrapped my unfortunate sister in a cloak, thereby extinguishing the flames. She was, however, severely burnt ; for some days it was hoped that she might recover, but she was too delicate to bear the shock, and she died shortly afterwards.*

My mother was at this time confined to her bed, and gave birth to a little girl, my sister Gabrielle, who only lived a few days.

It was necessary to conceal from my mother the death of my eldest sister ; she was always asking to see her, but Dr John, who was her physician, did not allow her to leave her bed. Every day she wrote to her daughter and insisted on her being allowed to come into her room, so that at length Dr John was obliged to tell her the truth. The news brought on

---

* In the Czartoryski Museum at Cracow there is a little book of 24 pages containing a poem on the death of this princess, entitled 'Thérèse Czartoryska,' by J K. L. (supposed to be Lavater), and published at Zurich on the 22nd of September, 1780.

an attack of paralysis of the side, and for a long time afterwards my mother had to walk with crutches. It was only by the application of electricity that she recovered the use of her leg.

I also was recovering from a serious illness which caused much anxiety. For some time my sister's death was concealed from me, and my man-servant, who pretended to ask for news of my sister, told me that she continued in the same state. I was deeply attached to her, and when I learnt the truth I for the first time shed tears of real grief. I still often think of her, so good, so amiable, and with so fine a soul that her parents and the younger members of the family were deeply attached to her.

My father was at this time at Wilna, where he was President of the Judicial Court. When he came back to Warsaw for the holidays he did not know anything of what had happened. As he was crossing the Vistula on the ferry-boat between Praga and Warsaw, he asked the ferryman for the news, and was told of my sister's death. My father refused to believe him, but was convinced when further details were given him by my grandfather Augustus. He nearly fainted, leaning for support against the wall of the room; and I saw a flood of tears flow from his eyes.

My sister's cottage was moved into the wood, and was kept there in remembrance of her. Each Thursday, the day of her death, was for a long time given up to mourning and pious meditation, and my mother consecrated it by a good action.

The Princess Anna Sanguszko, daughter of the

Princess Sapieha, *Chancelière* of Lithuania, also belonged to the colony at Powonzki, and later on it was joined by Madame Sewerin Potocka. My mother often went into their house, where there were amusements of all kinds. There was a performance of an opera called *Zémire et Azor*, in which two of my sisters and Mademoiselle Narbutt appeared in an enchanted palace, striving to calm the grief of Zémire. After my sister's death this opera was performed at the Warsaw theatre; my mother wished to be present, but she was so affected at the scene above described that she had to quit the theatre in a fit of despair, in spite of the efforts of the Princess Sanguszko to console her. I was a witness of this painful incident.

After a time everything resumed its usual course, as generally happens in this world; the fêtes were revived and new members were admitted into the colony. A great friend of my mother's, the Countess Tyszkiewicz, *née* Kinska, daughter of the Princess Poniatowska, and niece to the King, was received with great ceremony. She had lost an eye through an illness in early youth, and had replaced it by one of glass; still she was very pretty, and was fond of active sports, such as hunting and riding.

Being desirous of returning my mother's politeness, the Countess Tyszkiewicz had a comedy played in her house under the title of '*L'amoureux de Quinze Ans*.' She herself took the part, dressed in man's costume, of the lover, and my second sister played the heroine. The theatre was in the sheepfold, and the Countess went to it on horseback, in the costume in which she was to act.    After the play there was a collation.

There were also theatrical representations in the house of the *Chancelière* Princess Sapieha.    One of the pieces that were played there was an opera, '*La Colonie*,' in which the performers were the Princess Radziwill, *née* Przezdiecka, who often came to Powonzki and had a fine voice; my mother; M. Wojna, who was afterwards ambassador at Rome; and General Brühl, of the artillery.

On another occasion they played '*Andromaque*.' The leading part was taken by the young Princess Sanguszko, who had just married; she was very pleasant and good-natured, but a little frivolous, and she had taken lessons of a celebrated tragic actress from Paris.    The part of Hermione was played by another Princess Sanguszko, who was afterwards Princess of Nassau; that of Orestes, by Prince Casimir Sapieha; that of Pyrrhus, by a Swiss named Glaize; and that of his confidant, by Prince Calixtus Poninski.    This tragedy did not produce any impression upon me; I only recollect that Prince Sapieha was dressed in a Greek costume, and M. Glaize in a Roman one.

When we were at Warsaw I was often sent, according to the custom of that time, to assist at my grandfather's toilet.    When I went to him they had to put pomatum on my hair, and to powder and curl it, which was very unpleasant to my mother, who did not like to see me thus disfigured.    On one of these visits it was Corpus Christi day, and there was an altar in the courtyard.    The Bishop, a *protégé* of my grandfather's, was under the canopy, and my grandfather assisted at the mass. Shortly after my grandfather died,* and all amusements ceased. He was buried in the church of the Holy Cross, and his death caused general regret—especially to his daughter, the Princess Lubomirska, who was at Warsaw at the time, and did not leave him until the last moment.

He died simply and naturally, without the least desire to attract remark. Every day after dinner he used to play at a game called 'tryset,' which was very like whist, and was played by four people; the Pope's Nuncio generally joined in the game. The Prince kept up this habit to the last, and although he was very weak, he had himself dressed to go to the card-table. On the very day of his death he came as usual, bowed to the Bishop Archetti (who afterwards became a cardinal), and apologised for coming a little late. As his sight was failing, he asked why they had not lit the candles, although the room was lighted up as usual. Meanwhile the Princess Lubomirska was in her apartments in deep grief, and could not come down into the room, where my mother was with the whole family. All the people of the house, down to the lowest servant, were assembled in profound silence. The Prince, who was in an invalid chair, turned to Dr Bart, who never left him, and asked him in German: 'Wie lange wird's dauern' (How long will it last)? The doctor felt his pulse, and replied: 'Another half-hour, I think.' The Prince then apologised for not being able to play any longer

* On the 4th of April, 1782. (See preceding Chapter).

with the Nuncio, and had himself taken into the
bedroom; the prelate followed him, and began to
read the psalms for the dying. While he was reading
he held the Prince's hand, and as he spoke the words
of the Psalmist: 'My God, I give up my soul to
Thee,' the Prince pressed his hand and gave up his
last breath. The crowd which had penetrated into
the palace, hitherto respectfully silent, then burst into
tears and sobs.

At the time of my grandfather's death, my father
was still at Wilna, where he was for the second time
President of the Chief Tribunal of Lithuania. He
entirely devoted himself to his functions in this
capacity. Several magistrates were accused of having
done injustice to individuals either through indulgence for others, or from motives of personal revenge. I heard people say that while my father
was in office, an action was brought against my
grandfather by a gentleman who had a claim on
his estate, and that my grandfather was condemned
in costs.

There was much talk at this period about a crime
which had been committed some years earlier, but
the author of which could not be discovered. By a
singular accident the first trace of the criminal was
found in 1781, and it drew suspicion upon a man
named Ogonowski, who had become a priest and was
protected by the Bishop of Wilna, Massalski, well
known for his dissolute life. My father, who was
then President of the Court, used all his influence to
have the culprit brought to trial.

The Abbé Ogonowski, who had rapidly passed

the various ecclesiastical grades which lead to final ordination as a priest, hearing that he was in danger, took refuge in a convent, under the protection of Bishop Massalski. A detachment of troops belonging to the Lithuanian Guard, of which my father was in chief command, was ordered to surround the convent during the night, and succeeded in getting the doors opened, notwithstanding the resistance of the priests. Ogonowski was found with some difficulty in a cell, and taken to prison in spite of his protests and those of the clergy. He was convicted of murder and other offences, after a very long and careful trial, and was condemned to death and executed.

Several old cases were settled while my father was in office, and the procedure became much more regular than had previously been the case. He finally withdrew from his post in 1782, and hastened to return to Warsaw to take part in the Diet which had been opened under the presidency of Colonel Krasinski. This was the first meeting of the Diet at which I was present. My tutor and myself frequently went both to the senate and to the Chamber of Deputies. I was struck by the grave and imposing presence of Prince Lubomirski, Marshal of the Crown, who, as I have heard other people say, was eminently fitted to keep order at the meetings of both Houses.

The most important matter that was considered at this Diet was the withdrawal by the chapter of the Cathedral at Cracow (with the support of Prince Poniatowski, Bishop of Plock) of Monsignor Soltyk,

Bishop of Cracow, from the adminstration of that diocese, on the pretext of mental incapacity.

The anti-Russian party defended the bishop, who had been one of the most valiant members of the Confederation of Bar.*  The party of the King and of Russia strove to maintain and justify the act of violence committed against Monsignor Soltyk, and being the most numerous, succeeded in obtaining a majority in favour of the measure.

The opposing parties spoke with much passion, endeavouring to prove on the one hand that the Bishop of Cracow was perfectly sane, and on the other that he was mad.  One of the most moving and eloquent of the speeches was that of the Castellan Ankwicz, who was at that time regarded as an exemplary patriot, but afterwards passed over to the Muscovite party.  He was one of the victims of Kosciuszko's revolution ; the people of Warsaw themselves executed the sentence which had been pronounced against him.

During his year's residence in Lithuania, my father had gained the sympathies of the citizens of that province, and he thought that he would have the majority of the Lithuanian votes at the Diet in favour of the party of which he was one of the chiefs; but the fear of Russia and the King's presents decided otherwise.  Many of the Deputies found reasons to avoid the inconvenient results which

---

* The originators of the Confederation of Bar were two bishops, Soltyk and Krasinski.  The object of the Confederation, which was formed by Casimir Pulaski on the 29th of February, 1768, was to deliver Poland from the domination of Russia. The confederates maintained their ground by extraordinary feats of arms against the Russian troops for five years, and were finally crushed by Souvaroff in 1772, a few months before the first partition of Poland.  (See the previous Chapter).

would ensue from an open rupture with the King and the Russians.

The Diet having thus come to a close in so unfavourable a way for our party, my father determined to visit the estates which he had inherited in Volhynia and Podolia.

# CHAPTER III

## 1783



BEFORE leaving for Volhynia, I went with my tutor to pay a visit to Prince Lubomirski. This was the last time that I saw him; he did not long enjoy the fortune which his wife had inherited, and died in the same year, universally regretted. He lived in the palace which afterwards became that of the Tarnowskis, and belonged by right to the Czartoryskis. The Princess and her husband were very sensible people, but as often happens in the marriages of great families, their characters were not suited to each other. The Prince left heavy debts which his widow admitted and scrupulously paid. His sallies and repartees were characteristically Polish. My mother esteemed him greatly, and he was a true friend to her. I do not know on what occasion he once said to her that he would come to see her after his death, and for a long time she feared he would keep his word. These apprehensions recurred nightly, when everybody was asleep; the slightest noise recalled to her the promise of her deceased friend.

We left for the estates in Podolia with a large suite. My father at that time had a very numerous court, chiefly composed of noblemen's sons, many of whom came even from Lithuania. The rendezvous was at Pulawy, from which place we started. Dozens of carriages followed each other in line, and we travelled at the rate of not more than six miles* a day. After breakfast we proceeded to the next stage, where we dined ; the food and wine always preceded us. There were a great many led horses, and we often mounted them to get over a stage more quickly. One of the principal officials of the court always went on beforehand to get our quarters ready. We were accompanied by several young pages dressed after the Polish fashion ; and before we left Warsaw, the major-domo thought proper, as a prudential measure, to administer some corporal discipline to them. My father, as he was coming out of the house, perceived traces of tears and vexation on their faces, and asked what was the matter. ' See how the major-domo has punished us,' they answered. My father then asked the major-domo what they had done, to which the latter rejoined that it was a good thing to prepare them in this way for their journey.

We stopped on our way at the houses of several landowners, many of whom joined our party, which increased the number of our led horses and carriages ; we had also brought some camels with us, as my father wished to introduce them into general use. The caravan stopped at Klewan, the first of my father's estates in Volhynia. We next arrived on the property

* A Polish mile is equal to five English miles.

of Prince Sapieha, who received us with the amplest hospitality. The Prince suffered much from gout, and this was attributed to the custom, which at that time was very general, of always drinking with a visitor. Prince Sapieha came every evening leaning on a cane to look at the brilliant illuminations in the garden. Our next halting-place was Mikolajew, in Podolia. There were not enough rooms here for the whole of our party, which had become very numerous, and many of us slept in tents.

Among the many friends who accompanied us on this journey was Niemcewicz,* my father's aide-de-camp. Opportunities were frequently taken of embarking on various love adventures, in allusion to which one of the poets of our party wrote a song of which the first couplet was as follows :

'Beautiful Tomira, this is probably the last of our pleasant evenings ; I am with you to-day—to-morrow I shall be alone, and woods and streams will separate us. But when I shall no longer be there, remember I was the first to love you.'

Niemcewicz was very assiduous in his attentions to the sex. One of the houses where we stayed the longest was that of M. Onufry Morski. This gentleman had a very important position in Podolia, and was a friend of my father's, for whom he had a great liking. He had a very handsome wife, of whom he was jealous, and he did not trust the friendship of Niemcewicz. One day the comedy of '*Le Joueur*,' which my father had translated from the French, was

* An eminent Polish writer, best known for his ' Historical Songs ' and his excellent translations from various English poets. He was born in 1757, and died n exile at Paris in 1841.

performed at his house, and his wife took a part in it. He himself played the hero, and had to address her in a speech full of ardent love, to which she listened with the greatest coldness, as I remarked at each performance. Morski's younger brother was afterwards the ambassador of the King of Saxony and Grand-Duke of Warsaw at Madrid. His elder brother, the canon, was passionately fond of dancing; I still remember with what *entrain* he danced the mazurka at a masked ball at Siedlce, and he was not a man of very rigid morals.

Among the more intimate guests at my father's house was Colonel Molski, a wag fond of bon-mots and good eating. He once made a bet that he would eat an enormous dish of *pirogi** alone, without hurting himself. He gained his bet, and drank some punch to wash the *pirogi* down.

At Miendzyboz we met a large detachment of Cossacks, which gave us the idea of constructing a sort of fortress and feigning attacks upon it. My tutor shut himself up in the fortress with my brother ; the besiegers were under the command of Colonel Molski, to whom I acted as aide-de-camp. When the day for the attack came, there was much noise and fighting on horseback. M. Siehen, mounted on a very spirited horse and riding at full gallop, encountered one of the Cossacks, and the shock was so violent that Siehen fell from his horse and became insensible. When he recovered consciousness, he had completely lost his memory, and he did not recollect what had happened until several days afterwards. The Cossack

* Small meat puddings.

escaped with a few contusions.  Soon after there was almost a real battle between the Cossacks and the inhabitants of the village, a detachment of whom were in the fortress where we were to breakfast.  The besieged at last ate the food that had been prepared for us, and an arrangement was then made to prevent further accidents.  I assisted at this fight on horseback, and it greatly interested me.

From Miendzyboz we went to Kamieniec, where was M. Witt, the father of General Witt, whose wife was the beautiful Greek that afterwards married Felix Potocki.  At that time she was in all the freshness of her beauty, and shortly after she travelled all over Europe, her charms attracting universal admiration.  She did us the honours of her house at Kamieniec, surrounded by people distinguished by their youth, their birth, or their talents.  All paid her implicit obedience, and besides her beauty she attracted by a sort of originality proceeding either from a feigned naïveté or from ignorance of the language.  I was told that when people admired her beautiful eyes, or when she spoke of them herself, she used to say in French: 'mes beaux yeux,' thinking that this was a single word.

M. Witt took me and my tutor over the ramparts of the fortress to show us that it was impregnable.  The rock on which it is built is surrounded by a moat, on the other side of which is another rock, containing vast casemates to hold troops for the defence of the place.  The only channel by which the inner rock communicates with the outer one is very narrow, and is provided with very solid ramparts.

From Kamieniec we went to Chocim, which at that time belonged to Turkey, and where the officer in command was a pasha who displayed much luxury and politeness in receiving my father as general of the Podolian territories. After handing round chibouks and coffee, the pasha's son, a tall young man, approached me and my brother and invited us to visit the harem with his father's permission. We followed him, a *portière* was raised and then drawn down behind us, and we entered the seraglio.

I saw through the doors of the rooms looking into a passage some women, who seemed much astonished and alarmed at our presence. We went to a place where was the young man's mother, the pasha's wife, surrounded by several female attendants; this was a sort of kiosk erected in a corner of a rectangular garden. We did not like these women, and thought them very untidily dressed. They received us very amiably, examined us with much curiosity, and asked us some questions; but the conversation was neither long nor animated.

We returned to Miendzyboz, which was the last stage of our journey, for to my great regret we did not go as far as Cracow.

We travelled through Galicia, and after stopping at Oleszyce, Sieniawa, and Jaroslaw, we arrived at Pulawy, where we finally took up our residence.

[On the 27th of October, 1784, Prince Adam's sister Marie was married to Prince Louis of Würtemberg, the brother of the wife of the Grand-Duke Paul of Russia (afterwards the Emperor Paul) and a relative of Frederick the Great. The newly-married pair went to Berlin, and soon after Prince Adam's mother paid them a visit. Here she had an interview with Frederick, which she thus graphically describes in a manuscript diary preserved in the Czartoryski archives :—

'The King of Prussia always lived at Potsdam, and only received on certain days which were fixed beforehand. It was not without a certain degree of fear that I made myself ready to visit him. Having from my childhood constantly been told of his genius and great deeds, I had formed in my mind so high an idea of him that I felt timid. I hoped I would be admitted to his presence with many others, and be lost in the crowd; but Madame Voss, the Queen's lady-in-waiting, took me alone into the drawing-room, and directly I entered, the door opposite me opened, and the King came in also alone. Madame Voss merely mentioned my name and withdrew. I thus remained *tête-à-tête* with a man who filled me with fear, and whom I believed to far exceed in genius and learning all those whom I had yet seen. I was so dazed that if I had at once left the room, I could have sworn that Frederick was at least six feet high. He took my hand kindly, and said : "I am old, and my sight is bad; allow me, Princess, to take you to the window, so that I may have a good look at you." This completed my confusion ; tears were in my eyes, and I trembled like a leaf. The King, no doubt to give me courage, then himself began the conversation, still holding my hand. "You have given us an angel, Princess," he said. "I saw her yesterday, and she inspires me with the greatest interest." I then ventured to look at the man who had called my daughter an angel. To my surprise I saw not a giant, but a little man, shorter than myself, rather crooked, and in a shabby uniform covered with snuff. He had beautiful blue eyes, a mild but penetrating glance, and a manner which inspired confidence. Seeing that I was looking at him, but that I did not yet venture to open my lips, he continued : " Your angel will always find in me a friend. She has married my nephew, but I must plainly tell you that they are not made for each other, she is an angel and he*—" The King did not finish the phrase, but added, " Anyhow you know him and will do him justice ; all I will say now is that this cannot last, but let her boldly come to me whenever she finds it necessary." These words calmed my anxiety, and there remained only a feeling of gratitude which it was easy for a mother to express when speaking of her daughter. The interview lasted over an hour. Frederick II afterwards spoke of many other things. He asked me about Poland and our King. This was a very delicate subject, as he had only recently plundered our King with the help of his allies, who had shared in the spoil. Among the questions he addressed to me I remember his asking whether Stanislas Augustus wore a military uniform. I felt the irony of this question, as our army had at that time been so reduced that we hardly had any troops at all. I answered, as was the fact, that the King wears the uniform of the School of Cadets.

* Prince Louis of Würtemberg was afterwards deprived of his command in the Polish army for declining to fight against Russia, and his wife, the Princess Marie, then refused to live with him.

"He is right," observed Frederick; "*c'est vraiment un roi à l'école.*"   I felt indignant at this remark, which seemed to me quite uncalled for.   I turned red, the tears again rose to my eyes, and I exclaimed without thinking: "*Sire, vous lui avez donné une leçon cruelle et peu méritée.*"   When I came in I did not dare to raise my eyes to him; afterwards, when he began to speak of my daughter, I felt bolder, and I was thoroughly roused when he spoke slightingly of my unhappy country and King, whom he had humiliated after plundering him.   After I had spoken I felt frightened, but Frederick thus went on, as if he had not heard what I said: "I have often remarked that in Poland women should govern; if they did, everything would be better there, and our conversation to-day has confirmed me in that belief."   He then bowed to me politely and respectfully, again saying that my daughter could always reckon on his protection; and with this our first interview ended.']

# CHAPTER IV

## 1784-1787



At Pulawy we[*] began an existence which was entirely new to us, and we entered on our studies seriously and regularly.

Up to that time we had only been taught elementary knowledge, and our lessons were frequently interrupted, while now they became almost our sole occupation. M. Lhuillier taught us mathematics and universal history; Colonel Ciesielski, the history of Poland; Kniaznin, literature and Latin. Our classical master was at first a Dane named Schow, and afterwards Groddeck, who subsequently became a professor at the University of Wilna.

I do not quite remember whether it was then or later on that my father appointed as our tutor M. Dupont de Nemours, a member of the National Assembly, who was much esteemed in France for his ability and character. He had with him a secretary named Noyer, a very importunate man who paid

[*] The author and his brother Constantine. The Bohemian traveller Tanner, writing in 1678, says of this magnificent country seat of the Czartoryski family :—' Prospeximus hic a dextra fluminis parte Pulavii castrum splendidum, et a circumjacentium hortorum amœnitate deliciosum.'

marked attention to Madame Petit. One day he knocked at her door, and not knowing any other way to get rid of him, she told him she was not at home. M. Dupont did not stay long with us; he returned to France, and I saw him in Paris at the time of the Restoration. He introduced himself to me as my old tutor, but I had entirely forgotten him.

There was a fencing-master at Pulawy who gave us a lesson every morning in the garden after we got up, which was very early, and then we passed to other studies. The company used to be very large at dinner, as all the persons in the service of the family were present.

Besides our studies, we had various pleasures, such as hunting, excursions to the house of M. and Madame Filipowicz, the steward of the Pulawy estates at Konska Wola, country rides, and especially coursing. I was very fond of this pastime; in a wood in the vicinity there were hares on the hills, and a brood of foxes which we amused ourselves by driving out of their holes with dogs.

This was for us children what I may call 'the Pulawy period.' My father's stay in Lithuania attracted to our house a great number of citizens of that province; several young men also came from Lithuania to be educated at our house, and they amused the company during the hours which were not given up to study.

Our daily fencing-lessons took place in the garden during the summer. Although accustomed to the use of the foil at the school of Cadets, Rembilinski, one of our tutors, was once hit in the eye, and on another

occasion, as he was fencing with me, my foil pierced
his mask and wounded him in the mouth. He was
much frightened, and his first thought was to ascertain
whether his second eye had not been hurt. I was
profuse in my apologies, and thanked God that my
awkwardness had not had any more serious consequences.

We used to hold meetings like those of the Diets,
at which we discussed public questions. I recollect
that at one of these meetings the question discussed
was, which was the best government, one in which
political power was distributed among the people, or a
government in which all power proceeded from a
central authority. I advocated the greatest possible
liberty, while to my great surprise Rembilinski declared himself in favour of a central and paternal
government. His speech was so eloquent that I
could not find words to answer him, which greatly
dissatisfied me. I was beaten, but not convinced.

# CHAPTER V

## 1786



A HOLIDAY IN GERMANY.—WIELAND.—GOETHE.—A POLISH
CARNIVAL.—VISITS TO ENGLAND.

In 1786, I first went to travel abroad ; I was accompanied by my tutor, who had been ordered to take the waters at Carlsbad. Madame Oginska, the hetman's wife, my father's cousin and my mother's aunt, started for Carlsbad at the same time as we did, accompanied by a numerous suite, as was then the custom. We visited several German towns where I came into contact with many eminent men. I cannot say that I made their acquaintance, for my mind was as yet not sufficiently developed ; but I still remember having met them.

My father had invited to Pulawy a professor of Latin and Greek who had been recommended to him by Steine, the celebrated professor of Göttingen. He was a young Dane and an enthusiastic admirer of the beauties of ancient literature, like all who came from that university. I shared this enthusiasm —a little childishly, but very sincerely—under the influence of Kniaznin, who taught us Polish and

Latin literature.   I neglected the tedious though indispensable study of grammar, and tried to understand the classic poets, which gave me the appearance of knowing much more than I did in reality ; and I paraded my knowledge in the presence of the German *savants* whom I met on my travels.   At Prague I made the acquaintance of Meissner, professor of Greek literature and author of several German works. His reputation, which at that time was very great, did not survive him.   I recollect with pleasure the conversations I had with him, and I was much astonished to find that I was able to quote to him from memory some verses from the Greek poets.

We passed through Gotha, where, thanks to a letter of introduction from my father, we made the acquaintance of Baron Frankenburg, Minister to the Duke of Gotha.   He was an intelligent, amiable, and cultivated man, and he placed us in relations with other celebrated and interesting persons.   He gave us letters with which we went to Weimar, already known as the German Athens, where I saw Wieland and Herder, with whom my father kept up a correspondence.

Wieland's appearance was anything but poetical ;. he was short, rather stout, somewhat advanced in years, wrinkled, and wearing a sort of nightcap which he seldom took off.

Baron Frankenburg also enabled us to make the acquaintance of Goethe, and I was admitted with my tutor to a private house where the poet read to some friends his play of ' Iphigenia in Tauris,' which he had just finished.   I listened with great enthusiasm. Goethe was then in the brightest period of his youth; he was tall, and his face was handsome and imposing, with a piercing look, sometimes a little disdainful, as if he were looking down upon the horizon of humanity. This slight tinge of arrogance was also visible in the smile on his beautiful mouth. He hardly remarked the admiration of a youth like myself, for this was a homage to which he was accustomed. When he afterwards became Minister to the Grand-Duke of Weimar he no longer showed the same disregard of official favours and decorations; but he always retained in his face and demeanour a sort of grandeur which made people compare him to Phidias's statue of the Olympian Jove.

At length we arrived at Carlsbad, where we found Madame Oginska, whose presence greatly contributed to our pleasure. She had with her several young ladies, the daughters of her major-domo Siedlecki, and also Dr Kittel, who was young and very handsome, and was consequently much in request with ladies whose health required, or seemed to them to require, a doctor's care.

There was at that time at Carlsbad a very brilliant casino, where the whole society of the place assembled, and where there was dancing almost every evening. One of the ladies was said to be much admired by the Archduke Leopold, whose weakness for the sex was notorious, and who ascended the throne some years later. I was struck by the beauty of the features of this lady, and especially by the extraordinary vivacity of her movements.

We returned home in the autumn, and the winter

of 1786 to 1787 was passed partly at Pulawy, partly at Siedlce. We continued our studies at Pulawy without much regularity, but with great interest and diligence, and passed the carnival at Siedlce, where there was a numerous and brilliant gathering of visitors. Madame Oginska, who held her Court there, was very pious, but her sole anxiety was to amuse her guests and make them merry. She had in her house a great many charming young ladies belonging to noble families. When her toilet was over, her guests were admitted into her apartments, and these young ladies were to be seen taking to her some article of dress—a flower, a ribbon, a veil, or a bonnet—which was to be worn in the course of the day. Afterwards everybody went into the drawing-rooms, where amusements of all kinds were constantly going on.

Madame Oginska was very fond of playing at cards, and invited the best players to Siedlce. This was not perhaps very praiseworthy, but it contributed to our amusement for part of the day. In the evening there was dancing and drawing-room games; in the summer we walked about in a large garden which was called Alexandria, and which Madame Oginska had decorated in the English fashion; in the autumn we went out shooting, and she used to join our party, firing from her place at the birds as they flew by.

It was difficult to suffer from *ennui* at Siedlce, and the natural consequence was that romantic adventures frequently occurred, in which I sometimes played a part. I had found some books which fired my imagination; I read them during several nights, when I should have done better to devote the time to study. One of the young ladies at Siedlce, Mademoiselle Marie Niczabitowska, became the object of my 'sighs,' which I did not venture to communicate to her without great hesitation. To enter into the young ladies' room was beyond my power, and often I used to stand near the door, fearing to cross the threshold. At length I got over my timidity, and my usual place was on a box in the young ladies' room.

To make love or fall in love was the lot of every young man at Siedlce, and I had some rivals, among whom was Niemcewicz. Mademoiselle Niezabitowska was one of the prettiest of the young ladies there, and she was also endowed with other qualities by Nature which distinguished her from other women during her long life. Poets wrote verses to her, and I remember that one of these effusions ended by deploring her severity to those who surrounded her. It was indeed difficult to secure her good graces, and she treated her admirers with much rigour.

Some cases of scarlet fever having broken out in the ladies' apartments, my mother recalled me to Pulawy.

*      *      *      *      *      *      *

[Here there is a break in the Memoirs, which are not resumed until the year 1795, when Prince Adam Czartoryski proceeded with his brother Constantine to St Petersburg. In 1789, when he was nineteen years of age, he went with his mother to Paris and then to London, where he stayed for some weeks

with Lord Mansfield, to complete his political education by studying the English constitution. During
this time he witnessed the trial of Warren Hastings;
and afterwards he visited Scotland and the principal
manufacturing towns in England. One of his English
acquaintances of that period, Dr Currie of Liverpool,
thus describes, in a letter to Mr F. Creevy, M.P.,
dated the 31st of October, 1803, his impressions of
the Prince in 1790 :—'I dined yesterday by special
invitation with Prince William of Gloucester. There
was a good deal of talk about the Northern coasts,
where the Prince and several of his suite were last
year, and I was a good deal interested to hear that
the politics of Russia were led by Prince Adam
Czartoryski, the Secretary of State. The Prince
said that he was a most agreeable, accomplished man,
but decidedly in the French interest, a Jacobin, etc.
etc., and that his influence was the great bar to
England resuming her proper weight at the Court
of St Petersburg. Now you must know this Czartoryski is an old acquaintance of mine—was a cor-
respondent, and might have been so yet, but for my
own neglect, for he wrote me several letters since
I ceased to write to him. He made the tour of
the island along with his mother in grand style, some
time in the earlier and better stages of the French
Revolution. He was then about twenty or twenty-
one, and a very fine young man indeed, full of great
expectations of happy changes in society ; full of
ardour, benevolence, and adventure. He had passed
the preceding winter at Paris, in close attendance on
the National Assembly in the most brilliant days of

Mirabeau. He had afterwards been a close attendant on the debates in our own Parliament, at that time so interesting. He seemed to me extremely capable of appreciating the great talents then displayed on the theatres of both nations, and was very fond of comparing the statesmen and orators of France and England. Mirabeau and Fox were his heroes—but he preferred the latter. He was absolutely as great an idolater of Fox as you are of the General [Sir John Moore], and seemed to me to have that simplicity and elevation of soul which is necessary to appreciate our incomparable Charley. I took to Czartoryski extremely, and he used to ride out with me and walk with me during the fortnight he stayed here, as you do. He is an English-looking man, a black fellow, very tall and handsome—spoke our language and loved our country. I had several letters from him during his tour in Scotland (where I introduced him) and mean to have a search for them. He was very deeply interested in the Revolution in Poland, in which I think his mother played a principal part. She was with him, and took the direction of him—a woman then still handsome, and said to be of great address of every kind, but perfectly intelligible and feminine. When I revolve all these things, Sheridan's scheme of sending Fox to St Petersburg struck me as a noble thought. Depend upon it, if it could be accomplished, that his influence there would be speedily felt. For this Czartoryski is a virtuous man, and, if we knew how to approach him, neither is nor can be the tool of Bonaparte.'

Prince Adam returned to Poland in 1791, and

entered the army under the command of his brother-in-law, the Prince of Würtemberg.   It was in this year that the famous Reformed Constitution of the 3rd of May, which was afterwards made by Russia and Prussia the pretext for a second partition of the country, was passed by the Grand Diet (known as 'the Four Years' Diet') at Warsaw.*   This Constitution was regarded

* 'It was the deliberate and systematic policy of Russia and Prussia to maintain anarchy in Poland, in order that it might never rise to prosperity or power or independence.   With this object they agreed, at the beginning of the reign of Stanislas Poniatowski, that they would maintain by force the existing Constitution, and oppose any attempt to abolish the *Liberum Veto*, or to make the monarchy hereditary.   A strong and earnest effort was, notwithstanding, made to effect the former object, and the reform was so powerfully supported that it would have undoubtedly succeeded had not Russia again interfered, and re-established, with the concurrence of Prussia, *Liberum Veto* in its full stringency.   The jealousy of three great powers alone for a time saved Poland.   At last they agreed upon their share of the spoil.   In 1772 they signed 'in the name of the Holy Trinity,' treaties for the plunder of Poland, and in a few months the first partition was easily effected.   It was justified at the time, and has been defended by some later historians on the ground of that very anarchy which it had been for many years a main object of two of the plundering powers to foment and to perpetuate.   Prussia solemnly guaranteed the integrity of Poland.   She promised to assist her against all hostile attacks, and all interference with her internal concerns.   The King of Prussia not only fully recognised the right of the Polish people as an independent nation to revise their Constitution, but he also strongly urged them to do so.

'The Prussian policy of detaching Poland from Russia was, however, perfectly successful, and, relying on Prussian support, the Polish Diet, which first met in September 1788, and which was confederated for the emergency, carried a series of reforms which totally changed the constitution and condition of Poland.   It was decreed that the army should be raised from 20,000 to 100,000 men.   The system of taxation was thoroughly revised.   A considerable representation was given to the trading towns.   The excessive powers of the Dietines were abolished.   The *Liberum Veto* was swept away, and finally on May 3, 1791, a new Constitution was voted, in which, after the reigning King, the crown was offered to the Elector of Saxony, and to his heirs for ever.   It was certain that Russia would resist bitterly what was done, and she early announced to the Diet that she would permit no change whatever in the Constitution of 1775.   The King of Prussia expressed his satisfaction at what had occurred, to the Polish Minister at his Court, to the King of Poland, and the Elector of Saxony.   He urged the Elector to accept the Polish crown: he offered him his warm alliance, and he professed himself fully determined to fulfil his own treaty obligations.

'As for the policy of Russia towards Poland, it was one of cynical, undisguised rapacity.   The course of events depended largely on the King of Prussia.   That sovereign, as we have seen, had first induced the Poles to assert their independence of Russia.   He had himself urged them to amend their constitution.   He had been the first to congratulate them on the constitutional reform of May 1791.   He had bound himself before God and man, by two solemn and recent treaties, to respect the integrity of Poland; to defend the integrity of Poland against all enemies; to oppose by force any attempt to interfere with her internal affairs.   Yet, as we have

by the greatest statesmen and political writers of the
time as the highest step yet attained in the science
of government. Burke said that it was 'a glory to
humanity' and 'the noblest and greatest benefit shed
upon the human race.' Fox described it as 'a work to
which all the friends of freedom should be sincerely
attached,' and Volney remarked that Poland was the
only country of Northern Europe which had amelio-
rated the hard lot of its peasantry.

In 1792, Prince Adam took part in the campaign
against the Russians, who had invaded Poland in consequence of the issue of the new constitution; he
fought in the battle of Granno, and was decorated by
the King for his bravery.

In 1793, he again went to England, and entered
into close relations with nearly all the politicians of
note in that country.* It was while he was still
staying there in 1794 that the Kosciuszko insurrection
broke out. Directly he heard the news, he hurried
back to join the insurgents, but was stopped at
Brussels and put in arrest under orders from the
Austrian Government. Meanwhile the insurrection
was suppressed, and the third partition of Poland took
place. Soon after the Prince rejoined his parents at
Vienna, where the Emperor Francis intervened with
the Empress Catherine of Russia to cancel the confis-

also seen, he had resolved as early as March 1792, not only to break his word and to
betray his trust, but also to take an active part in the partition of the defenceless
country which he had bound himself in honour to protect.' (Lecky, *History of
England in the Eighteenth Century*, Vols V and VI.)

 * There are in the Czartoryski archives several bulky manuscripts written by the
Prince during his stay in England at this time. Two of these, in the English
language, are treatises on English law and on the system of police and civil
administration generally; a third, in Polish, is on the judicial administration in
England.

cation of the estates of the Czartoryski family, ordered by her in consequence of their participation in the insurrection.    The Empress insisted, as a condition of her entering into negotiations on this subject, that the two young princes should go to St Petersburg to enter the Russian service, and after much deliberation at a family council this condition was accepted.]

# CHAPTER VI

## 1794-1795



IT was the 12th of May 1795, when my brother and I arrived at St Petersburg. In order to form an idea of our feelings on entering that city, it is necessary to know the principles in which we were brought up. Our education had been entirely Polish and Republican. The study of ancient history and literature, and of the history and literature of our country, had occupied the years of our adolescence. Our minds were full of Greeks and Romans, and, following the example of our ancestors, we thought only of perpetuating the ancient virtues on the soil of our fatherland. With regard to political liberty, more recent examples, taken from the history of England and France, had up to a certain point rectified our ideas, without in any way diminishing their energy. The love of our country, of its glories, its institutions, and its liberties had been inculcated into us by our studies, and by everything we had seen or heard around us. I should add that this feeling, which penetrated the whole of our moral nature, was accompanied by an invincible aversion to all who had contributed to the ruin of the fatherland which we so much loved.

This two-fold sentiment of love and hatred dominated me so entirely, that I could not meet a Russian either in Poland or elsewhere without feeling a rush of blood to the head—without blushing or turning white with anger—for every Russian seemed to me an author of the misfortunes of my country.

My first task was promptly to replace on a satisfactory footing the affairs of my father. Three-fourths of his fortune, all consisting of land situated in the provinces seized by Russia, had been sequestrated. These estates were mortgaged to a considerable extent, so that not only my father's own property, but also that of a great number of our countrymen, was in question. The representations made in my father's favour by the Court of Vienna had had no result. Catherine was provoked by the patriotism of my father and mother, and their sympathy with the Kosciuszko insurrection. 'Let their two sons come to me,' she said, 'and then we will see.' She wished to keep us as hostages.

Our departure for St Petersburg was thus indispensable. Our father, kind and considerate as ever, did not venture to demand this sacrifice from us; and it was the fact of our knowing this that prevailed over every other consideration. Our fatherland was lost: were we also to condemn our parents to want, and make it impossible for them to discharge their debts? We did not hesitate an instant. At the same time we knew well that to go to St Petersburg, far from all our connections—to give ourselves up as prisoners, so to say, into the hands of the most detested of our enemies, of the executioners of our country—was in our situation the most painful sacrifice we could make to paternal affection ; for to do this it was necessary to act in opposition to all our sentiments, all our convictions, all our plans—to everything that was nearest to our hearts and minds.

I described with all the ardour of a youthful poet my state of mind at this time, in some verses entitled ' The Song of the Bard,' which I composed during my stay at Grodno.  When I left that town I sent the manuscript to our friend Kniaznin, and it was often read with tears of sympathy by my family.

We bade adieu to our parents (who at that time were residing at Vienna), in the month of December 1794.  After sadly passing a few days at Sieniawa,* we proceeded on our journey at the beginning of January, and stopped at Grodno (where the King Stanislas Augustus then lived under the surveillance of Prince Repnin), until we received permission, which did not arrive till the following spring, to go on to St Petersburg.  The Empress at first refused to give this permission, and we were shown a note in her own hand in which she stated as the reason of her refusal that my mother had, as in the story of Hamilcar and Hannibal, made us swear eternal hatred to Russia and her sovereign.  While at Grodno we often went to see the King, and we were witnesses of his grief and bitter self-reproaches at not being able

* In Galicia, now the country residence of Prince Ladislas Czartoryski.

either to save his country or to perish in fighting for her.

Since my first arrival at St Petersburg my feelings have never changed, but their outward expression has necessarily been modified by events. The same juvenile ardour which made us regard our departure as a heroic sacrifice to paternal affection, made the detested position in which we were placed more tolerable. When one is young, there are few things that cannot be borne ; one is strong enough to contend with every kind of adversity and even of misfortune. New scenes, new impressions, though painful, yet hitherto unknown, always distract the mind in the end even if they do not change it.

We were received in St Petersburg society with much consideration and good-will. Our father, who had lived in the Russian capital at the time of Elizabeth, of Peter II, and of the accession of Catherine, was well known and respected there by the older inhabitants. His letters, which we brought with us, procured us a favourable reception. The injustice with which we had been treated by the Cabinet, elicited a sympathy in our favour which was not entirely barren, as it was openly and fearlessly expressed. I have no doubt, remembering the compliments which were paid to us, that the courtiers of whom St Petersburg society was at that time almost entirely composed, knew beforehand that their politeness to the disinherited of Poland—the foster-children of liberty—could not compromise them at Court. Perhaps they had even received a hint that this conduct on their part would be pleasing to the

Empress. After a few weeks we had made many acquaintances, and we received invitations every day from the members of the aristocracy. Dinners, balls, concerts, soirées, private theatricals, succeeded each other without intermission.

We were everywhere accompanied by M. James Gorski, who had been requested by our father to be our friend and guide, and to assist us by his advice. No better mentor could have been selected. Easy-going, merry, tolerant, a genial and witty companion, and at the same time scrupulously honourable and never hesitating to tell an unpleasant truth, he was the very man to keep us in the right way without alienating us by excessive severity. We were very happy in the society of this excellent friend, and I only satisfy the demands of my conscience in here expressing our gratitude to him and our grief at his unexpected loss. He encouraged us to take advantage of the friendly reception given to us, by entering into relations with the persons who were ultimately to bring about the restitution of our fortune. Gorski spoke French with a strong Polish accent, but this did not in any way disconcert him. All he said and did was marked by a laconic precision which was thoroughly in accordance with his character and appearance. He held his head high, and had a proud manner and a brief and decided way of speaking, always, however, within the limits of politeness. Although he did not much esteem the majority of his acquaintances, they were devoted to him. He was very fond of pleasure and good living, and persuaded us to go into society, which perhaps our melancholy, and also a little natural indolence, would otherwise have prevented us from doing. He never lost sight of the object of the journey we had undertaken, and he never neglected any means calculated to achieve it. He always urged us to pay visits and take steps which were inexpressibly disagreeable to us, and it was to his persistence in this respect that our success was mainly due.

This period of our youth was a decisive one for the rest of our career : for, thus suddenly introduced into a state of things entirely foreign to us and contrary to our ideas, we saw all our plans disappear and our future changed and broken in opposition to our wishes and our convictions. As regards myself this phase of my life produced deep and painful results. The misfortunes of my country, of my parents, and of many others of my countrymen, the defeat of justice and the triumph of violence and crime, had unhinged my mind. I began to doubt the ways of Providence. I saw only contradictions and aimless struggles ; nothing seemed to me to deserve any serious attention ; I was absorbed by a feeling of scepticism, of cold and despairing indifference. I have since more than once relapsed into these attacks of despair. But although, seeing nowhere any solid basis of action, and suspecting everybody, I looked upon men and things with contempt, an interior voice suggested to my reason that virtue and charity were indubitable realities that were worth living for, and that even if this were not the case, they were to be preferred to anything else. This debate of my conscience alone saved me from the fatal effects of universal doubt. The first germs of belief, though weakened, still remained in my soul.

Compliments and pleasures always produce their effect on a youthful mind, though they do not prevent, and indeed sometimes promote, a feeling of scepticism. Our souls retained their wounds, but we felt some change on the surface. We found that, according to the proverb, the devil is not so black as he is painted, especially if he makes himself amiable ; that it was not just, notwithstanding the outrages that had been committed on our country, to accuse the whole Russian nation of them—to include in our detestation of the Government, individuals who had nothing in common with it ; that the appearances of things change according to the condition and status of persons, and that to arrive at a sound judgment of their private, and still more of their public, conduct, one should put one's self in their place and have regard to the circumstances by which they are surrounded. By degrees we came to the conviction that these Russians, whom we had instinctively learnt to hate— whom we indiscriminately classed as malignant and sanguinary beings, with whom we were to avoid every contact, and whom we could not even meet without disgust—that these Russians were much like other people ; that there were among them young men who were witty and courteous, and even kind, so far at least as could be judged from their words ; that Russian ladies were very amiable ; that, in a word, one could live among Russians without repulsion, and even sometimes feel obliged to give them one's friendship and gratitude.

I only make these self-evident remarks to show that we were in no way prepared for the transition, and that, passing so suddenly from one extreme to the other, we felt as if we had been cast from a precipice on a sea where, not being able to land, we were obliged to direct our course as best we could. We were young, and we met with dangerous and insidious acquaintances and amusements. The society of St Petersburg was on the whole brilliant, animated, and full of variety. Many houses of different kinds were open to us, and strangers were everywhere received with eagerness.

The salons of the Princess Basil Dolgoroukoff and those of the Princess Michael Galitzin, both of whom have since become well known in Paris, were distinguished by their elegance. These two ladies rivalled each other in wit, beauty, and amiability. It was said that both had been admired by Prince Potemkin. The unfortunate adorer of the Princess Dolgoroukoff was at that time Count de Cobentzel, the Austrian ambassador, while the Princess Galitzin had enchained Count de Choiseul-Gouffier, known by his mission to Constantinople and the narrative of his travels in Greece. He had converted the Princess's palace into a sort of art museum, though she herself did not much care for art.

The Narishkin palace was of quite a different kind. With all its anachronisms, it was a true Russian building of the Asiatic type, and the young ladies there, who were less looked after than they usually are in Russia, were said to have been also distinguished by Prince Potemkin. The doors were open to everybody, and Cossacks, Tartars, Circassians, and other Asiatics were among the guests. The owner, Leo Narishkin, gay, affable, good-natured, an old favourite of Peter III, and afterwards a courtier of the Empress Catherine, always ready to please her favourites, with all of whom he was on good terms, spent enormous sums as Grand Equerry in balls and receptions, and yet, though he had been doing this for ten years, did not manage to get through his fortune. I do not know if his heirs, who had the same taste for lavish expenditure, have been more successful.

At the Golowin palace there were not daily soirées, as elsewhere, but little coteries like those got up in Paris, to perpetuate the ancient traditions of Versailles. The mistress of the house, whose two daughters have since married MM. Fredro and Potocki, was very witty, talented, sentimental, and fond of art.

Another house which had a peculiar character of its own was the palace of Count Strogonoff. The Count had lived for a long time in Paris, and had contracted habits there which were in singular contrast to the old Muscovite customs. He and his friends talked of Voltaire, of Diderot, of the Parisian stage, and discussed the merits of the pictures of the old masters, of which the Count had a rich collection; and while this conversation was going on, a huge table was laid, with a barbaric disorder betraying the origin of his Siberian riches, at which people dined without being invited and were waited upon by a crowd of serfs.

I will not sketch in detail the society of St Petersburg; I have to speak of more serious subjects. I will only add that Russian society was at that time, as it probably is still, only a reflection of the Court. It might be compared to the vestibule of a temple, where no one has eyes or ears for anything but the divinity within. Every conversation, I had almost said every phrase, always ended in a reference or question relating to the Court—what was said or done there, or what was intended to be done. Every important impulse came from the Court; this deprived society, it is true, of any distinctive character, yet it seemed to be animated and gay.

The Empress Catherine, the immediate author of the ruin of Poland, whose very name inspired us with horror, and who was cursed by everyone with the heart of a Pole—who, in the opinion of people outside her capital, neither had virtue nor even womanly decency—had nevertheless succeeded in gaining the veneration and even the love of her servants and subjects. During the long years of her reign the army, the privileged classes, and the administrators had their days of prosperity and lustre. There can be no doubt that since her accession the Russian Empire had gained in prestige abroad and in order at home far more than during the preceding reigns of Anne and Elizabeth. People's minds were still full of the ancient fanaticism and of a servile feeling of adoration for autocrats. The prosperous reign of Catherine had confirmed the Russians in their servility, though some gleams of European civilisation had already penetrated among them. Thus the people,

great and small, were not in the least shocked at the
depraved tastes of their sovereign or the murders and
other crimes which she committed.  Everything was
allowed to her.   Her luxuriousness was a sacred thing,
and no one dreamt of condemning her debaucheries ;
it was like the pagans respecting the crimes and the
obscenities of the gods of Olympus and the Cæsars of
Rome.

The Muscovite Olympus had three stages.  The
first was the so-called ' young court,' occupied by the
young princes and princesses, all of whom were graceful and cultivated, and promised well for the future.
The second was held solely by the Grand-Duke Paul,
whose sombre character and fantastic humour inspired
terror, and sometimes contempt.  At the top of the
edifice was Catherine, with all the prestige of her
victories, of her prosperity, and of her confidence in
the love of her subjects, whom she could always lead
according to her caprices.

All the hopes that could be based on the ' young
court' belonged only to a distant future, and did not
in any way diminish the general affection for the
supreme authority of the Czarina, especially as the
' young court' was regarded only as a creation of the
ruling power.   Catherine reserved to herself exclusively the care of the education of her grandchildren ;
and their parents were forbidden to exercise any
influence in this respect.  Directly they were born
the princes and princesses were taken away from their
parents, and they grew up under the eyes of the
Empress, to whom alone they seemed to belong.

The Grand-Duke Paul was the shadow in the

picture, and augmented its effect.    The terror which he inspired greatly strengthened the general attachment for the rule of Catherine.    Everyone wished that the reins of government should long remain in her strong hands ; and as all feared Paul, they admired the more the power and the great abilities of his mother, who held him in dependence, far from a throne which by right belonged to him.

This rapid sketch will explain the idolatry of the inhabitants of St Petersburg for their female Jupiter. It was in some sort a reproduction of the adoration of Louis XIV before death had carried away his numerous descendants.

It would have been very difficult, if not impossible, for a stranger arriving at St Petersburg to resist impressions and prejudices so deeply rooted.    Once he entered the Court atmosphere and the society which depended upon the Court, he was imperceptibly carried away by the same ideas, and generally ended by joining in the concert of praise which was continually rising around the throne.    As a proof of this, illustrious travellers might be cited, such as the Prince de Ligne, the Counts de Ségur and de Choiseul, and many others.    In the group of strangers and natives who slandered their acquaintances, who would sacrifice anything to a *bon mot*, and who had no reason to mistrust us, there was not one who, so far as I knew, ever ventured to make a joke at the expense of the Empress.    They respected nothing and gossipped about everything ; a disdainful and mocking smile often accompanied the name of the Grand-Duke Paul ; but if that of Catherine was mentioned, all men's faces at once put on an air of seriousness and submission. There were no more smiles or jests; no one dared even to murmur a complaint or a reproach, as if the most unjust and outrageous actions, when committed by her, were decrees of fate, to be accepted with respectful submission.

Catherine was ambitious, spiteful, vindictive, arbitrary, and shameless; but her ambition was combined with love of glory, and although when her personal interests or passions were concerned everything had to give way, her despotism was in no way capricious. Her passions, disorderly as they were, were dominated by her reason and her abilities. Her tyranny was not the fruit of impulse, but of calculation. She did not commit crimes which were of no advantage to her. She even consented sometimes to be equitable in matters to which she was indifferent, in order that the glory of justice might increase the splendour of her throne. Moreover, being jealous of every kind of fame, she aspired to the title of a legislator, in order to give herself, at least in the eyes of Europe and of history, a reputation for statesmanship. She knew only too well that sovereigns cannot dispense with appearing just, even if they are not so in reality. She was anxious to gain over public opinion to her side so long as it did not run contrary to her views; otherwise she disregarded it. The political crimes which she committed in Poland, she explained as necessary for the security of the State and as adding to its military glory. She seized the estates of the Poles who had shown most zeal for the independence of their country, but in distributing these

estates she benefited the great Russian families, and
the bait of an illicit gain induced all around her to
flatter her taste for a criminal, pitiless, and conquering
policy.

Much astonishment was expressed when General
Fersen, the winner of the battle of Macieyovice,*,re-
fused the confiscated estates of the Czacki family, and
asked as his reward some bonds of the Imperial
domains. No one else would have ventured to make
so legitimate a request, as every order of the Empress
was received with blind submission. Her wish, even
if it entailed a revolting act of injustice, was not to be
discussed: to do so would have been a proof of unexampled boldness. People held that her acts were
not to be judged by ordinary standards, and that even
the principles of equity were subject to her decrees.

I will quote an example of this which made some
noise at the time. The Princess Schakoffskoy, who
had a colossal fortune, had married her daughter to
the Duke of Aremberg. This had happened abroad.
Catherine, indignant at her consent not having been
asked, ordered the princess's goods to be confiscated.
The mother and daughter came to implore the
Empress's pardon, but Catherine was deaf to their
prayers. She cancelled the marriage, saying that it
was invalid, as it had been contracted without her
permission. The mother and daughter quietly submitted, and the public took this iniquitous decision as
a matter of course; at least nobody said a word about
it. Some time after, the young princess was per-

* The battle in which Kosciuszko's insurrection was finally suppressed, and
Kosciuszko himself was wounded and taken prisoner (10th of October 1794).

suaded to contract a second marriage; but being sincerely attached to her first husband, and stung by remorse, she killed herself.

There was also an analogy between the Court of the Empress Catherine and that of Louis XIV in so far that his mistresses played exactly the same part at Versailles as her favourites did at St Petersburg. As to the immorality, the license, the intrigues, and the baseness of the Court of St Petersburg, they are rather to be compared to what we read of the courts of the Byzantine Emperors; while for a parallel to the submission and the veneration of the people we must look to the fascination exercised upon the English nation by Queen Elizabeth, who, equally cruel and ambitious, was endowed with greater talents and a masculine energy.

Even the libertine spirit of Catherine, which often prompted her to improvised amours, was of service to her with the army, the Court, and the privileged classes. Every subaltern, every young man who possessed physical attractions, aspired to the favours of his sovereign; and although she descended from her Olympus only too often to visit ordinary mortals, her subjects did not the less respect her power and her authority; on the contrary, they were always admiring her discretion and cleverness. Those who approached her, of whatever sex, and who had enjoyed her benefits, were truly attached to her, and were never weary of praising her goodness and amiability.

For some time we were forbidden to see this source of favour and power, whose rays dazzled all eyes. In other words, we had not received permission to present ourselves at the Imperial Court, which as usual occupied the Tauris Palace from the beginning of spring. The only members of the Imperial family we had seen were the young princes, who were in the crowd on the day of our arrival, the 1st of May according to the Russian calendar, when nearly the whole of the population goes to the promenade of Catherinenhoff. Some time after, when we were already received in society, we were invited to assist at a fête which was to last about twenty-four hours, for it was to begin with a breakfast, to continue with a dance, walks, and the theatre, and to end with a supper. This fête was given by the Princess Galitzin in honour of the 'young court.' We had not been as yet presented ; but the Princess Galitzin, following the instructions she had received from the Countess Schouvaloff, her mother, who had been given a hint by the Empress, had invited us, and this gave us a certain position in society. It would be impossible to see a handsomer couple than the Grand-Duke Alexander, who was then eighteen, and his wife, who was only sixteen. Both beamed with youth, grace, and goodness.

The evenings were passed in the amusements I have described, but during the day, which is so long in that climate, the whole bitterness of our situation forced itself upon our minds. We had to visit, to solicit, to humble ourselves. It was hard, and we should have had much more difficulty in doing it if Gorski had not been there to keep us up to the work. He exercised all his authority over us ; he did not leave us a moment's relaxation, repeating that the effects of our neglect would fall upon our parents, and that the only object for which we were at St Petersburg was to replace them in their estates.

Plato Zuboff was at that time the most powerful of the Empress's favourites, and we had to go to him first. We came to his apartments in the Tauris Palace at the appointed hour. He had a brown coat on, and was leaning on a piece of furniture. He was under middle age, with a good figure and an agreeable countenance; his dark hair was curled and brushed up into a tuft; his voice was soft and clear. He received us with an air of benevolent protection. Gorski acted as our interpreter, and hastened to reply to the questions which Zuboff addressed to us; his French was not correct, but his mien was always imposing. Zuboff assured us that he would do all he could to help us, but added that we must not be under any illusions, that everything depended on her Majesty's favour, and that neither himself nor any one else was able to influence her decisions. He added that we would soon be admitted to her presence.

Prince Kourakin, brother to the future ambassador, who had undertaken to protect us, had taken us to Zuboff; but at the moment when we entered he disappeared, or rather stayed behind in the ante-chamber. He rejoined us as we were going out, and listened with a smile of curiosity to our account of what had happened. All his questions proved that he was convinced that we had just left the most powerful man in Europe.

But there was another man equally important;

this was Valerian Zuboff, Count Plato's younger brother. His more masculine face and figure made him more attractive than his brother, and it was said that the Empress liked him so much that if he had presented himself first he would have become the favourite. As it was, the fact of his being Count Plato's brother, and his personal qualities, gave him great influence over the mind of the old Czarina. We were therefore obliged to pay him a visit. By a singular coincidence, Valerian Zuboff had been the commander of the detachment which had sacked Pulawy* in the previous year. The horrors which marked the passage of the Russian troops through Poland are well known, and though Zuboff did not preside in person over the pillage of Pulawy, it can hardly be credited that the most savage soldiery would have acted in so outrageous a manner without their commander's consent. If, as is probable, they acted under orders from above, a man of honour would have taken care to show that it was with reluctance that he acquitted himself of such a mission, and would have at least moderated the execution of it. No such moderation, however, was shown; and we, the victims of the pillage, had to ask the spoiler (for such we thought him) for his protection. We were even obliged to request his intercession to be admitted into the presence of his brother, and it was to him that we owed the special honour of a private reception.

In the opinion of the Russians, however, Valerian Zuboff was a young man of loyal and noble sentiments. All that was said against him was that he

* See note on page 42.

was too fond of pleasure; his honour was believed to be untarnished. He was at that time engaged in a love intrigue with Madame Prot Potocka, who had followed him to St Petersburg, where she lived in concealment: this, however, did not prevent him from making other *liaisons*. He had lost a leg in a skirmish, before Praga* was taken by assault, and his crutches seemed to add to his charms in the eyes of the Empress and other ladies. On examining him more closely one saw the nonchalance of a young man spoiled by fortune and by women. His rooms were always full of flatterers of all kinds. In the interest of our parents, our worthy friend Gorski took us there also, much against our will. When, by repeating our visits, our relations had developed into a sort of familiarity, we still felt them to be inexpressibly tedious; there were no points of sympathy between us, and it was impossible to enter into any conversation. Count Valerian usually began by assuring us that he and his brother did not possess anything like the influence they were supposed to exercise over Catherine's mind, and that very often she did the very opposite to that which they wished her to do. I believe, however, that Count Valerian Zuboff was the only one who had our interests at heart. Whether as a matter of conscience, or from a desire to retrieve his reputation, he urged his brother to help us, and he pleaded warmly to the Empress in our behalf.

The principal favourite acted very differently.

* A suburb of Warsaw, captured in 1795 by Souvaroff, who put its inhabitants to the sword. This event was followed by the capitulation of Warsaw, the abdication of King Stanislas Augustus, and the third partition of Poland.

Count Plato Zuboff, as I said above, had granted us the honour of a special audience, and, like other applicants, we had to remind his Excellency of our existence in order to obtain his protection. Every day about eleven o'clock he had a levee, in the literal sense of the word. An immense crowd of petitioners and courtiers of all ranks hastened to assist at his toilet. The street was full of carriages with four or six horses, exactly as at the theatre. Sometimes, after a long period of waiting, the crowd was informed that the Count would not see them on that day, and they then dispersed to come again on the morrow. If Zuboff was disposed to see them, the folding doors were opened, and generals, high civil functionaries, Circassians, and merchants with long beards, crowded into the room. Among the applicants were many Poles who came to claim the restoration of their estates, or redress for some grievance. One of these was Prince Alexander Lubomirski, who intended to sell his estates in order to save the remains of his fortune, which had been involved in the ruin of the country. There was also the Metropolitan of the United Greeks,* named Sosnowski, who came to bow his venerable head to the favourite in order to obtain the restitution of his property and save his church, which the Russian Government had already begun cruelly to persecute. M. Oskierko, a young man of interesting appearance, came to ask for an amnesty for his father, who had been imprisoned or banished to Siberia, and whose fortune had been confiscated.

---

* The union of the Roman and Greek churches in Poland was effected in the 1434.

The number of persons who had been thus treated was immense;* the proportion of them who would be able to avail themselves of the doubtful chances of the so-called amnesty was very small. Some were in chains, others in Siberia; and it was not every one who could get permission to go to St Petersburg. All complaints were suppressed, and the Government officials, who constituted a hierarchy of fabulous extent, did not give the required permission unless they themselves derived some advantage from it. And even when all difficulties had been overcome, and the petitioner had obtained admission to the Russian Court, the usual answer was that given to the Metropolitan of the United Greeks—that the Empress's decrees, whether just or unjust, were irrevocable, that complaint was useless, and that what had been done could not be undone—especially as official avidity closed the doors to every appeal.

To return to the assemblages in the favourite's rooms. Each suitor showed in his face what he wanted. Some expressed grief and a simple desire to defend their property, their honour, and their existence; others betrayed a design to seize somebody else's property, or to keep it if they had already obtained it. Thus some were led by misfortune, others by greed. Others again only came to prostrate themselves before the rising star. It seemed almost impossible to be humiliated on finding one's self in a crowd composed of the first dignitaries of the

* Many of these exiles, being deprived of all means of communication with their friends and relatives in Poland, remained in Siberia for the rest of their lives. There are thousands of Polish families now in Siberia which are descended from the confederates of Bar and men who took part in subsequent Polish insurrections.

Empire, men of the most illustrious names, and generals in command of our provinces, who placed everybody in their districts under tribute and inspired universal fear, and who, after coming in all humility to bow their heads before the favourite, either went away without obtaining a look from him, or stood waiting like messengers while he changed his dress reclining on a sofa.

The following was the usual course at these receptions. When the folding-doors were opened, Zuboff slowly entered the room in a dressing-gown, with scarcely any underclothing, and after nodding slightly to the suitors and courtiers, who stood respectfully in a circle, began his toilet. The servants approached him to dress his hair and powder it. Meanwhile other applicants came in ; they also were honoured by a nod when the Count perceived them ; all watched carefully for an opportunity to catch his eye. We were among those who were always received with a gracious smile. Everybody remained standing, and none dared to speak. It was by his gestures, by an eloquent silence, that each person advocated his cause before the all-powerful favourite. Only those spoke to whom the Count addressed himself, and on these occasions he never talked of the subject of the application. Often he did not say a word, and I do not remember his having ever offered anybody a seat except Field Marshal Soltykoff, who was the chief personage at Court, and had, it was said, made the Zuboffs' fortune ; it was through his intervention that Count Plato had succeeded Mamonoff. The despotic pro-consul Toutoulmin, who at that time was the terror of Podolia and Volhynia, having been invited by one of the servants to take a seat, only ventured to sit on the edge of a chair and got up directly afterwards.

While the favourite was having his hair dressed, his secretary, Gribovsky, usually brought him papers to sign. The applicants used to whisper to each other the sum that was to be paid to induce him to get his master to look favourably on their requests, and he took these presents with as much pride as Gil Blas. When the hair-dressing was over and the papers were signed, the Count put on his uniform or his coat and withdrew into his apartments. All this was done with a nonchalance which he tried to pass off as gravity and dignity; but there was too much artifice in it. When the Count had disappeared, all went to their carriages, more or less discontented at their reception.

We did not plead our case before any Minister, as in Gorski's opinion it was better to rely on the protection of Zuboff alone. We were introduced, however, to several other eminent persons. One of the most important of these was Count Bezborodko. He was a native of Little Russia, and had begun his career under the orders of Marshal Romantzoff. Having been recommended to the Empress by his chief, he soon obtained by his talents, his great aptitude for work, and his extraordinary memory, rapid promotion both as regards fortune and dignities. He was appointed a member of the Committee of Foreign Affairs, and was employed by Catherine in the most secret negotiations. With the outward appearance of a bear, he had a keen wit, a lucid intelligence, and a rare power of mastering a subject. Lazy to a degree, and given up to pleasure, he never set to work till the last moment: but then he worked very rapidly and without stopping. This gained him the esteem of the Empress, who loaded him with rewards. He was the only man of any distinction at Court who did not flatter the Zuboffs; he did not even visit them. All admired his courage; but no one imitated it.

The old Count Osterman, Vice-Chancellor and senior member of the Committee of Foreign Affairs, looked like a figure in a piece of old tapestry. Long, thin, pale, dressed in the ancient fashion with cloth boots, a brown coat, gold buttons, and a black ribbon round his neck, he represented the period of the Empress Elizabeth. He was quoted as an example of honesty, a rare quality in those days; he was grave in manner, and without saying a word he would wave his visitors to their seats with his long arm. He now only appeared at solemn dinners on great occasions, when there was a question of a final despatch or declaration to which his name was to be signed at the head of those of the other members of the Committee. Though advanced in years and of moderate capacity, Count Osterman was valued for his high principle, his good sense, and his great experience. He was the only member of the Council that had opposed the partition of Poland; he represented that such an event would rather be of advantage to Austria and Prussia than to Russia. His advice was not taken, but he should have the credit of it. Since then his influence declined daily, and although still the titular head of the department

of Foreign Affairs, he was really shelved; this, however, did not prevent Catherine from treating him
with every consideration.

At the time of the accession of the Emperor
Paul, Osterman retired to Moscow, with the title
of Chancellor of the Empire. His elder brother,
the Senator, known for his absence of mind, also
lived there. These two old men were still in existence at the time of the coronation of the Emperor
Alexander. As they did not leave any direct heir,
they adopted as their successor Count Tolstoï, who
assumed the name of Tolstoï-Osterman, and afterwards distinguished himself by his bravery at the
battle of Culm, where he lost a leg.

Count Samoïloff, Procurator-General (an office
which at that time comprised the direction of the
Ministries of the Interior, of Justice, and of Finance),
although he was a nephew of Potemkin, was one of
the most assiduous of the flatterers of the Zuboffs,
who, as everybody knew, were declared adversaries
of his late uncle. Samoïloff was not remarkable for
ability, and indeed he made himself ridiculous by his
foolish pride. He was not ill-natured, but, as was
well said by Niemcewicz, he committed evil actions
by his want of discernment, his meanness, and his
pusillanimity, rather than by inherent wickedness.
In making use of him, Catherine wished to prove to
the world that she could govern her immense empire
even with an incapable minister. She took a pride
in showing that she was thoroughly acquainted with
legislation in everything that related to the conduct
of the affairs of the country, and one must in justice

admit that its internal organisation was visibly improved under her reign.    Samoïloff, however, had really no preponderant position in the Government, and any one who had to do business with him generally found reason to regret it—not because he wished to do harm, but because he was incapable of understanding anything clearly, and was at the same time too vain to admit it.    Prince Alexander Lubomirski, who negotiated with him for the purchase of his estates, and our unfortunate fellow-countrymen who were locked up in prison, had only too much reason to know this.

Days and weeks thus passed in constant movement—various scenes, sometimes disagreeable, sometimes unimportant, succeeding each other and at least giving variety to our lives.    But neither our constant anxiety as to the recovery of our parents' fortune, nor the splendour of the society into which we were thrown, effected any change in the deeper sentiments of our hearts.    When we returned to our rooms we always thought of our parents, our sisters, our country, and of the sad position in which we were placed. What we felt most bitterly was that, at the moment when we were passing our time at balls and entertainments, the most heroic of our countrymen were in prison.    It was very difficult and dangerous to get news of them; but fortune favoured us in this respect. After the second partition, when part of the Polish army in Podolia and the Ukraine was forced to enter the Russian service, two young men put on the Russian uniform and managed to obtain places in the service of Plato Zuboff.    One of these was Komar, afterwards the possessor of millions in Podolia, who was not unknown to us, as his father had been employed by my grandfather to manage his affairs; the other was Poradowski, afterwards a valiant general, killed in the war of 1812.

Poradowski had been an officer in the regiment of my brother-in-law, the Prince of Würtemberg; we were thus old acquaintances. These two gentlemen, Poradowski especially, found means of obtaining some news for us about the prisoners. We learnt in this way that Niemcewicz, Konopka, and Kilinski were shut up in the casemates of the fortress; that Kosciuszko had been removed from them and confined somewhere else, and that he was treated with every consideration and generally respected. He was placed in charge of Major Titoff, who, was much attached to him and related various anecdotes of him which were very insignificant (the Major was very rough and ignorant), but, being about such a man as Kosciuszko, were repeated from mouth to mouth. Potocki, Zakrzewski, Mostowski, and Sokolnicki were confined in a house in Liteïna Street. Not being able to do anything for them, we at least gave ourselves the pleasure of often going through this street, either in a carriage or on foot, in the hope of seeing them. Sometimes we succeeded in catching a glimpse of them passing like shadows before our eyes; but they probably never perceived us, as the house was very strictly guarded both within and without. Our hearts beat fast, however, when we raised our eyes to the windows behind which the prisoners were confined. Except Marshal Potocki, they were not personally known to us ; but they had become dear to the heart of every good Pole by the great deeds which they were being made to expiate by sufferings equally cruel and unjust.

When we came back in the evening we used to talk of the impressions of the day. Our worthy friend Gorski did not spare his epithets with regard to those whom he had been obliged to treat with consideration in public. Whenever the name of any of these people (except a few whom he really respected) was pronounced, he immediately added : 'Yes, he is a villain, a rascal,' and so on. These expressions he used particularly with regard to Poles of an equivocal or tarnished reputation. People unfortunately were to be found daily, who thought that their indifference to the fate of their country and their treasonable practices would gain them the favour of the Ministers and the Court. If their former services did not seem to them to have been sufficiently rewarded, they tried to show themselves more base in order to get a larger reward. We had more than once to blush at this disgraceful conduct on the part of some of our countrymen. We were not, however, confounded with them ; the Poles at St Petersburg were divided into two classes, entirely distinct by their qualities, their manners, and their sentiments.

There was no Pole whose society we enjoyed more than that of Prince Alexander Lubomirski. He was a good patriot and a wise and worthy man; the turn of his mind was both tranquil and gay, so that he sometimes evoked merriment out of the saddest events. He often went with us on our visits.

Between one visit and another we gave free course to our observations and criticisms, as sometimes happens when men who are tired of concealing their thoughts, and of feigning to agree by a gesture to what they do not approve, can afterwards, when they are in the society of people with whom they are intimate, freely express their true opinions, and thereby compensate themselves for the constraint and humiliations they have been obliged to suffer.

Notwithstanding these moments of confidential talk, the sad necessity of concealing our sentiments and our sufferings, of dissimulating our thoughts, the impossibility of declaring aloud what we felt— were most painful to us; and they influenced my character and my intellectual faculties in the most disastrous manner. This clog on my frankness made me sombre, extremely silent, and reserved, and I seldom made any remark except to myself. It may be that I was by nature inclined to reticence, but more propitious circumstances would perhaps have made this inclination disappear or might have diminished it, while my position at St Petersburg only aggravated it. During the whole of my life I have not been able to master this tendency, imposed on my youth by an inevitable fate.

At length, after waiting for several months, we were informed that we were to be presented to the Empress at Tsarskoe-Selo, the summer residence of the Court. This was a decisive moment for us, for until that time we had not had the slightest idea of what was to be the result of my father's memorial announcing that he had sent us to St Petersburg and asking for the restitution of his estates. We were advised to come early : the presentation was to take place after church. Meanwhile we went to General Branicki, who was married to a niece of Potemkin's, and had rendered great service to Catherine in the affairs of Poland ; he was still in high favour with her, and an apartment was reserved for him in all the Imperial Palaces. It was very unfortunate that he should have degraded himself by assisting in the ruin of his country. A courtier stained with misdeeds, ambitious, unprincipled, and greedy of wealth, he yet felt himself a Pole at heart, notwithstanding his family relations with the Russians ; and he would have preferred to satisfy his tastes and his ambition in Poland rather than in any other country. He was still proud of the Poland he had lost ; he regretted her and suffered at her humiliation. He detested the Russians, whom he knew well, and he revenged himself upon them by silent contempt and mockery of their faults. On the other hand, his heart was open to some old friends to whom he could speak without fear. His lively, essentially Polish mind and his witty remarks made his conversation gay and interesting. Though very fond of describing his experiences, he avoided all allusion to the fatal league of Targowitza.* He also liked to talk of old times, and then he assumed a *grand seigneur* air which entirely disappeared when he was in the crowd of courtiers whose nothingness he felt, or in the presence of Catherine, who often invited him to play cards with her.

---

* This League, formed by Branicki and others at the instigation of the Empress Catherine, was the precursor of the second partition of Poland.

He seemed really attached to our parents, with whom he had passed many long and eventful years; but he could only help us by advice, which might be expressed in the words 'patience and submission.' He told us of all that passed, and offered us a room at Court on the audience-days, when people had to wait a long time. We accordingly went to him on arriving at Tsarskoe-Selo to wait for the hour when we should be presented. He gave us his instructions, and when we asked whether we were to kiss the Empress's hand, he replied, ' Kiss her where she likes, so long as she gives you back your fortune.' He also showed us how to bend the knee.

The Empress was still in the chapel when those who were to be presented to her went to the reception room. We were first presented to Count Schouvaloff, Grand-Chamberlain, formerly the favourite of the Empress Elizabeth ; he was at that time all-powerful, and was known for his correspondence with D'Alembert, Diderot, Voltaire, and other eminent writers who solicited his favour. It seems that it was by Elizabeth's orders that he engaged Voltaire to write the life of her father Peter, and Catherine, who was then young, also strove to gain his good-will. Count Schouvaloff was now old, but still vigorous, and insisted on performing the functions of his office. We were placed by him in a line near the door through which the Empress was to come. The mass being over, the procession passed two abreast. First came the gentlemen of the chamber, the chamberlains, and the great dignitaries ; then the Empress herself, accompanied by the princes, the princesses, and the ladies of

the Court.   We had no time to look at her closely, for
it was necessary to bend the knee while she pronounced
our names.   Then we stood in a circle with the ladies
and other Court personages, and the Empress walked
round addressing a few words to each person.

She was well advanced in years, but still fresh,
rather short than tall, and very stout.   Her gait, her
demeanour, and the whole of her person were marked
by dignity and grace.   None of her movements were
quick ; all in her was grave and noble ; but she was
like a mountain stream which carries everything with
it in its irresistible current.   Her face, already wrinkled,
but full of expression, showed haughtiness and the
spirit of domination.   On her lips was a perpetual
smile, but to those who remembered her actions, this
studied calm hid the most violent passions and an
inexorable will.   In coming towards us her face
assumed a gentler expression, and with that sweet
look which has been so much praised, she said : ' Your
age reminds me of that of your father when I saw
him for the first time.   I hope this country suits you.'
These few words sufficed to attract to our side a
crowd of courtiers, who began to lavish upon us
compliments even more flattering than those we had
previously received.   We were invited to occupy seats
at the table under the colonnade ; this was a particular honour, as the Empress never gave such invitations but to her private friends.

Our reception by the Empress and the society of
St Petersburg was, considering our age and position,
evidently only the last echo of old traditions relative
to Poland—of the high opinion still held by the

Muscovites as to our leading men. Our family especially, which during the previous century had unfortunately been forced into frequent relations with Russia, was better known than the others. My grandfather and my father were generally respected in Russia, and we met at St Petersburg the two Narischkins and their wives, who had known my father when he was in great favour with Peter III, and with Catherine at the time of her accession.

We were presented on the same day to the Grand-Dukes. Paul received us coldly, but with dignity; his wife, the Grand-Duchess Maria, showed us much consideration, chiefly on account of her brother, whom she wished to reconcile with our sister.* The younger Grand-Dukes received us frankly and graciously.

The wealthier classes at St Petersburg pass the summer in country-houses in the vicinity. Every great nobleman has one, and lives in it as luxuriously as in the capital. As the fine season is short, every one tries to use it to the best advantage, so that for some months the town is deserted. Our visits consequently had to be paid in the country, and as we were always travelling we often returned to town very late. There is scarcely any night in the summer, and the recollection of our moonlight nights in Poland made us sad. Gorski allowed us no breathing time; we had to renew our journeys daily, and neglect no opportunity of multiplying our relations. This was, indeed, the only means of attaining our object, for in spite of our flattering reception at Court, and the repeated recommendations of people

* See note on page 40.

in power, our business was still in suspense.   Catherine, who was well informed as to everything that was going on, knew that we were popular in the capital, and the praise that was lavished upon us could not fail to produce a good impression upon her.

Besides our journeys to the country villas, which were in themselves very fatiguing, we had to go every other Tuesday and on each holiday to Tsarskoe-Selo to assist at Zuboff's toilet.   Having been presented, we were also qualified to go to the Palace, and on these occasions we were usually invited to dine at the principal table.   At the head of this table sat the Empress and the Imperial family, but people of all the higher classes were admitted to it.   We were also advised to take part in the evening entertainments, which in fine weather took place in the garden. The Empress walked there with the whole of her Court, or sat on a bench surrounded by the older courtiers, while the young Grand-Dukes and Grand-Duchesses, with the younger ladies and gentlemen of the Court, played at various games before her on the grass.   The Grand-Duke Paul never took part in these amusements, for when divine service or dinner was over he went to his residence at Pavlovsk. While playing at these games we became more closely acquainted with the Grand-Dukes, who were most amiable to us.

It was the custom for certain of the elect, ourselves included, to go after dinner to Zuboff's rooms. This was not a ceremonious visit; one was supposed to be admitted to a certain familiarity, and to form part of a friendly meeting.   The favourite used to wear a loose coat, and was more nonchalant than ever; he would ask his visitors, who usually were not numerous, to sit down, and would then stretch himself at full length on a sofa. The conversation was characteristic of the host: it was sometimes brightened by Count Cobentzel, the Austrian Ambassador, or by Count Valentine Esterhazy, afterwards master of the ceremonies at Vienna. The latter was a welcome guest at Tsarskoe-Selo, having by his good stories, and a bluntness of manner which is best suited to every kind of flattery, insinuated himself so far into the good graces of Zuboff and the Empress that he obtained some considerable estates in Volhynia. Neither Count Esterhazy nor his wife had any nobility of character or appearance, yet the latter was on a very intimate footing with Catherine. Their scapegrace of a son, a spoilt child brought up in the palace with a Calmouk girl, and amusing by his tricks, greatly contributed to the good fortune of his parents.

It was whispered at the Court that while Count Plato Zuboff was being loaded with favours by his septuagenarian mistress, he paid court to the Princess Elizabeth, the wife of the Grand-Duke Alexander, who was at that time only sixteen. This aspiring and chimerical pretension covered him with ridicule; people were surprised at his having dared to nourish such a thought under the very eyes of Catherine. As for the young Grand-Duchess, she took no notice of him whatever. It seems that he was seized with a love-fit generally after dinner, and he then did nothing but sigh, lie on a sofa with a sad air, and look as if he were oppressed by a heavy burthen on his heart. Nothing would please him but the melancholy and voluptuous sounds of the flute, and he had all the appearance of a man seriously in love. It is said that he had imparted the secret to some of his confidants, who professed to sympathise with his sorrows without appearing to have guessed their cause. His servants alleged that whenever he returned to his rooms after a visit to the Empress, he was prostrate with fatigue and pitiably sad; he then used to pour scent on his handkerchief and receive intimate visitors with an air of depression which was the subject of general remark. Yet he refused to take any rest, alleging that sleep deprives us of some of the most beautiful moments of our lives.

In this manner the summer season of 1795 passed away. In the autumn the Court returned to the Tauris Palace, and our morning visits to the favourite recommenced with more frequency than ever, as the day was approaching when our case was to be decided. The Zuboffs constantly repeated to us that their good-will was not sufficient, and that they could not do all they wished. No good augury was to be discovered in these words. Meanwhile, the suitors became more and more pressing: some sought to recover their estates, while many others set every engine in motion to obtain part of the sequestrated estates for themselves. From the highest to the lowest, each wished for a share of the spoil: for Catherine had not yet said anything as to what she would do with the immense private estates, crown domains, and church property, which she had seized.

The crisis was very interesting, and its solution was looked forward to on all sides with anxiety. How many Russians founded upon it their hopes of enlarging their estates and increasing the number of their serfs or ' souls,'* as they called them ! This gave a new stimulus to sycophancy, not only with regard to the favourite, but to his secretaries, who aped his ridiculous morning receptions, and rehearsed his arrogance before the stupid mob that crowded their ante-chambers. Among the speculators who, like pillagers on a battlefield, sought to enrich themselves at the expense of the vanquished, there were unfortunately some Poles unworthy of the name they bore. Appealing to their services, to their treason to the fatherland, they chose their victims among those who had been convicted or even suspected of patriotism. The more they increased the number of these victims, the greater were their chances of plunder.

Our parents, pressed by their creditors, and anxious about their fate, were still more so for us, as at the time when we were informing them of the friendly receptions we had met with at St Petersburg my mother had received an anonymous letter, written in excellent French, describing in exaggerated language the effect we had produced in society and our favourable reception at Court, but adding that what was most to our credit was that, insensible to all cajoleries, we remained steadfast in our love for our country and our hatred for the Empress Catherine. As it was known that all letters to my family were opened at

---

* Serfage properly so called, *i.e.*, the right of selling a peasant as part of one's property, never existed in Poland ; it was a purely Russian institution.

the post-office, my mother's distress on receiving this communication may easily be imagined.   It was evident that the anonymous letter had only been written with the intention of awakening Catherine's suspicions, and preventing the restitution of my father's estates. It will be recollected that during our stay at Grodno, Prince Repnin had shown us the autograph of a note from Catherine, with regard to an oath of hatred to Russia and the Empress which I was supposed to have taken before my mother.   This story was probably also manufactured by one of our countrymen ; it was absurd to suppose that such a theatrical demonstration should be necessary to inspire us with hatred for such enemies.

The only means left to us for obtaining the recovery of our parents' estates was to resign ourselves to entering the Russian service.   This was the *sine quâ non*, the completion of our sacrifice, the inevitable consequence of our journey to St Petersburg.   At one of our evening visits to Tsarskoe-Selo, Zuboff had told us that the Empress intended to give us commissions as officers of her guard ; and that it was the greatest piece of good fortune that could happen to us that we should thus become part of a glorious and irresistible army, which was strong enough to march across the world without being stopped by any obstacle.   This was indeed the prevalent idea among the officers in the Russian army, and they could not as yet rid themselves of it.   Although we were prepared for the proposal, our hearts failed us when it was made officially.   It was impossible, however, to refuse it, and moreover, having once determined to give ourselves up to the Russians, the form which the sacrifice should take was a matter of very little importance. We considered that it would be unworthy of us to propose the slightest compromise, or to show the least anxiety to obtain any higher position. The highest rank would be as insupportable to us as the lowest; any discussion on this point would show that we attached importance to the proposal, while the fact was that it was to us a matter of perfect indifference.

With bowed heads, feeling like victims, we were ready to accept any suggestion that might be made to us, without enquiry into its consequences. A traveller suddenly placed by some chance in Central Africa, would not attach the least importance to the forms, distinctions, or honours used among the savages, and this was precisely our case. Thrown out of our natural sphere by misfortune, surrounded by violence and compulsion, filled with disgust and despair, we thought it our duty not to express any wish whatever : it was not worth while.

At length came the long-expected ukase announcing the decision of the Government as to the confiscated estates. Catherine distributed a whole mass of them among her favourites, her Ministers, her generals, governors of provinces, and even subaltern officials ; also among some Poles who were traitors to their country. She did not restore my parents' estates, but without mentioning them she made a present of their fortune (amounting, according to the Russian mode of calculation, to 42,000 souls) to my brother and myself. The estates of Latyczew and Kamieniec, which formerly belonged to my father, fell to the lot of Count Markoff. The ukase did not mention my sisters; but this arbitrary and illegal act having always been regarded by my family as invalid, it remained without result both with regard to my sisters and my parents. The property really went back to them, as all we had to do was to send my father full power to dispose unconditionally of the fortune which had been ceded to us.

There had been so much uncertainty as to Catherine's final decision in this matter, that the result was received in society with general satisfaction. We were told that the loss of Latyczew and Kamieniec should be regarded as a fine, and that we had no reason to complain. We thanked Catherine with one knee on the ground, as required by the etiquette of the Court, and almost immediately after we had our uniforms on. Mine was that of the cavalry of the guard; my brother's, that of the Ismaïloff regiment of infantry.

It would not have been proper abruptly to cease our visits to the favourite, and Gorski was too much a man of the world to allow it. We also received several invitations to the concerts in the Tauris Palace, which was regarded as an extraordinary favour for officers of the guard who do not form part of the Court. These were further signs of the Empress's good-will; but they all ceased directly the Court moved to the Winter Palace. We were then classed as officers of the guard, who only go to the palace on Sundays and holidays, when they have to stand at a door next to the diplomatic corps as the Empress goes by. She merely gratified us with a look as she went to the chapel and returned from it. The Grand-Dukes always bowed to us with much grace.

It was for these dress receptions, which were repeated on every Sunday and holiday, that the dandies of the barracks put on their best uniforms, tightened their waists, put pomatum on their hair, and placed themselves in line with the hope of attracting the eyes of the Empress and fascinating her with their tall stature and broad shoulders. It is said that some of them used in days gone by to be promoted to her favour on these occasions; but she was now too old to indulge in such fancies.

The military service in the Guards' regiments was at that time much neglected, but it was necessary to attend drill at least once a year. Some officers really liked the service and performed it, but this was because they chose to do so, and their zeal was thought rather ridiculous by young men of fashion. The generals who commanded us did not take any pains to make us work. We were seldom on guard in the palace, and my turn only came once. As to my brother, being an infantry officer, he was on duty with a detachment of his regiment, which always had to guard the castle at night. The Empress having perceived him, said that now he was on guard she would sleep in peace.

An amusing adventure happened at this time to my friend Gorski. The ukase relating to my father's family had been published, but the order for handing over the property to us had not yet appeared. Plato

Zuboff was entrusted with the task of communicating
the order to the Governor-General Toutoulmin, who
was then at St Petersburg, hoping to participate in
the act of spoliation and to derive illicit advantages
from it; but Zuboff did not hurry. We were therefore obliged to continue to assist at his toilet. One
day the favourite, who had on his shoulders a white
towel, beckoned to Gorski to come to him. The
latter came up at once, and listened with such
attention to Zuboff that he allowed some snuff to drop
from his nose and stain the favourite's towel. The
audience expected some tragical *dénoûment*, but
Gorski, who never lost his presence of mind, finished
what he had to say and returned to his place as if
nothing had happened.

On New Year's Day we were appointed Gentlemen of the Chamber. Court appointments were at
that time held in much higher estimation than they
are now. Ranks at Court stood on the same footing
as corresponding ranks in the army, and took preced-
ence of ranks in the civil service; the consequence
was that families with a great name, or with great
interest, always placed their sons in the Guards, and
tried at the same time to obtain for them an appointment at Court. Being thus raised in the hierarchy
of the *tchin*, they afterwards passed into the civil or
military service with the rank to which they had
been promoted.

Catherine wished the Grand-Duke Constantine to
marry while she was still living, and all preliminary
preparations were made for the establishment of his
household. People intrigued for places either for

themselves or for others, and lists were formed of the gentlemen of the chamber and the chamberlains, the former with the rank of brigadier, and the latter with that of major-general. The Duchess of Saxe-Coburg, accompanied by her three children, had just appeared at St Petersburg, and it is from that time that the elevation of this princely family began. Whenever a princess was wanted at Moscow, a diplomatic agent was sent to the capitals of the small German princes who had pretty daughters to marry, and made a detailed report on the qualities of these princesses, and the moral character and blood-relations of their parents. After reading these reports, the Empress designated the princesses whom she wished to see at St Petersburg, in order to make her selection. She had in her time herself undergone an examination of this kind, and did not think that she was inflicting any humiliation on these ladies by subjecting them to the same ordeal. Indeed all the German princesses were very glad to get a summons of this kind for any of their daughters, and felt very flattered when one of them was chosen as the bride of a Grand-Duke. During the past century Russia had perhaps more prestige—in Germany at least—than she has now, and the young princesses who were destined for that country looked forward to a life the prospect of which singularly pleased their old mothers. They were like the Circassian women who think their fortunes made when they are taken as slaves to inhabit the harems of Turkish pashas. The mothers looked upon the brilliant position of Catherine as a presage for their daughters, and were not repelled by any thought of possible sacrifices, or else only looked upon them as difficulties from which the young Grand-Duchesses could easily extricate themselves, and which therefore need not cause them any anxiety. It was Baron Budberg, then a diplomatic agent, and afterwards Minister of Foreign Affairs, who procured for the Duchess of Saxe-Coburg the happiness of bringing her three daughters to St Petersburg.

The Duchess was very clever, and her daughters were all pretty. It was painful to see this mother offering her daughters like goods for sale, and watching anxiously to discover on which of them would fall the eye of the Empress and the handkerchief of the Grand-Duke Constantine. There was something so humiliating in this conduct that we tried not to notice it, especially as the Duchess and her daughters were in all other points very amiable and worthy of respect. Various anecdotes about the Grand-Duke Constantine were current which were far from confirming the hope that the match would be a happy one. These stories ought to have opened the eyes of the daughters and their mother, but perhaps they thought that as they had come from so far it was too late to go back, or maybe their eyes, fascinated by the splendour of greatness, did not see things in their right light.

Catherine had received the mother and her daughters with open arms; she was continually with them, and while she talked with the mother, her grandsons had plenty of opportunities of becoming acquainted with the daughters, as there were fêtes, soirées, balls, and promenades every day. The Grand-Duke Constantine had received orders from his grandmother to marry one of these princesses ; he was only allowed to choose from among the three. Constantine was then seventeen years old. When he was older, and indeed during the whole of his career, he always proved by his conduct that his passions were independent both of his will and his reason. It was not therefore probable that at so early an age he should have consulted either; he simply obeyed the orders of his all-powerful grandmother.

It was thought in the capital (we did not yet belong to the Court) that the Grand-Duke would select the youngest of the three sisters. The eldest had managed to withdraw by frankly declaring that her heart was not free ; and she was the only one who could congratulate herself on her courage. She had accepted the addresses of a young Austrian officer (afterwards a general) ; her parents, not wishing to oppose her inclinations, finally gave their consent, and she alone of the three sisters was happy.

The appointments of officers of the Guards and of Gentlemen of the Chamber were both sinecures. At the same time this combination of military rank in the Guards regiments, to which no duty was attached, and of honorary rank in the Court, was not without its advantages. It furnished a career of adventure and emotion to young men who were ambitious, rich, and fond of pleasure. They were admitted to the games, dances, soirées, and theatrical performances of the Court—into the interior of that sanctuary in the midst of which people who had real duties to perform could not penetrate unless they had attained the highest ranks. It seemed strange that men without any personal merit should find the gates of the palace open to them, while generals of long service mixed with the crowd in the ante-chambers. We had at least some satisfaction in seeing the terrible Governor-General of a province totally eclipsed in the capital, barely obtaining a look from the favourite, and not daring to show himself in any distinguished society. There was some sweetness in this little revenge; but, the sentiment of social superiority apart, all other relations remained the same; for this governor, who was treated with contempt in the capital, indulged in the same tyranny as before directly he returned to his province : he compensated himself over and over again for the humiliations he had had to put up with, and, sure of impunity, inflicted rapine and persecution on the members of families which he dared not visit at St Petersburg. It was difficult, if not impossible, to obtain justice with regard to the permanent abuses of discretionary power, so long as these abuses were not too revolting—revolting in a country where nothing shocks !—and were covered by certain forms. In the provinces everything was done by officials and secretaries who had no access to society, still less to the Court, and who decided every case in the name of their chiefs, most of whom were either indolent or stupid. To have on one's side the clerks was a sure way of success, for the provincial oppressors and pillagers kept up so close an understanding with the underlings of the senate and the ministerial departments that the truth could not come out any where.

Our appointment as Gentlemen of the Chamber

initiated us into the private habits of the Court, and enabled us to make a closer acquaintance with several high dignitaries and with some young men whom we met in the salons and who became our comrades. It also had the effect of bringing us nearer to the Grand-Dukes.

I will first speak of the ceremonies which attended the marriage of the Grand-Duke Constantine. His choice was well known to the public. The young Princess Julia, who, as the future Grand-Duchess, was to assume the name of Anna, was already being taught the Russian catechism, and was preparing to change her religion. It is said that German princesses who had any chance of marrying a Russian Prince, did not receive any special or profound instruction as to the dogmas which mark the line of distinction between the various Christian religions. This precaution was taken by the prudent parents so that the princesses might change their religion without much conscientious scruple. Be this as it may, the facility with which they adopted the Russian faith certainly gave the statement a colour of truth. They were mostly quite indifferent to religious dogmas, or if not, they adhered secretly to the religion which they had publicly disowned.

The day of renunciation and baptism—for even if you are a Christian you have to be baptised over again when you embrace the Russian religion—came first. The Imperial family and all the courtiers proceeded in splendid dresses to the chapel, which was already occupied by the bishops and the clergy. It was painful to see the young princess advancing in a dress of cloth of gold laden with diamonds, like a victim crowned with flowers, to bow her head to images which were in no way sacred to her, to submit to the exigencies of a ceremony which was opposed to her convictions and her sentiments. It was evident that she did this simply out of deference, knowing opposition was useless, and without attaching the slightest importance to the ceremony.

The Russian rite reminds one rather of pagan than of Christian observances. The bishops and popes, all with long beards, involuntarily recall to one's mind the high priests of antiquity. Everything is calculated for external pomp and to appeal to the senses; there is no provision for that religion of the heart, lifting up the soul to the Creator, which demands tranquillity and reflection. Preaching is a mere form; I have never heard a good sermon in a Russian church either at Court or elsewhere. Moreover, the clergy never preach except on grand occasions. Their sermons are, both by habit and obligation, borrowed to a great extent from the writings of the primitive Slavonic church; this always makes their eloquence subtle and pompous rather than instructive or convincing. Hymns and ceremonial take up the whole time of the service, so that there is none left for doctrine. The services are, in fact, theatrical representations copied direct from those of idolaters. The chalices carried on the acolytes' heads, the opening and closing doors of the sanctuary, the worship before images, the censers constantly in motion, present a scene very like those we read of in connection with pagan sacrifices. One would look in vain for the simplicity and instruction to be found in Protestantism, or the devotion and the tender aspirations of Catholicism ; these bear the stamp of civilization, while the Russian rite is Asiatic and barbarous. There is something strange even in its manifestations of devotion. Thus everybody—young or old, elegant or shabby—takes the sacrament. People who belong to the churches of Western Europe often do not wish or do not dare to approach the holy table, yet they often have more faith and true piety ; their abstention from the sacrament, though sometimes blameable, is accompanied by respect for their religion, and may be merely a consequence of it. In Russia, on the other hand, religious ceremonies are often performed not in satisfaction of one's moral aspirations, but merely as a matter of custom, and the people who go to church turn the hymns and prayers sung by the popes into ridicule. At confession the priest reads to the penitent or penitents (for sometimes several confess their sins at the same time) a list of sins, and the penitent usually does not answer aloud, but when some sin is mentioned of which he is guilty, he murmurs long prayers, often without seeming to pay attention to them, and then goes to take the sacrament.

These reflections occurred to me when I saw the young princess, endowed by nature with gaiety and charm, accepting the new religion without foreseeing her destiny—which, however, it was easy to guess at ; while those of her family who were present seemed to beam with happiness.

Some days afterwards the marriage took place. The princess was given to a youth barely entering manhood, but with a violent temper and savage caprices which had already furnished many a topic of conversation. The ceremonious dinners, balls, entertainments of all kinds, and fireworks lasted for several weeks; but as usual all these noisy diversions, splendid as they were, did not inspire mirth. The marriage ceremony always has a tinge of melancholy; it is a solemn moment which decides the whole future of the persons who are united by it, and those who witness it cannot help reflecting on the fact that at that moment the happiness of two human beings is at stake. This was especially the case at the marriage of the Grand-Duke Constantine; a sinister veil of sadness hovered over the ceremony and the fêtes which followed it. It was a mournful spectacle, this handsome young princess, come from so far to adopt a foreign religion on a foreign soil, to be delivered up to the capricious will of a man who it was evident would never care for her happiness. These fatal presentiments were soon confirmed by the confidential avowals of the Grand-Duke himself. What he related to those with whom he was intimate about his honeymoon was marked by an unexampled want of delicacy towards his wife. She and the wife of the Grand-Duke Alexander became friends. Being both German and both far from their respective families, they were naturally inclined to a mutual confidence which might be their consolation in case of adversity, and might double their happiness if their marriages should prove a success. The Grand-Duchess Elizabeth, who was destined to a more elevated position, and was incomparably more fortunate in the character of her husband, seemed to be the supporter and protectress of her sister-in-law, and a substitute for her mother and sisters, who were soon to leave St Petersburg. The inequality of their respective positions drew the bonds between them still closer.

When the fêtes were over, and the Coburg family had gone, the Court resumed its normal life. Sledging parties were organized; the Empress sometimes wished them to take place in the morning, and the Gentlemen of the Chamber who were on duty were then called to accompany her. On one of these occasions I saw Catherine in a morning négligé and Zuboff coming familiarly out of her room in a pelisse and kid boots—which did not disconcert either the Empress, her favourite, or the bystanders.

In the Winter Palace, so called because the Court inhabited it at that season, the evening assemblies used to take place in a room known as the *salle des diamants*, because the crown jewels were kept in it in glass cupboards. This room communicated on one side with the bedroom and other private rooms of the Empress, and on the other with the rooms allotted to her servants. The throne-room, which was regarded as belonging to the private apartments, separated the servants' rooms from the drawing-rooms beyond. The *chevaliers-gardes*, a detachment of officers selected for their stature and merit, used to sit at the entrance to the throne-room. They were the direct descendants of the famous company of grenadiers who had placed the Empress Elizabeth on the throne, and had been rewarded for this service by all of them who were soldiers being promoted to the rank of officer and made her private guard. This guard was maintained on the same footing until Catherine's death, and it always kept its rich costume.

The ordinary Court assemblies used to take place in the *salle des diamants;* one only saw there people who were on intimate terms with the Imperial family and officers on duty. The Empress used to play cards with Zuboff and other dignitaries. It was remarked that the favourite did not pay much attention either to his sovereign or to the game; he was often absent-minded, and his eyes were constantly turned to the table where the two Grand-Duchesses were with their husbands. It was surprising that the Empress did not notice what was evident to every one else. These evenings would have been terribly dull in any other place, and even in the Empress's salon people were glad they were so short. The Empress did not wait for supper, but used to leave early and withdraw into her room. She bowed with dignity to the princesses and the members of the Court, the folding-doors of her room opened, and then Zuboff, bowing like the Empress, used to go in with her and the doors were shut. The Grand-Dukes and Grand-Duchesses withdrew at the same time as the Empress.

Two snow hills were sometimes erected in the vicinity of the Tauris Palace. The princesses and the whole *personnel* of the Court used to go there to descend in sledges according to the Russian custom. People were very merry at these entertainments, the young men having young and pretty ladies as their partners. One day young Strogonoff gave the officer of police, who wished to prevent his passing, a box on the ear. Strogonoff was reprimanded, and there was an end of the matter. Some excellent concerts were given in the Grand-Duchess's apartments, and at the Hermitage Palace French plays and Italian operas were admirably performed. The Austrian Ambassador, Count de Cobentzel, usually conversed with the Empress; besides these the only persons present were the Grand-Dukes and Grand-Duchesses and people belonging to the Court. These performances took place twice a week, and were very pleasant as there was no constraint of any kind. I still see the audience as it then appeared to me. In front of the stage was the Empress, occupying a double seat owing to her size; next to her was the Count de Cobentzel, with his squint, and his bald head covered with a thick coat of powder, approving everything she said. On either side were the Imperial family, all fresh and pretty faces, except that of the Grand-Duke Constantine; and the rest of the society occupied seats raised in the shape of an amphitheatre.

The Empress was quite satisfied at her second grandson's marriage, and she seemed to revel in the leisure which was given her by the favourable turn in foreign politics. Everything went smoothly: the affairs of unfortunate Poland had been settled according to her wish, the King of Prussia was about to cede the city of Cracow to Austria in compliance with her orders, and all the European monarchies were at her feet, approving and flattering her plans. This was because England and Austria wished to procure her active assistance against France, while Naples, Rome, and Sardinia, fearing the republican movement, sought the same object. The King of Prussia took care not to oppose her in anything. But while Catherine issued the most vehement diplomatic notes against the Revolution and the French Republic, and fomented the whole of Europe against them, she prudently avoided war, observing the vicissitudes of the fortunes of the allies, and taking care not to allow her troops to intervene. While the others were exhausting themselves in sanguinary battles, she twice* robbed Poland of territory and distributed fragments of the booty among her accomplices; she was supreme over the whole of Northern Europe, the terror of the Turks, and proud of the universal homage paid to her. Tranquil at home, she sent troops to Persia under the orders of Valerian Zuboff, for her feminine instincts were always mixed up with the masculine, or rather Macchiavellian, enterprises of her policy. These were the last of her happy days. The victories of Buonaparte in Italy and the conduct of the young King of Sweden were soon to fill with bitterness the last year of her life.

* In the partitions of 1773 and 1792.

# CHAPTER VII

## 1796



BEFORE the break-up of the ice on Lake Ladoga, which generally occurs towards the end of April, St Petersburg usually has a few days of fine weather, with bright sun and a moderate temperature ; and the quays are then full of gaily dressed people walking and driving. The Grand-Duke Alexander was often there either alone or with his wife ; and this was an additional incentive for high society to assemble. I used also to come with my brother, and whenever the Grand-Duke met one of us, he stopped to talk, and showed us particular attention.

These morning meetings were, so to say, a continuation of the Court soirées, and our relations with the Prince daily became more intimate. In the spring the Court moved as usual to the Tauris Palace, where the Empress Catherine professed to live in greater retirement, and only admitted very select company in the evening. The Grand-Duke still came occasionally to the quay ; he told me he was sorry to see me so

seldom, and asked me to come to him to the Tauris
Palace for a walk in the garden, which he wished to
show me.  Spring had already begun, and as generally
happens in this climate, nature had made up for lost
time, and vegetation had rapidly developed itself in a
few days; the trees and fields were green and covered
with flowers.  I went on the day and hour fixed by
the Prince.  I am sorry I did not take note of the
exact date, for that day had a decisive influence on a
great part of my life and on the destinies of my
country.  Thenceforward I became devoted to the
Grand-Duke, and I may say that our conversation
then led to a mutual friendship, followed by a series of
fortunate and unfortunate events, whose results still
make themselves felt and will be perceived for many
years to come.

As soon as I came in, the Grand-Duke took me
by the hand, and proposed that we should go into the
garden, in order, he said, that he might enable me to
judge of the skill of his English gardener.  We walked
about in every direction for three hours, keeping up
an animated conversation all the time.  The Grand-
Duke told me that my conduct and that of my brother,
the resignation we showed in a position which must
be painful to us, and the calm indifference with which
we had received both the smiles and the frowns of
fortune, had gained us his esteem and confidence; that
he divined and approved our sentiments; that he had
felt it necessary to let us know what he really thought,
and that he could not bear the idea that we should
judge him otherwise than as he really was.  He
added that he did not in any way share the ideas and

doctrines of the Cabinet and the Court; and that he was far from approving the policy and conduct of his grandmother, whose principles he condemned. He had wished for the success of Poland in her glorious struggle and had deplored her fall. Kosciuszko, he said, was in his eyes a man who was great by his virtues and the cause which he had defended, which was the cause of humanity and of justice. He added that he detested despotism everywhere, no matter in what way it was exercised; that he loved liberty, to which all men had a right; that he had taken the strongest interest in the French Revolution, and that while condemning its terrible excesses, he wished the French Republic success and rejoiced at its establishment. He spoke to me with veneration of his tutor, M. de la Harpe, as a man of great virtue, of true wisdom, of strict principles, and of energetic character. He owed to him all he knew and any good qualities he might possess—especially those principles of truth and justice which he was happy to bear in his heart and with which M. de la Harpe had inculcated him.

While we were walking about in the garden we several times met the Grand-Duchess, who also was taking a walk. The Grand-Duke told me that he confided his thoughts to his wife, that she alone knew and shared his sentiments, and that I was the only person besides herself to whom he had dared to speak of them since his tutor had gone; that he could not mention them to any Russian, as none were as yet capable even of understanding them; and that I must therefore feel how great a pleasure it would be for him to have in future some one with whom he could talk openly and in entire confidence.

This conversation was, as may be imagined, occasionally interrupted by demonstrations of friendship on his part, and of astonishment, gratitude, and devotion on mine. He bade me farewell, saying that he would try to see me as often as possible, and urging on me the greatest circumspection and secrecy, though at the same time he authorised me to communicate to my brother the subject of our conversation.

I was deeply moved, and could hardly believe my ears. That a Russian Prince, Catherine's successor, her grandson and her favourite child, whom she would have wished to see reigning after her instead of her son, and of whom it was said that he would continue her reign, should disavow and detest his grandmother's principles—should repel the odious policy of Russia—should be a passionate lover of justice and liberty—should pity Poland and wish to see her happy—seemed incredible. And that such noble ideas and great virtues should be able to grow and flourish in such an atmosphere and with such surroundings, was surely little less than a miracle.

I was young, full of exalted sentiments and ideas; extraordinary things did not long astonish me, for I readily believed in anything that seemed to me great and virtuous. I was subjugated by a charm which it is easy to understand: there was so much candour, innocence, resolution which seemed unshakeable, and elevation of soul in the words and countenance of this young prince, that he seemed to me a privileged being whom Providence had sent to this world for the happiness of humanity and of my country. My attachment to him was boundless, and the feeling with which he inspired me at that moment lasted even after the illusions which had given birth to it successively disappeared; it resisted the attacks which Alexander himself made upon it, and it never died in spite of the many events and sad misunderstandings which might have destroyed it. I told my brother of our conversation, and after giving a free rein to our surprise and admiration, we plunged into reveries of a radiant future which seemed to be opening before us. It should be remembered that at that time so-called liberal opinions were much less prevalent than they are now, and had not yet penetrated into all the classes of society and even into the Cabinets of sovereigns. On the contrary, everything that had the appearance of liberalism was anathematised in the Courts and salons of most of the European capitals, and especially in Russia and at St Petersburg, where all the convictions of the old French régime were grafted in an exaggerated form on Russian despotism and servility.

It was assuredly a most fortunate and important incident that in the midst of these elements there should be a prince, the future ruler of Russia, who would necessarily exercise immense influence in Europe, holding such decided and generous opinions entirely opposed to the existing state of things. Now that I look back, forty years afterwards, upon the events which have taken place since that conversation, I see only too well how little they have realised the picture that our youthful imaginations had drawn.

Liberal ideas were at that time in our eyes still surrounded by an aureole which has paled since they have been tested by experience; their realisation had not yet produced the cruel deceptions which have so often disheartened us. That period, in the years 1796 and 1797, was the most brilliant one of the dawn of liberal ideas: the cycle of the French Empire had not yet chilled and dispersed the warmest partisans of the Revolution.

Our Polish sentiments, our wishes, our inexperience—our faith in the ultimate success of justice and liberty—will explain how at that moment we abandoned ourselves with joy to the most seductive illusions. For some days after this remarkable conversation we had not an opportunity of talking with the Grand-Duke; but whenever he met us we exchanged friendly words and sympathetic gestures.

Soon after, the Court left for Tsarskoe-Selo. All the cavalry officers of the guard had to go there on Sundays and holidays to attend at mass, at dinner, and in the evening; some even resided there, either in one of the very inconvenient little houses which surrounded the courtyard opposite the palace, or in the village, where the discomfort was equally great, but where the officers were less under constraint.

Alexander at first urged us to come often, and then to stay at Tsarskoe-Selo, in order, as he said, to have an opportunity of being more with him. He liked our society and wished for it, as it was only with us that he could speak unreservedly. We had a right to come into the Imperial apartments when the Empress went there in the evening, to take part in the promenades and games which took place every fine day, and to join the courtiers who met under the colonnade, a part of the palace which the Empress liked best, and which was close to her apartments. The officers did not on ordinary days dine at the Empress's table unless they were on duty. This happened to me once; I was placed opposite to Catherine and had to wait upon her, which I did with some awkwardness.

We often returned to Tsarskoe-Selo, and soon after we settled there for the season. Our relations with Alexander naturally aroused much interest: it was a kind of freemasonry, but the Grand-Duchess was let into the secret. An intimacy whose object was at that time so recent and so ardently discussed furnished material for conversations which were suspended only to be resumed on the next opportunity. Political opinions which now seem trite and hackneyed were at that time startling on account of their novelty, and the mystery we had to preserve, the idea that we were expressing these opinions under the eyes of a Court encrusted with the prejudices of absolutism and of Ministers puffed up with their supposed infallibility, added interest and piquancy to these relations, which grew more frequent and intimate every day.

The Empress Catherine looked favourably upon the connection which was establishing itself between her grandson and ourselves; she approved it, of course without guessing at its true motive or at its probable consequences. Probably, with her old ideas as to the splendour of the Polish aristocracy, she thought it would be useful to attach an influential family to her grandson. She in no way suspected that this friendship would confirm him in the opinions which she detested and feared—that it would be one of the thousand causes of the progress of liberty in Europe, and of the re-appearance—only for a time, alas!—of Poland, which she had thought she had buried for ever, on the political scene. Her approval of the marked preference shown us by Alexander closed the mouths of all objectors, and encouraged us in continuing our relations, which were so attractive to us in all respects.

The Grand-Duke Constantine, from a spirit of imitation, and seeing that his doing so pleased the Empress, now made great professions of friendship to my brother, invited him to his rooms, and admitted him to the intimacy of his family; but there was no question of politics in this connection. My brother was not in this respect as fortunate as I was; none of the motives which had bound us to Alexander existed in the case of Constantine, and his capricious and violent character, not admitting any impression but that of fear, rendered all intimacy with him undesirable. Alexander, however, requested my brother to take Constantine's overtures in good part, at the same time charging him not to reveal the secret of our political conversations.

At first Alexander was quartered in the palace, and did not yet live in the separate building in the park which the Empress had ordered to be built for him, and which had just been completed. We used to go there for our afternoon walks until

Alexander established himself in the new building, when he was much more free to see us. He often had either my brother or myself to dinner, and a day seldom passed but one of us supped with him also, when the rooms at the palace were quite finished. In the morning we used to take long walks together; the Grand-Duke was very fond of walking and of visiting the villages in the neighbourhood, and it was especially on these occasions that he used to talk of his favourite subjects. He was under the charm of early youth, which creates images and dwells upon them without being checked by impossibilities, and which makes endless projects for a future which seems to it eternal.

His opinions were those of one brought up in the ideas of 1789, who wishes to see republics every-where, and looks upon that form of government as the only one in conformity with the wishes and the rights of humanity. Although I was myself at that time very enthusiastic—although born and brought up in a Republic where the principles of the French Revolution had been accepted with ardour—yet I had constantly to moderate the extreme opinions expressed by Alexander. He held, among other things, that hereditary monarchy was an unjust and absurd institution, and that the supreme authority should be granted not through the accident of birth but by the votes of the nation, which would best know who is most capable of governing it. I repre-sented to him the arguments against this view, the difficulty and the risks of an election, what Poland had suffered from such an institution, and how little

Russia was adapted to or prepared for it.  I added that now at any rate Russia would not gain anything by the change, as she would lose the man who by his benevolent and pure intentions was most worthy of acceding to the throne.  We had incessant discussions on this point.  Sometimes during our long walks we talked of other matters.  We turned from politics to nature, of whose beauties the young Grand-Duke was an enthusiastic admirer.  One had to be a great lover of nature to discover its beauties in the country we walked in; but everything is relative in this world, and the Grand-Duke flew into ecstasies about a flower, the greenness of a tree, or the view over an undulating plain.  There is nothing uglier or less picturesque than the neighbourhood of St Petersburg. Alexander loved gardens and fields, and was fond of agriculture and the rustic beauty of village girls; the occupations and labours of the country, a simple, quiet, and retired life in some pretty farm, in a wide and smiling landscape—such was the dream he would have liked to realise, and to which he was always returning with a sigh.

I knew well that this was not the thing best suited to him; that for so high a destiny more elevation, force, ardour, and self-confidence were necessary than Alexander seemed to possess; that it was not right for a man in his position to wish to rid himself of the enormous burthen which was reserved for him, and to yearn for the pleasures of a quiet life.  It was not enough to perceive and feel the difficulties of his position; he should have been filled with a passionate desire to surmount them.  These reflections occasionally presented themselves to my mind, and even when I felt their truth, they did not diminish my feelings of admiration and devotion for Alexander. His sincerity, his frankness, his self-abandonment to the beautiful illusions that fascinated him, had a charm which it was impossible to resist. Moreover, he was still so young that his character might yet gain the qualities in which it was defective; circumstances and necessities might develop faculties which had not the time or the means of showing themselves; and although he was afterwards much changed, he retained to the last a portion of the tastes and opinions of his youth.

Many people—my countrymen especially—in later years reproached me for having placed too much confidence in Alexander's assurances. I have often maintained against his detractors that his opinions were sincere. The impression produced by the first years of our relations could not be effaced. Assuredly, when Alexander, at the age of eighteen, spoke to me with an effusiveness which relieved his mind, about opinions and sentiments which he concealed from everybody else, it was because he really felt them, and wished to confide them to someone. What other motive could he have had? Whom could he have wished to deceive? He certainly followed the inclination of his heart and expressed his real thoughts.

Besides our political discussions, and the ever-welcome topic of the beauties of nature, and the dream of a quiet country life after the destinies of free Russia should have been secured, Alexander had also a third object to which he ardently devoted himself, and which was not at all in accordance with the others, namely, the army, which was his hobby, as it was that of his father, the Grand-Duke Paul. This prince lived during the summer in his country-house of Pavlovsk, half-a-league from Tsarskoe-Selo. The Empress Catherine had allowed him to keep there for his amusement some battalions of marines. He was Grand-Admiral, and this honorary title gave him certain privileges. The Empress pretended not to perceive that Paul made too large a use of them, and that following the example of Peter III, his unfortunate father, he had created for himself a sort of little army, which he clothed and endeavoured to drill according to the system he had observed in Prussia when he visited Frederick the Great at Berlin. This army was, I believe, composed in all of twelve very small battalions, some cuirassiers, dragoons, and hussars, and some guns; and all promotions in this force were in the Grand-Duke's hands. The uniforms were very eccentric in cut, and were in striking contrast to the uniforms of the Russian army in this respect; they were a caricature of the uniforms of the troops of the Great Frederick. Many people of society and of the Court had obtained permission to wear these uniforms, and they were the only courtiers whom Paul allowed to attend at his country-houses. Among them was M. Rostopchin, who played an important part after Paul became Emperor, and was afterwards much talked about at the time of the fire of Moscow. These courtiers took their uniforms with them whenever they went to Pavlovsk or to Gatchina, another country-house belonging to the Grand-Duke, or even to his soirées in the Winter Palace, for Paul never went to his mother's in the evening. People only appeared in this costume, however, in Paul's apartments; everywhere else it was tabooed so long as Catherine lived, and people laughed at it with impunity.

The two young Grand-Dukes had commands in Paul's army. They gave themselves up to their duties with the zeal of young men who are for the first time given something to do, and the Court and the public compared them to children playing at soldiers. This, however, produced no impression upon them; all they thought of was to obey the wishes and even the eccentricities of their father.

There occurred at the parades and manœuvres of this miniature army grave events, defeats, ups and downs of favour, misfortunes or successes, which sometimes caused the deepest consternation, at others the greatest joy. I heard of them from the two brothers, who took a pleasure in relating all the vicissitudes of the Court of Pavlovsk. To these young princes it was an active life which gave them importance, in a restricted circle no doubt, but where they played a part which, while it flattered their vanity, contented their juvenile activity without much expenditure of thought. The regulated uniformity of their grandmother's Court, on the other hand, where they had no serious occupation, was often inexpressibly tedious to them. Their bodily fatigues, the necessity of keeping out of the way of their grandmother when they returned tired from their drill, in a dress which they had to take off at once—even their father's scoldings, which they greatly feared—gave attractions to this mode of life, which was very different from the one which the public of St Petersburg and the views of Catherine had marked out for them.

The Empress did not know how to appeal to the imagination of her grand-children or how to give them active and varied occupation. Their father was more successful, and this was a great evil which had unfortunate consequences. The young Grand-Dukes thought themselves, and were in reality, more a part of the army of Gatchina than of the Russian army. Gatchina was Paul's favourite Palace and his residence during the autumn; he was there at some distance from St Petersburg, and could give himself up without constraint to his hobbies. The Grand-Dukes regretted not to be able to go there, but they liked to imitate the manners of Paul's troopers, and, in speaking of what was done in his little army, to say, 'That is our way, after the fashion of Gatchina' (*Po naszemu, po Gatchinski*).

I recollect that the Empress one day thought of sending Alexander with General Kutuzoff, to inspect the fortresses on the Swedish frontier. The young Prince did not seem to like the idea, and it was consequently abandoned. The minutiæ of the military service and the habit of attaching extreme importance to it gave an unfortunate turn to Alexander's mind; he took a liking for it of which he could not afterwards rid himself, even after he had perceived its absurdity. During the whole of his reign he had a mania for parade which made him lose much precious time while he was on the throne, and prevented him during his youth from working usefully and acquiring indispensable knowledge. This was also the bond of union between Alexander and Constantine, and it often gave the latter too great an influence over his brother, for Constantine was well versed in military science so far as mere drill is concerned, and his brother could not help having a great idea of him in this respect. It was the constant subject of their most animated conversations.

The Empress Catherine saw the understanding between Paul and his sons with displeasure, though she did not foresee all its consequences, for if she had, she would probably have prohibited it. Alexander said to me one day as he was returning from Pavlovsk: 'They do us the honour of fearing us,' meaning that Catherine was beginning to be anxious at the maintenance of the troops at Pavlovsk, and at the sort of concert which had been established between Paul and his sons. Alexander was flattered at the thought of having inspired some fear in the Empress; but I doubt whether she really felt any such sentiment; if she did so it was very occasionally and to a very slight extent. Catherine knew too well the cowardly spirit of her son, the ridiculous appearance of his troops, and the disfavour with which they were regarded by the public and the rest of the army, to trouble herself by fearing them. She remained in peace under the protection of a single company of Grenadiers, while Paul was manœuvring with his little army half-a-league off.

The Empress Elizabeth had done the same at Peter-hoff with Peter III, who lived at Oranienbaum, surrounded by a corps of devoted Holsteiners; she also knew the extreme pusillanimity of her successor, and perhaps also his kind heart. Various rumours have been current as to the legitimacy of Paul I; but those who saw the extreme resemblance of character and conduct between him and Peter III, could have no doubt that he was really Peter's son.

During this year an event occurred which had vast consequences for Europe and terrible ones for Poland. The Grand-Duchess Maria gave birth to a son. The baptismal ceremony took place in the chapel of Tsarskoe-Selo; the whole Court attended in full dress in the spacious hall which precedes the chapel. The ceremony, as was to be expected, was a most sumptuous one. The ambassadors were present, and some of them held the child at the baptismal font as the representatives of their respective sovereigns. He was named Nicholas! Looking at him then in his swaddling clothes as he moved about impatiently while the long baptismal ceremony of the Russian Church was being performed, I little thought that this weak and pretty child would one day become the scourge of my country.

Among the motives which attracted the young Grand-Dukes to their father was one that was more noble and sensible than those above mentioned. They were painfully impressed by the cruelty of Catherine in not allowing her sons and their wives to enjoy the company of their children even in extreme youth. As soon as the Grand-Duchess Maria could leave her bed, her child was taken away from her to be brought up with his brothers and sisters under the eyes of their grandmother. Not one of them was, so long as Catherine lived, left to the care of its parents or remained with them. Such injustice revolted the young princes and alienated them from the Empress. Moreover, Alexander's views as to his grandmother's policy did not make him disposed to follow her wishes when he could do otherwise. He always found some objection to raise, and showed nothing but *ennui* and indifference when he was called upon to take part, however little, in a government which was not at that time at all in accordance with his opinions. Constantine, who did not share his brother's liberal views, yet agreed with him in his disapproval of the manners and character of Catherine. I have heard him more than once speak about his grandmother, even after she was dead, with outrageous rudeness and in the coarsest terms.

The stay of the Court at Tsarskoe-Selo was drawing to a close. This gave us a feeling of sadness : we regretted our unceremonious meetings, our daily conversations, our long walks in the gardens and in the country. We had gathered the first flower of youthful and confiding affection—we had enjoyed the dreams with which it is soothed. Whatever we may do, we do not again find sensations so strong and fresh ; as we advance in life they become more and more rare.

The Court proceeded as usual to the Tauris Palace for the season which precedes the winter. Alexander was not so often visible, and could not have us so often with him at his meals. Yet our relations, the partial interruption of which caused us much regret, continued to be the object of our constant pre-occupations.

# CHAPTER VIII

## 1796



THE FATE OF THE PRISONERS.—REFLECTIONS ON ALEXANDER'S EDU-
CATION.—ARRIVAL OF THE KING OF SWEDEN.—FAILURE OF THE
NEGOTIATIONS FOR HIS MARRIAGE WITH THE GRAND-DUCHESS
ALEXANDRA.—DEATH OF CATHERINE.

OUR friendship with Alexander had not helped us to
improve the condition of our countrymen who were
imprisoned in the town or the casemates of the fortress.
We often talked of them and of Kosciuszko; Alexander
always spoke with enthusiasm of the devotion and
the great deeds of these martyrs of patriotism, and
was indignant at the unjust tyranny of which they
were the victims.   But, bound by his position, and
timid from a consciousness of his youth and inexperience, he took no part in affairs of State, and did
not even think he ought to seek to interfere in them.
He accordingly had no influence or even contact with
those who had the management of affairs.

It is certainly astonishing that Catherine, who
took pleasure in the thought that Alexander would
continue her reign and her glory, did not think of
preparing him for this task by familiarising him in
his early youth with the various branches of govern-

ment.   Nothing of the sort was attempted.   Perhaps
he would not have acquired very correct information
on many things, but he would have been saved from
the want of occupation.   Yet it would seem that either
the Empress and her council had no such idea, or that
the former did not at least insist upon its being carried
out.   Alexander's education remained incomplete at the
time of his marriage, in consequence of the departure
of M. de la Harpe.   He was then eighteen years old ;
he had no regular occupation, he was not even advised
to work, and in the absence of any more practical
task he was not given any plan of reading which
might have helped him in the difficult career for which
he was destined.   I often spoke to him on this
subject, both then and later.   I proposed that he
should read various books on history, legislation, and
politics.   He saw that they would do him good, and
really wished to read them ; but a Court life makes
any continued occupation impossible.   While he was
Grand-Duke, Alexander did not read to the end a
single serious book.   I do not think he could have
done so when he became Emperor, and the whole
burthen of a despotic government was cast upon him.
The life of a Court is fatiguing and yet idle.   It
furnishes a thousand excuses for indolence, and one
is constantly busy in doing nothing.   When Alexander
came to his rooms it was to take rest and not to
work.   He read by fits and starts, without ardour
or zeal.   The passion of acquiring knowledge was not
sufficiently strong in him ; he was married too young,
and he did not perceive that he still knew very little.
Yet he felt the importance of useful study, and

wished to enter upon it; but his will was not sufficiently strong to overcome the daily obstacles presented by the duties and unpleasantnesses of life. The few years of his early youth thus passed away, and he lost precious opportunities which he had in abundance so long as Catherine was alive, and of which he might have recovered a part even under the Emperor Paul.

While he was Grand-Duke, and even during the first years of his reign, Alexander remained what his education had made him, and was very different from what he became later on when he followed his natural propensities. It must be concluded that nature had endowed him with rare qualities, as notwithstanding the education he had received he became the most amiable sovereign of his age and the cause of Napoleon's fall. After having reigned for some years, and acquired the experience entailed by the necessity of at once taking the management of important affairs of State and by constant intercourse with men in office, people were surprised to find him not only an accomplished man of the world, but an able politician, with a penetrating and subtle mind, writing without assistance excellent letters on complicated and difficult subjects, and always amiable, even in the most serious conversations. What would he have become had his education been less neglected and more adapted to the duties which were to occupy his life? M. de la Harpe was the only man that can be mentioned with praise among those to whom the education of the two Grand-Dukes was entrusted. I do not know exactly who were the persons directed by Catherine to select their tutors; probably they were some encyclopædists of the clique of Grimm or the Baron d'Holbach.

M. de la Harpe does not seem to have directed Alexander into any serious course of study, though he had acquired so much influence over the Grand-Duke's mind and heart that I believe he could have made him do anything. Alexander derived from his teaching only some superficial knowledge: his information was neither positive nor complete. M. de la Harpe inspired him with the love of humanity, of justice, and even of equality and liberty for all; he prevented the prejudices and flatteries which surrounded him from stifling his noble instincts. It was a great merit in M. de la Harpe to have inspired and developed these generous sentiments in a Russian Grand-Duke, but Alexander's mind was not penetrated by them; it was filled with vague phrases, and M. de la Harpe did not sufficiently make him reflect on the immense difficulty of realising these ideas—on the thorny task of finding means to obtain possible results. He was, however, merely charged with Alexander's literary education; the choice which was made of those who were to look after his moral training was extraordinary. Count Nicholas Soltykoff, who was a subaltern during the Seven Years' War and had not since seen any active service (which did not prevent him from attaining the highest rank in the army), was the superintendent of the education of the two Grand-Dukes. Short, with a large head, affected, nervous, and of health so delicate that it required constant attention (he could not wear braces,

and constantly hitched up his breeches like a sailor)
he had the reputation of being the most astute
courtier in Russia.  When Catherine discovered that
her favourite Momonoff had formed intimate relations
with one of her maids of honour, she ordered the
culprits to come before her, had them married, and
then expelled them from her Court; after which
Soltykoff at once introduced to her Plato Zuboff, who
speedily became Momonoff's successor.  The elevation
of Zuboff so angered Prince Potemkin that he declared he would go to St Petersburg to extract this
tooth (*zub* means tooth in Russian); but he died
before he could carry out his intention, and Soltykoff
remained in high favour with the Empress.  He was
not only the channel by which her messages and
admonitions were conveyed to the young princes; he
also acted as intermediary whenever Catherine had
anything to communicate to the Grand-Duke Paul.
Soltykoff used to omit or soften any words which
seemed too disagreeable or severe in the orders or the
reproaches of his Imperial mistress, and he did the
same with regard to the replies he had to convey to
her.  This gave satisfaction to both sides; he alone
knew the truth, and took good care not to tell it.
There was perhaps some merit in doing this success-
fully, but Count Soltykoff was certainly not the man to
direct the education of the young heir to the throne,
or to make a salutary impression on his character.

Besides Count Soltykoff, each of the two princes
had a special director of studies with assistants.  The
selection of the two directors was even more extraordinary than that of the chief superintendent.  The

one attached to Alexander was Count Protasoff, whose only merit was to be the brother of the *demoiselle à portrait*,* an old favourite of the Empress as to whose functions, though she was a good woman at heart, there were all sorts of extraordinary anecdotes. Constantine's special director was Count Sacken, a weak-minded man who was the object of incessant ridicule on the part of his pupil. Count Protasoff may justly be said to have been a complete imbecile; Alexander did not laugh at him, but he had never the smallest esteem for him. The assistant directors were selected solely by favour, with the exception of Mouravieff, whom Alexander when he ascended the throne made his secretary for petitions, and afterwards appointed curator of the schools of the Moscow district. He was a worthy man and was said to be well-informed, but he was so timid as to be almost incapable of transacting business. I should also not omit Baron Budberg, who some years later succeeded me as Minister of Foreign affairs.

Such surroundings could only produce a bad effect on the young princes, and the qualities displayed by Alexander are the more astonishing and praiseworthy, as he developed them notwithstanding the education he had received and the examples which were before his eyes.

At the close of the stay in the Tauris Palace in 1796, the last year Catherine was there with her Court, the chief topic was the approaching arrival of

---

* A decoration which gives the rank of Field Marshal. Three ladies under Paul, and one under Nicholas, obtained this rank.

the young King of Sweden, who came to marry the eldest of the Grand-Duchesses. The Empress directed the ladies of the Court to learn the French *contre-danse*, which was then the favourite dance at the Court of Stockholm, and this was the daily occupation of all at Court who were dancers. The King of Sweden was received with exquisite politeness. He came with the Regent, his uncle, Duke of Sudermania, and with a numerous suite. The Swedish costume, which resembled that formerly worn in Spain, produced a fine effect at the receptions, balls, and other fêtes which were given to the young King and his suite; all the Court entertainments were for them. The Grand-Duchesses only danced with Swedes, and never did a Court show more courtesy to strangers.

While the fêtes were going on at the Winter Palace, and balls, concerts, and *montagnes Russes* were daily repeated at the Tauris Palace, the King of Sweden was admitted to the presence of the Grand-Duchess Alexandra as her future husband. She was of rare beauty and sweetness of character; to know her was to admire her, and his daily interview with her could only add to the motives which seemed to prompt the King of Sweden to unite himself by family ties with the House of Romanoff. The Duke of Sudermania was strongly in favour of the match, and had urged his nephew to go to St Petersburg so as to leave no doubt as to his intentions. All that remained was to agree as to forms and the treaty to be drawn up between the two powers; and this did not seem of a nature to cause any difficulty.

As both parties were said to be agreed, no negotiation seemed requisite, and the task of framing the necessary documents was entrusted to Count Markoff, whom the Zuboffs were putting forward in order to eclipse Count Bezborodko, who, though he had refused to cringe to them, yet kept his place and his credit with the Empress.

After some gay and brilliant weeks the day of the betrothal was fixed; the ceremony was to take place in the evening. The Archbishops of St Petersburg and Novgorod, with a numerous suite of clergy, went to the chapel where the ceremony was to take place. The whole of the Court, the Ministers, the Senate, and many generals were assembled in the waiting-room. We waited for several hours. It was getting late, and people observed whisperings among those who were likely to be well informed, and movements to and fro of persons proceeding to the Empress's apartments, all of whom came out at a quick pace. At length, after four hours of suspense, we were told that the ceremony would not take place. The Empress sent to apologise to the Archbishops who had come in their pontifical robes, to the ladies in panniers, and to the rest of the Court, and announced to them that the ceremony had been postponed owing to some unexpected difficulties.

Soon after it became known that the marriage was broken off. Count Markoff, frivolous through self-sufficiency, and inattentive through pride and disregard of all but himself, was persuaded that all was arranged without troubling himself to put the arrangement in writing and get it signed. It was when the signature was required that difficulties arose. King Gustavus IV wished to limit the liberty which the Russian princess who was to be his queen should enjoy in following the rites of her religion. The Swedes, who are staunch Protestants, had made objections on this subject, but Count Markoff took no notice, and proceeded to act as if the matter had already been decided, thinking that the Swedes would not dare to withdraw at the last moment, and that the Grand-Duchess's beauty would succeed where the ability of the Russian Ministers had failed. But he was wrong in his calculations. The young King was the most zealous Protestant in his kingdom, and he would never consent to his wife having a public Russian chapel at Stockholm. His Ministers, his Councillors, and the Regent himself, fearing the consequences of an affront to the Empress, pressed him to yield or to seek a compromise, but in vain. Instead of inclining to the Russian demands, Gustavus IV, in the prolonged conversations which he had with the Grand-Duchess, strove to convert her, and almost made her promise that she would adopt the religion of her husband and of the country in which she was to reside.

The King obstinately rejected all the proposals which Count Markoff made to him with the view of overcoming the difficulty; he was told in vain that he would expose himself to a war with Russia, if after having gone so far, he broke off the marriage just as it was about to be concluded. All was useless— even the fixing of the day, the presence of Catherine in her Imperial robes, and the convocation of the clergy and the whole Court, failed to move the Swedish King.

The young sovereign's obstinacy at first made the Swedes anxious, then frightened them, but finally pleased them; they were proud at their King having shown so much character. As for the Russians, all the excitement produced by the appearance of the King of Sweden in their capital was changed into a sombre silence of disappointment and vexation. The next day was the birthday of one of the little Grand-Duchesses (afterwards the Queen of Holland), and there was a Court ball in honour of the occasion. The Empress appeared with her eternal smile, but her eyes had a sombre expression of sadness and anger; people admired the impassive dignity with which she received her guests. The King of Sweden and his suite showed constraint, but not embarrassment; there was a stiffness of manner both on their part and on that of the Empress which communicated itself to the whole company. The Grand-Duke Paul expressed great irritation, though I suspect he was not really displeased at the blunder made by the Cabinet. As for Alexander, he was indignant at the insult which had been offered to his sister, but cast the blame of it on Count Markoff; and the Empress was very glad to see her grandson share her indignation.

The Swedish cloaks and plumes seemed no longer to float in the air with the same grace as before and shared in the general constraint; they were no longer the fashion. Some minuets were danced with even more gravity than usual. My brother was one of the dancers, and he acquitted himself very well.

Two days after the King left with his suite, and St Petersburg remained gloomy and silent. People were astounded at what had happened; they could not believe that a 'little kinglet' should thus dare to insult the Sovereign of all the Russias. What would she do now? It was impossible for Catherine II to pocket the affront and not take her revenge. So at least people said. As for the Court, the Grand-Duke Paul was at Gatchina, while the Empress remained in her apartments; and it was thought that she was preparing some resolute step which would make the King of Sweden repent his obstinacy. But it was Catherine herself that succumbed.

It was November; the weather was cold and foggy, and harmonised with the appearance of the Court and the Winter Palace after the fêtes which had animated them. Alexander continued his walks on the quays, and one day he met my brother. After having walked for some time, they stopped at the door of the lodgings where we lived. I had just come down and we were talking together, when a footman of the Court who was looking for Alexander came to tell him that Count Soltykoff wished to see him as soon as possible. Alexander immediately followed the man, not guessing the cause of this urgent message.

The Empress had had an apoplectic stroke. Her feet had for sometime been much swollen, and she had not done anything that her physicians had prescribed, but had taken some quack remedies which her chambermaids had recommended to her. The humiliation inflicted upon her by the King of Sweden was too hard a blow to her pride, and it may be said that Gustavus IV shortened her life by several years. She got up the same day, to all appearance in good health, and remained in her dressing-room longer than usual. The valet in waiting, not seeing her returning, went to the door, and opening it softly saw the Empress lying unconscious. When Zuboff came, she opened her eyes, placed her hand on her heart with an expression of extreme pain, and then shut them for ever. This was the only and the last sign of life and consciousness which she gave. The physicians hastened to the room and for three days used all the resources of their science, but in vain.

Next day the news of the Empress's fatal illness spread in the town. Those who had the entry to the Court went there with a feeling of terror, of anxiety, and of doubt as to the future. Both the town and the Court were in the greatest confusion. Most of those who were present in the room expressed sincere grief; the pale and distorted features of many betrayed a fear of losing the position they enjoyed and perhaps of being obliged to render an account of their administration. My brother and myself were among the spectators of this scene of regret and of terror. Zuboff, with his hair dishevelled and an air of consternation on his face, attracted all eyes. Both himself and all those whose fortunes he had made were naturally in despair. At one time he was busy burning papers which might have compromised him; at others he came to see if the remedies tried by the physicians gave any hope. All was disorder, and etiquette was abandoned.

We entered the room where the Empress was lying on the ground on mattresses, lifeless, like a machine whose movement has ceased.

When Zuboff learnt from the physicians that there was no longer any hope or possibility of her reviving, he sent his brother, after destroying a number of papers, to the Emperor Paul at Gatchina to inform him of his mother's death. Although Paul had for some time thought of the chances of this event soon occurring, he was thunderstruck, and arrived at St Petersburg much troubled with the uncertainty of what was awaiting him, and doubting whether his mother would not recover after all. So long as her body moved, although she had completely lost consciousness, Paul did not make use of the power which had already accrued to him, and remained concealed in his mother's room, or in his own apartments. He came with the whole of his family to see the lifeless body, and repeated this lugubrious visit twice a day.

# CHAPTER IX

## 1796-1798



NEVER was there any change of scene at a theatre so
sudden and so complete as the change of affairs at
the accession of Paul I. In less than a day costumes,
manners, occupations, all were altered. Under
Catherine we had worn our collars so high as to cover
the lower part of the face ; we now had to wear them
narrow and turned down, showing thin necks and
prominent jaws which until then had remained unseen.
The hair was dressed *en pigeon* in the Parisian
fashion ; it was worn flat and long behind, with two
very stiff curls above the ears, and a pigtail, all well
pomatumed and powdered. Hitherto the dandies had
endeavoured to give a more graceful cut to their
uniforms, which they often wore unbuttoned, while
now the Prussian uniform of Frederick the Great,

already used by the troops of Gatchina, was adopted for the army generally. The military parade became the chief occupation of each day; it was then that the most important events occurred, making the Emperor either indulgent and lavish of his favours, or severe and even terrible, for the rest of the day.

Soon the little army of Gatchina made its solemn entry into St Petersburg. It was to be a model for the Guards and the whole Russian army. The Grand-Dukes were much agitated, for they had been ordered to place themselves at the head of these troops and take them to the capital. They had to appear before a public which had hitherto been ill-disposed, and, which was more difficult, to give satisfaction to the Emperor. But all went off well. The Gatchina troops were placed in battle array on the great square of the Winter Palace, in the midst of a timid crowd astounded at the sight of soldiers entirely different from those it had been accustomed to see. The troops defiled in good order before the Emperor, who expressed to his sons his satisfaction at the manner in which they had carried out this first manifestation of his rule. They were much pleased at the Emperor's words, and the new comers were at first quartered on the inhabitants, who hastened to give them a friendly reception. In the evening grenadiers with pointed hats like Prussians, whose hosts had freely treated them with wine and brandy, were to be seen staggering about dead drunk in the streets.

During the long years of his retirement Paul had

planned out everything he proposed to do directly he should come into power. Changes and novelties accordingly succeeded each other with extraordinary rapidity. The men of Gatchina were divided among the three regiments of foot guards and the regiment of horse guards. The regiment of cavalier guards was supplied with silver helmets and cuirasses which were manufactured for the occasion, as these articles of uniform had ceased to be worn in the Russian army. The officers of Gatchina were all promoted, and one soon saw old soldiers and courtly officers of the Guards obliged either to retire or to obey the commands of ill-bred braggarts, whose names they had never mentioned except to laugh at them.

In the midst of all that was eccentric and ridiculous about the first acts of Paul's reign, there was an element of seriousness and justice ; thus the Emperor ordered the young courtiers to choose some career and devote themselves to it. No one was allowed to join the Guards as an amateur; and the service became so severe that most young men preferred a civil career.

Scarcely had Paul come into power when his first thought was to render a striking act of homage to the memory of his father, and at the same time a sort of verdict upon those who were guilty of his death. During the first few days after the death of the Empress and the time necessary for embalming her body, the whole of the Court, including ladies and high functionaries of State, were ordered to watch by the body day and night in the Imperial apartments, and soon after the Emperor directed that his

father's remains should be exhumed and carried in
ceremony from the Nevski convent to the Winter
Palace to be deposited by the side of Catherine. There
were still living three or four of those who had been
accused of complicity in the murder of Peter III.
They were at that time privates or sub-officers in the
Guards; they were now great nobles with large
incomes. Among them was the Court-Marshal,
Prince Bariatynski, who was disliked because he was
rude, ill-bred, and ill-tempered, and Passeyk, Governor-General of White Russia, who was the Empress's
aide-de-camp. There were very few who possessed
this title, and it gave very high rank and great
privileges. When the Imperial aide-de-camp was
present he alone held a cane, commanded at the
palace, and watched over the safety of his sovereign.
Passeyk disappeared on the day of Catherine's death,
and Prince Bariatynski almost died of fear. He and
some of his accomplices were forced to watch at the
coffin of Peter III and follow his body in the funeral
procession. Count Alexis Orloff, one of the principal
assassins of the late Emperor, was the only one who
walked with a firm step and a countenance apparently
tranquil.

The Emperor Paul had the two coffins placed
together on a bier, where they were exposed (that of
Catherine was open) to the sight of the crowd. The
high functionaries and ladies of the Court continued
their service by the side of the bodies night and day
for six weeks; this gave rise to singular meetings,
and created friendly relations among people who had
previously been almost strangers. Others, after pass-

ing twenty-four hours together at a stretch, and finding each other amiable and pleasant companions, never saw their fellow-watchers again.

The burial of Peter and Catherine took place six weeks after; they were interred in the same vault of the Nevski convent. All the troops of the garrison of St Petersburg and of its neighbourhood accompanied the procession, and all who belonged to the Court or Government went on foot to the convent, which is at the other end of the town. Neither the men nor the women were allowed to wear powder, and as they had not altered their way of dressing the hair, this was very unbecoming. Mourning was strictly prescribed and observed; and as the funeral procession was extremely long, the ceremony lasted a whole day.

The Emperor kept the apartments at the Winter Palace which he had occupied when he was Grand-Duke. The waiting-room was usually filled by those who were admitted to his presence. People sometimes passed the whole day there, and went as if to a diverting entertainment. There was incessant agitation and excitement: footmen and aides-de-camp in thick boots ran about knocking against each other, some carrying the Emperor's orders, others looking for some one they were sent to summon to his presence. Those who were called ran up breathless, not knowing what was to be their fate; many entered the room and left it immediately after with radiant faces and a red or blue sash across their chests. One of those whom I saw coming out of the room was Count Nicholas Züboff, appointed Grand-Equerry

and decorated with a blue ribbon for having been
the first to bring Paul the news of his accession.
Changes were occurring daily. Nearly all that
had been great and distinguished under Catherine
became neglected and insignificant under Paul. New
persons were constantly coming forward and being
advanced with extraordinary rapidity, and almost all
the Ministers were changed.

Plato Zuboff, who looked like a dethroned
sovereign, went to his estates in Lithuania, a vast
domain which Catherine had given him (and the
desire to acquire which was one of the causes of the
two last partitions of Poland), sufficient to furnish
him with ample means to defray the expense of his
travels. He visited several towns in Germany.
Some women of ready wit and easy virtue made him
lose that air of languid dignity which he usually wore.
He recognised the advantages of an independent
existence, but soon his ambition and vanity, leading
him to believe that he was destined still to play a
great part, brought him back to St Petersburg, and
rendered him more guilty and unfortunate than he
had ever been before.

The only one of Catherine's Ministers whom Paul
adopted was Count Bezborodko; this was because of
his remarkable talents, his high reputation, and perhaps also because he had neglected Zuboff when he
was at the height of his favour with the Empress.
Paul felt that while he was still inexperienced in the
art of government he needed Bezborodko's services,
and he loaded him with distinctions of all kinds. He
made him a prince, consulted him when he wanted to

carry out some of his hobbies, and doubled his property by grants of land and of considerable sums in cash.

The Emperor's choice of his Ministers was always directed by one dominant idea—that of surrounding himself with servants on whom he could entirely rely; for from the moment of his accession he foresaw and dreaded a Palace revolution. He raised to the highest positions persons who were quite insignificant and often the least capable of performing their new duties. They were chiefly taken from among those (or their descendants or relations), whom he had employed at Gatchina, and who had given proofs of fidelity to his father. He persecuted and dismissed those who had been in favour with his mother; this alone made him suspect them. The fear of treason was continually present to his mind during the whole of his reign. He erred in the selection, and especially in the extent, of the means which he employed to save his life and his power; they only precipitated his deplorable end. Among the men whom he suspected, he persecuted some with implacable rigour, while he retained others at their posts and endeavoured to secure their fidelity by presents; this, however, only made them ungrateful. Never was there a sovereign more terrible in his severity, or more liberal when he was in a generous mood. But there was no certainty in his favour. A single word uttered intentionally or by accident in a conversation, the shadow of a suspicion, sufficed to make him persecute those whom he had protected. The greatest favourites of to-day feared to be driven from Court on the morrow, and banished to a distant province. Yet the Emperor wished to be just. Notwithstanding his capricious and disorderly impulses, he had a profound feeling of equity, which often caused him to perform praiseworthy actions. It often happened that after he had dismissed some one whom he had badly treated, he called him back, embraced him, almost asked his pardon, confessed that he was wrong, that he had unjustly suspected him, and gave him presents to make up for his past severities. He inspired all the officials of his empire with the terrors which he often felt himself, and this universal fear produced salutary effects. While at St Petersburg and at the centre of Government the uncertainty of the morrow tormented and agitated people's minds, in the provinces, the civil governors, the governors-general, and the troops, fearing lest the abuses they committed should reach the Emperor's ears, and they should some day be suddenly dismissed without any form of trial and banished to Siberia, paid more attention to their duties, treated their subordinates with more humanity, and refrained from abuses of a flagrant kind. In the Polish Provinces especially the inhabitants felt the change, and the reign of Paul is still mentioned there as a period when there were less abuses and acts of oppression and injustice than at any other time when Poland was under foreign rule.

One of Paul's first and most generous thoughts after his accession, was to liberate the Polish prisoners. Like his father, when he visited Ivan VI in his prison, Paul went himself to Kosciuszko and ordered him to be treated with the greatest consideration, telling him that if he had been on the throne at the time, he would not have consented to the partition of Poland, and that he regretted that so unjust and impolitic a deed had been committed; but that it was not now in his power to withdraw it. At Kosciuszko's request he liberated all the other prisoners, only requiring them to take the oath of allegiance. Whenever Paul did not grant a request made by Kosciuszko on behalf of his countrymen, he excused himself by alleging that he was obliged to pay attention to the representations of his Ministers, who prevented him from following his inclination in this respect. Kosciuszko, oppressed by a feeling of sadness, covered with wounds which were not yet healed, and bearing on his face an expression of despair, of touching resignation, almost of remorse at being still alive and having failed to save his country, greatly interested the Emperor and did not inspire him with the least fear or suspicion. He often used to visit Kosciuszko, accompanied by the whole of the Imperial family, which showed real interest and almost affection for the unfortunate patriot. Alexander no doubt felt these generous sentiments more than anybody, but his duties at that time entirely absorbed him, so that at first I could hardly see him. Since Paul's accession our relations had become more rare and more difficult, and his extreme fear of his father prevented him from expressing on his own account to Kosciuszko what he had long felt with regard to him.

We were each called to the palace to sign an assurance that Marshal Potocki would not enter on any enterprise prejudicial to the State, and to be guarantees for his conduct at our own risk. This obligation had to be expressed clearly and precisely in writing. The meeting was a numerous one. Prince Kourakin, the new Vice-Chancellor, was present, and was directed to see that each document clearly expressed the obligations undertaken by the signer of it. My brother and I signed without hesitation; we had long felt too much esteem and family attachment for the Marshal to hesitate to give this general assurance which alone could restore him to liberty. Some raised difficulties, others went away directly they learnt the object of the meeting. Among the latter was Count Irenœus Chreptowicz, the son of the Chancellor of that name who had done the most to induce King Stanislas Augustus to join the Confederation of Targowitza,* and who soon became entirely Russian. The number of signatures, however, was sufficiently large to induce the Emperor to liberate Count Potocki.

One may imagine how happy the prisoners were to see each other again after so long and painful a confinement, though their happiness was mingled with regret. The most illustrious members of the Grand Diet of 1788-92† were assembled there : Count Potocki, Count Thaddeus Mostowski, Julian Niemcewicz; Zakrzewski, mayor of Warsaw, known by his integrity, his patriotism, and his great courage ; General Sokolnicki, who voluntarily went to prison with him, not wishing to leave him ; and Kilinski and

* See page 84.

† The Diet which passed the famous Constitution of the 3rd of May 1791 (see page 52).

Kapostasz, worthy citizens of Warsaw, the first a master bootmaker, and the second a money-changer, who exercised great influence over the population of that city. We saw them every day. After having had the happiness of being liberated from prison and of seeing each other, they had to disperse in different directions. The Emperor lavished presents of money on Kosciuszko to make him independent, and the latter was obliged to accept them. When he arrived in America, however, he sent them back with a letter expressing his gratitude and that of the other prisoners.

On Twelfth-day, one of the most solemn festivals of the Russian Church, there was a great military parade in the Russian fashion, and the Emperor wished the day to be celebrated with all possible pomp. The Guards and all the regiments in the neighbourhood were posted on the banks of the Neva, between the Winter Palace and the Admiralty. The Imperial family alighted there, and the Emperor took the command of the troops in person; he liked to put himself forward on these occasions. He defiled at the head of the army together with the Grand-Dukes before the Empress and the Princesses. I thought this march past would never end. The cold was intense, and we were in Court dress, with silk stockings; although we wore warm coats, we were almost frozen. My arms and legs were numbed, and I and several others, feeling that our lives were in danger, stamped our feet and moved our arms about to keep up the circulation. I could not stand this martyrdom, and went home, where it took me some hours to get warm.   My fingers have since that day lost all feeling whenever there was the slightest cold.

Our King, Stanislas Augustus, with whom we had dined during our six months' stay at Grodno, was invited by Paul immediately after his accession to come to St Petersburg.   During Paul's journey abroad (in 1785 I think) with his wife, they had passed through Southern Poland, and King Stanislas Augustus had left Warsaw to meet them.   The principal reception took place in the Palace of Wiszniovice, which belonged to Count Mniszek, Grand Marshal of the Crown.   This palace was a princely abode that had belonged to the Wiszniowiecki family, now extinct, whose last heir had married a Mniszek, the descendant of the one whose daughter was for some time seated on the throne of the Russian Czars.*   The apartments of the palace were full of valuable historical portraits.   Among them was that of the famous Marina and of Dimitri; there were also pictures representing their consecration at Moscow.

It was in this beautiful palace that the King of Poland welcomed the Grand-Duke of Russia to his kingdom.   Stanislas Augustus had the gift of amiability, and Paul took a liking to him; he also made himself agreeable to the Grand-Duchess Maria. They had several confidential interviews, at which perhaps promises, or at least hopes, which were never realised, were expressed that when Paul should come into power, he would repay to his host a hundredfold the splendid reception given him in Poland.   It is

---

* Marina Mniszek, married to 'the false' Dimitri 18 May 1605.

said that Marshal Mniszek at that time hoped that the goodwill of Catherine's successor might one day bring them even to the throne, to which he might perhaps have thought he had a claim as the heir of Wiszniowiecki * and the descendant of the father of the celebrated Czarina. The story goes that in the course of a familiar conversation with him the Grand-Duchess, showing her diamonds to make her hosts remark the beauty of a diadem in precious stones which was in her jewel-box, placed it on the head of the King's niece, and then on that of the Grand Marshal. 'I accept the augury,' said the latter, carried away by an impulse of naïveté or of empty vanity which he probably regretted immediately afterwards.

By inviting to his Court the prisoner-King from his confinement at Grodno—an invitation in which the Empress Maria heartily concurred—Paul made some return for the hospitality he had received, and gladly found an opportunity of showing himself more generous than his mother had been. The King was received at St Petersburg with all the honours due to a sovereign. On approaching the capital he was met by chamberlains and other high dignitaries, who complimented him on behalf of the Emperor and the members of the Imperial family. Paul offered him one of his palaces, furnished it magnificently, and did all he could to make the King's stay at St Petersburg agreeable. There were mutual receptions and banquets, and at first no cloud obscured the friendly relations which seemed to be a continuation of those

---

* Michael Wiszniowiecki, King of Poland from 1669 to 1675.

of Wiszniowiec ; but there was no talk of Stanislas returning to his kingdom, except perhaps that the Emperor told him, as he had done to Kosciuszko, that it was impossible to undo what had been done, however unjustly, by the Empress Catherine.

The first years of Paul's reign were marked by a curious confusion ; they were a series of moving incidents and of singular and ridiculous scenes, which seemed to foreshadow the reversal of the existing state of things and the establishment of a new one, not radically, but only in outward form. The civil officials and generals were constantly changed, and promotion was given without any enquiry as to the capacity of those whom seniority placed in ranks to which they had never hoped to attain.

The Emperor's only consideration in the decisions he gave, was that his will, although the fruit of impulse and not of reflection, should at once be executed. The terror which he inspired ensured submission to his most unexpected and most eccentric commands. The parades daily gave rise to singular and provoking incidents. Generals and other officers of rank received for mere trifles, degradations or distinctions which only unpardonable faults or great services to the State could have justified.

Paul had forbidden round hats, which he regarded as a sign of liberalism. If a poor man, with an old round hat on his head, showed himself in the crowd which witnessed the parades, an aide-de-camp immediately pursued the culprit, who fled to avoid being bastinadoed at the first guard-house. The chase was often continued in the streets, to the great amusement of the people, who hoped the unhappy man would succeed in making his escape.

Lord Whitworth, the British Ambassador, was obliged to have a hat of peculiar shape made for him, so as to be able to walk about in the morning without contravening the Emperor's orders.

Paul drove through the town daily in a sledge or an open carriage, accompanied by one of his aides-de-camp. When he met a carriage it stopped, the coachman and footmen had to take off their caps, and the persons in the carriage had to alight and make a profound bow to the Emperor, who observed whether it was sufficiently respectful. Sometimes women, with their children trembling with fright, were seen descending into the snow in a hard frost, or into the mud during a thaw, to accomplish this salutation. Paul always thought that people wished to slight him as they did when he was Grand-Duke; he liked everywhere to meet with marks of fear and submission. When people went out into the streets in carriages or on foot, all took care to avoid meeting their Imperial master; they fled at his approach and went down a side street or hid under a gateway. Another dangerous person to meet was the terrible Archaroff, Grand-Master of Police, who also drove through the town to see that everything was being done according to his orders. He prohibited rapid driving in sledges, which is one of the greatest pleasures of a Russian; and when he perceived a sledge which seemed to go at a forbidden pace he at once ordered it to be seized, had the coachman flogged, and then appropriated both sledge and coachman to his own use for any period he pleased, while the occupant of the sledge had to walk home. This once happened to my brother. He had driven out in a sledge and met the Emperor, upon which he at once jumped to the ground. As he passed, Paul cried out to him, 'You might have broken your neck.' On his return, M. Archaroff sent by the Emperor's orders for my brother's horses and his sledge, and used them for a week, after which he returned them.

Both at Court and at parade the Emperor wished to establish strict exactitude in the ceremonies, in the way of approaching him and the Empress, and in the number and kind of salutations to be made. The Grand-Master of the Ceremonies, Natouyeff, treated the courtiers like recruits who do not yet know their drill and in what order they ought to march. Whenever they met the Emperor they had first to make a profound bow, and then, with one knee on the ground, apply a sounding kiss to the Emperor's hand while he kissed them on the cheek. The same genuflexion had to take place when they approached the Empress, after which they had to withdraw without turning their backs, which often caused confusion, as they trod on the toes of the other courtiers who were coming forward to perform the same ceremony. Thanks to the efforts of the Grand-Master of the Ceremonies, the courtiers at length learnt to go through this manœuvre without a hitch, and Paul, satisfied at the look of fear and submission which he saw on their faces, then made the etiquette less rigid. My brother and I had to go through this ordeal, and in doing so we nearly fell into disgrace. The

Emperor and Empress were once present at the christening of a child in the Chapel of the Palace. We were on duty together with two chamberlains, and we had to be ready to precede their Majesties as they left their apartments. We were late, and when the time for the ceremony came we were not at our posts. Paul, not seeing his escort as he came out of his room, flew into a terrible rage. We arrived breathless with haste, and found all the courtiers assembled at the closed door of the chapel, anxious to see what would happen. The door opened ; Paul came out and passed before us with a threatening look, making furious gestures and breathing hard as he generally did when he was angry and wished to inspire terror. Our punishment, however, was slight ; we were simply ordered to remain in our apartments and not leave them until further orders. Alexander interfered on our behalf, explained that we had not received our orders in time, and pleaded in our favour so effectively, with the assistance of Koutayschoff,* the Emperor's barber, that in a fortnight's time we were free. Soon after we entered the army, in conformity with the rule that every officer of the Court must take up an active career.

Our rank in the army was that of brigadier, the one usually given to gentlemen of the chamber ; and by a special favour due to the preference shown to us by the Grand-Dukes, I was appointed aide-de-camp to Alexander and my brother to Constantine. These appointments greatly pleased us, as they attached us more closely to the Grand-Dukes and relieved us of the functions of the Court, for which we had no vocation. Our duties consisted in accompanying the Grand-Dukes at military parades, and in standing behind them when the Emperor passed the officers in review. He used to address his sons by the title of Monseigneur, and then returned to place himself in the midst of the officers and superintend the drill which usually preceded the regular parade.

We constantly saw the Grand-Dukes in our capacity of aides-de-camp. Both of them were absorbed by their Court, family, and military functions, and by endless details connected with their command of the two regiments of the Guards. The whole morning was taken up by these occupations, which involved more bodily fatigue than mental work, although great attention was necessary not to omit any of the minute details of the service. Alexander almost always dined with the Emperor. The afternoon was the only time when one could speak to him more freely, but he was generally too tired by his work of the morning, and he took some rest until the evening, when he had to go to the Empress.

In the beginning of the spring of 1797 the Emperor went to Moscow for his coronation. All the society of St Petersburg followed him. It was still very cold, and the *habitués* of the salons of St Petersburg were to be seen passing each other on the roads, wrapped up in furs and reclining in sledges, all hastening to the ancient capital of the Empire. Moscow had at that time a characteristic appearance, which must have greatly changed since it was burnt down and rebuilt. It was like a collection of towns communicating with each other not only by gardens and parks, but by vast fields. People often had to drive for an hour to pay a visit in another part of the city. Everywhere, by the side of ugly huts, were sumptuous palaces, inhabited by the Galitzins, the Dolgoroukis, and other families with historic names— great noblemen who consoled themselves by the luxury in which they lived for the vexations and disappointments they had experienced at Court. In the midst of this vast city was the Kremlin, a sort of fortress surrounded by a crenelated wall, outside which the tradesmen had their principal shops in a series of bazaars. The ancient residence of the Muscovite Grand-Dukes, full of old associations, was the place where the ceremony of coronation was to be performed. It lasted several days. Paul had stopped for the night outside the barriers of the town, and made his solemn entry into the Kremlin on the following day, with an immense suite. He first went to the cathedral, where Plato, Archbishop of Moscow, who was regarded as the ablest and most learned prelate of the Russian Church, complimented the Emperor in biblical language. Then took place the coronation, the return to the palace with the same solemnity, and finally the Imperial banquet, at which the sovereigns and their families were served on a raised platform and under a magnificent canopy by the high officers of the Crown. Various minor ceremonies took place during the following days. The Emperor appeared in them all; he was passionately fond of display, and was proud of his figure and his grace. Whenever he appeared in public he walked with a measured step, and tried to look tall and majestic, though he was really short; it was only when he entered his apartments that he showed the fatigue which his efforts had cost him. Each ceremony was preceded by a dress rehearsal, in order that everybody should know where to place himself and what to do. My brother and myself of course had to take part in the ceremonies as aides-de-camp to the Grand-Dukes. The Emperor was as active and busy as a stage manager, and looked after the smallest details of costume and decoration. He liked to appear to the best advantage before the ladies, and once he stood at the head of his favourite battalion of the Guard with a halbert, to do honour to the Empress, whom he had crowned with his own hand.

Paul ordered the King of Poland to follow him to Moscow, and insisted on his being present at all the solemnities of the coronation. He had to join the brilliant suite which surrounded the Emperor and his family—a sad part for a King to play. During divine service and the ceremonies which preceded the coronation, and were very long and tedious, Stanislas Augustus was so tired out that he sat down in the tribune which had been assigned to him. Paul at once remarked this, and sent a messenger to tell him to stand up so long as they remained in the church; and the poor King had no alternative but to submit.

When the ceremonies were over, the Emperor and his family left the Kremlin to go to a more spacious residence, called the Petrovski Palace, in another quarter of the town. He gave up the rest of his time at Moscow to fêtes, parades, and military exercises.

There were fireworks and public banquets both at Moscow and at St Petersburg, and the nobility gave the Emperor a ball in a vast hall where they usually met. These fêtes were somewhat tedious, and did not give satisfaction either to Paul or to his hosts. Numerous deputations from all the provinces of the empire were ordered to salute the Emperor and present addresses of submission. The delegates from the Polish provinces had an air of great constraint and depression. All of them had been citizens of an independent Poland ; all had distinguished themselves either in their palatinates, at the last Diet, or in appointments of State. They saw their King relegated to a side gallery, and had to pass him to kneel before a foreign prince and declare themselves his subjects. I met several of my acquaintances, but could not feel any pleasure at seeing them again under such circumstances. I was struck by the change in their appearance ; they looked confused and humiliated. Among the delegates from Lithuania was Bukaty, who had for several years occupied the post of Polish Minister in England. He was a man of simple manners and great good sense, and had acquired the esteem of the English people and their Government. Several of his English friends gave as a token of their friendship their names to his children at their christening. I had often dined with him in London with my mother. He was at that time stout, in good health, and in excellent spirits. He was now thin, his face was pale and haggard, his clothes, which in England fitted tight to his body, now hung about him in loose folds ; he walked with bent head and an uncertain step—he was a picture of what Poland had become. No satisfactory or consoling word came from his mouth. Soon after his return to his home at Minsk he died.

The death of Catherine and the accession of Paul, which brought Alexander nearer to the throne, had so far in no way changed the latter's political opinions; on the contrary, all that had happened since these events seemed to confirm him in his views, and the resolutions he thought he could execute. When he had a few moments of leisure after his military labours, to which he devoted himself with zeal and with a desire to carry out the wishes of his father, he always spoke of his plans and the future he wished to prepare for Russia. The despotism of his father— sometimes eccentric, terrible, and even cruel—and its immediate and probable effects, produced a lively and painful impression on Alexander's generous mind, which was full of ideas of liberty and justice. He was at the same time appalled at the extent of the diffi- culties which awaited him and were rapidly advancing upon him. The ceremonies of the coronation, which he would have to undergo some day, and which were totally opposed to his principles and his natural tastes, contributed to strengthen him in his views.

My brother and myself having obtained three months' leave to see our parents in Poland, Alexander was uneasy at the prospect of remaining without any one who could understand him or in whom he could confide. His anxiety increased as the time for our departure arrived. He asked me to leave him a draft proclamation expressing his resolutions, in case he should be called to the throne during our absence. In spite of my objections he insisted upon my doing this, and I ultimately complied to quiet him. My draft set forth the evils of the régime under which Russia had up to that time existed, and the benefits of the one which Alexander proposed to introduce; the blessings of liberty and justice which Russia would enjoy after the obstacles to her prosperity had been removed; and his resolution to abdicate after having accomplished this task, in order that some one more worthy than himself to be in power should be called upon to consolidate and perfect the great work which he had inaugurated.

I need not say how little all these reasonings and fine phrases, which I endeavoured to bring into connection as much as possible, were applicable to the true state of affairs. Alexander was delighted at my work, which satisfied his fancy of the moment—a very noble, but at bottom a very selfish one, as while wishing to secure his country's happiness as he then saw it, he at the same time desired to be free to withdraw from a position which he feared and disliked, and to live quietly in retirement where he would enjoy at a distance the good he had done. Alexander put the paper in his pocket with great satisfaction and thanked me effusively for my work. It reassured him as to his future. He thought that with this paper in his desk he would be prepared for the events which fate might suddenly bring : a strange and almost incredible effect of the dreams and illusions which youth cherishes even in circumstances where experience soonest chills the heart! I do not know what became of the paper. I believe Alexander did not show it to any-body, and he never spoke to me about it again. I hope he burnt it, seeing how unreasonable was what he had asked me to write—which indeed I never doubted.

While we were talking about these chimeras a new incident gave a more practical character to Alexander's intentions. Since my arrival at St Petersburg, one of the houses which I most visited was that of Count Strogonoff. I had become, so to say, part of his family. The friendship, indeed the affection shown to me by the old Count has left me recollections which will be always dear to me, and which fill me with gratitude. I was on intimate terms with his son Paul and his friend M. de Novosiltzoff, said to be a distant relation of the family, both of whom were of about the same age as myself. The young Countess was a lady of much distinction, good, amiable and witty; without being exactly beautiful, she had more than beauty, the gift of pleasing and charming all who came near her. The old Count had long lived in Paris under Louis XV; like most Russian noblemen, he wished his son to be brought up by a Frenchman. He even sent him to France with his tutor, M. Romme, a man of ability, and, as I was assured, of high principle, but an enthusiastic admirer of Rousseau. He proposed to make an Emile of his pupil, a plan which did not displease the old Count, whose generous propensities and loving heart had inclined him to some of the doctrines of the philosopher of Geneva. Count Paul was accordingly placed in M. Romme's charge, and the latter made him go on walking tours and endeavoured to give him an education in which Rousseau's precepts were followed and perhaps too closely imitated. When the French Revolution broke out, and the revolutionists boasted that they were following Rousseau's teaching, M. Romme strongly sympathised with it, and wished to combine what he regarded as his duties as a citizen with those which he had undertaken with his pupil. Frequent occasions presented themselves of showing him in practice the principles M. Romme had inculcated in theory. Both master and pupil eagerly took part in the revolutionary scenes which were then succeeding each other in France with alarming rapidity, and joined the Jacobin club, whose meetings they regularly attended. Count Strogonoff was informed of this by the Russian embassy, which had not yet left Paris, and also, I believe, by the letters of M. Romme himself, who thought he could not complete the education of Count Paul more effectively than by making him take part in a practical course of his teacher's doctrines.

M. de Novosiltzoff was then sent to Paris to withdraw his young friend from the charge of a tutor whose zeal had become so dangerous, and he acquitted himself of his commission with great skill. He managed to overcome the resistance of M. Romme, and his regret at the separation of, as he said, two friends who understood each other so well. Notwithstanding the attachment of the young Count for his tutor, he was persuaded to return to St Petersburg, where he was soon made to perceive the danger to which he had been exposed. His opinions changed entirely, but he always retained in his character and his principles of action some traits of his first education.

The general tone of conversation in Count Strogonoff's house had always been, so to say, liberal and somewhat critical; the doings of the Court were a favourite topic. Yet the old Count was always on good terms with the Empress Catherine. She liked to see in him a man who had known her old friends the encyclopædists, and who was not a stranger to any of the doctrines or sayings of that sect. This permitted him sometimes to speak frankly even to herself or in her presence. He has often told me that being admitted to the Empress's toilet, a privilege granted only to the most distinguished noblemen of the Court, he was once there when she was preparing to give an audience to a deputation from the Confederation of Targowitza, which had come to thank her for the 'signal benefits' she had conferred upon Poland (in depriving her of the constitution of the 3rd of May,* and soon after taking her finest provinces at the second partition). When it was announced that the deputation had arrived, and that the Empress was about to enter the throne-room to listen to the false speeches which were to be addressed to her, Count Strogonoff laughed and said : 'Your Majesty will not have any difficulty in replying to the eloquent thanks of these gentlemen ; all you can say is that really they have nothing to thank you for.' This remark did not please the Empress. She took it in cold silence, and went out to receive homages

* See page 52.

the absurdity of which she probably felt.   Despotic
sovereigns should spare those whom they oppress the
necessity of telling them falsehoods by which nobody
is deceived.

The service rendered by M. de Novosiltzoff to the
Strogonoff family, by bringing back the young Count
to Russia, had strengthened the friendship for him
both of the father and the son.   He became the
adviser of the family in all circumstances, and took a
pride in having an independent character, in acting
according to fixed principles, and in not tolerating any
unjust constraint.   He had been attached as aide-de-
camp to the Prince of Nassau when he was charged
with the command of the Russian fleet against the
Swedes, and he had also accompanied him at the siege
of Warsaw in 1794.   He thought he had deserved
the military cross, and he indignantly refused the civil
cross of Vladimir with which the Empress wished
to decorate him.   He insisted on sending it back, and
it was only with great difficulty that he was appeased
on being shown the risks he would run by taking such
a step.   He finally consented to wear the cross, when
a knot of ribbon was added to it, signifying that it
was the reward of military prowess.

M. de Novosiltzoff had wit, penetration, and great
aptitude for work, but an extreme love of pleasure
and sensual enjoyments ; this had prevented him from
reading many books, and from acquiring any sound
knowledge of law, of legislation, or of political economy,
though he had studied all these subjects.   He had a
facile philosophy which strove to be free from all pre-
judice, but which did not seem to impair the clear and

decided qualities of his mind. These qualities were reflected as in a glass in the young Count Strogonoff. The opinions and feelings of these two young men had a spirit of justice, of sincerity, of European enlightenment which at that time was scarcely ever to be found in Russia, and which was the foundation of the intimate friendship and reciprocal confidence between us of which I have spoken. They often asked me questions about Alexander ; and I thought that while maintaining a certain reserve, I could without indiscretion communicate to them some of the statements he had made to me, and the generous projects which he entertained. They fully appreciated the extreme importance of what I told them.

I spoke of my two friends to Alexander ; he had already remarked Count Paul, and I told him that their convictions resembled his own, that he could rely on their sentiments and their discretion, and that they wished to see him in private, to offer him their services, and to ascertain what would have to be done to carry out his noble impulses. Alexander consented to their being informed of his secret plans and associated in his designs. I spoke to them on the subject at St Petersburg, immediately after Paul's accession, but the arrangement was not finally completed until after the coronation at Moscow. It was agreed that we should meet on a certain day and hour in a retired spot, and that Alexander should join us. Novosiltzoff prepared himself for the conference by translating into Russian a fragment of a French work whose title I do not remember, which related to advice given to a young prince about to ascend the throne, and desirous of making his country happy and of knowing how to set about it. The portion which Novosiltzoff translated was only the introduction, where the subject was treated generally, each special branch of Government being dealt with in detail in the body of the work. He was to translate the rest of the book, but he never did so. The succinct review, however, of the obligations of the head of a State and the labours which should occupy him was listened to by Alexander with much attention and satisfaction. It contained well-chosen views and general deductions as to the foundations of national prosperity, with a scheme of the measures necessary for promoting it. The author had introduced some eloquent passages which went straight to the young prince's generous and patriotic heart. Novosiltzoff wrote Russian with elegance; his style was clear and seemed to me harmonious. Alexander praised him highly, and assured both him and Count Paul that he adopted the principles expressed in the work, which were indeed his own. He urged Novosiltzoff to complete the translation and then forward it to him, in order that he might be able more maturely to consider its contents and some day put its theories into practice. From that day the young Count Strogonoff and Novosiltzoff shared in the confidence which Alexander had bestowed upon me, and were admitted to our understanding, so long kept a secret. This afterwards produced serious results, and the admission of two zealous Russian patriots to Alexander's confidence, naturally began to dissipate the illusions of our first dreams—so attractive to me as holding out the prospect of the independence of my country, and to Alexander as leading him to believe in the possibility of tranquil retirement from State affairs. These dreams were not, however, at once abandoned; we adhered to them in spite of hard facts which gradually destroyed them. Alexander constantly reverted to his plans, seeking in them consolation for a near future whose approach and whose burthens he already felt. He could not make up his mind to lose the hope of another future, more distant and more in conformity with his wishes; his imagination presented it to him under such attractive colours, that it was even after the conversation which I have described that he insisted upon having the draft proclamation which I mentioned above.

Alexander's new friends perceived his inclination for a quiet life, relieved of the cares which the Crown would impose upon him; they said with justice that this could neither promote his fame nor the happiness of his country, which should be his sole object. They took every occasion of opposing these egotistical leanings, while pretending not to know of them. I understood Alexander's views, and I could not entirely condemn them, though I did not conceal from him my belief that they were impracticable. The consequence was that his confidence in me grew stronger. It continued, after many vicissitudes, for a considerable time, and did not cease until after I had left St Petersburg.

At the conference which took place during the coronation it was decided that Novosiltzoff, who was in bad odour on account of the opinions he was supposed to hold and his known independent spirit, should leave Russia until it should be possible to recall him, and that he should pass the interval in England. Alexander obtained a passport for him through Rostopchin, the Minister for War, who was beginning to be in high favour with the Emperor. This Minister had been one of his most assiduous courtiers at Gatchina and Pavlovsk before his accession to the throne. He was, I think, the only able man who had attached himself to Paul's person before he became Emperor. Alexander, who during Catherine's reign was devoted to his father, had remarked Rostopchin, and had felt great esteem and friendship for him. These relations were afterwards converted by Court intrigues into coldness and opposition ; but at that time they still existed, and Rostopchin was also on friendly terms with Novosiltzoff, for both had found fault with the Government. Although, however, he had promised Novosiltzoff a passport, he did not at once carry out his promise, and when I reminded him of it, he expressed impatience and suspicion at the political importance which he said appeared to be attached to this journey. The passport came at last, and Novosiltzoff proceeded to St Petersburg and thence to England, where he remained during the whole of the period of Paul's reign. He completed his studies there, and entered into relations with English statesmen which were afterwards very useful to him.

Our leave having been granted, my brother and myself, accompanied by Gorski, left for Pulawy, where our parents were impatiently expecting us after an absence of two years which had given them much anxiety and care. The time we passed with them, in the place where we had lived in our happy youth, was one of great joy to us, though it was somewhat marred by the prospect of having soon to go back again to St Petersburg, where we knew that fresh trials and troubles were awaiting us. We talked of nothing but Alexander's good qualities and the hopes we had of him. Our parents listened with astonishment, anxiety, and doubt. I received at Pulawy several letters from Alexander full of friendly expressions; they were brought by various persons, among others by the Archduke Palatine, who had just married the Grand-Duchess Alexandra. This obtained for me a friendly reception from the Archduke when I passed through Pesth in 1812.

My mother was anxious for our safety. She feared lest we should be denounced and the object of our relations with Alexander be betrayed. This was the topic of all our conversations.

The Governor of Galicia, Count Erdödy, came at this time to pay my father a visit.* A Hungarian by birth, he was preoccupied with an idea which he was constantly talking about. He wished to prove to the Poles that the best thing that could happen to them would be to be united to Hungary; for, he said, the Emperor of Austria had only put forward his claims to Galicia as King of Hungary. This language on the part of a high Austrian functionary proved how much strength the Magyar element still possessed.

---

* Pulawy then formed part of Austria, together with Lublin, Sandomir, and Cracow.

The annexation of Galicia to Hungary, if it had been possible, would doubtless have brought great material advantages to Galicia, would have conferred upon her a free government, and would especially have protected her against the many evils which she suffered during the fifty years which preceded the year 1848. What would have been the immediate result of such an annexation at that period it is difficult to guess. In any case the Poles would have gladly fraternised with the Hungarians; yet public opinion and the Polish national spirit would probably have been opposed to such a measure, besides which I do not think the Austrian Government of that time would ever have agreed to it.

Pulawy was just then recovering from a two-fold pillage to which it had been subjected during the war of Kosciuszko. The first occurred under the command of Count Bibikoff, and its results were long felt by the inhabitants of the village; the second, which was chiefly directed against the Palace, was carried out by the advanced guard of a corps under the orders of Count Valerian Zuboff. The Palace was completely sacked. All the ornaments were broken and destroyed. Valuable pictures were cut in pieces; the books of the library were stolen and dispersed in various parts of the Empire, and the only room that was spared was one which, as it had gilt wainscots and pictures by Boucher over the doors, the Cossacks thought was a chapel. All the provisions in the house—oil, wine, sugar, coffee, spirits, preserved meats, &c.—were thrown pell-mell into a basin in the middle of the courtyard, which was then used by the Cossacks as a bath. When we arrived, people were still employed in cleaning the ruins, rebuilding damaged walls or partitions, and repairing the library. In the middle of the vast courtyard before the Palace there was a little hill, a sort of *Monte Testacio*, composed of débris covered with earth. When our parents returned to their home they had some difficulty in finding rooms fit to live in, and the works of restoration were not completed when we left.

About this time we lost our friend Gorski, who died of an apoplectic stroke. I found him one morning complaining of pains in the head and difficulty of speech; a surgeon was called to bleed him, and he was put to bed. Dr Goltz, who was absent at the time, came too late to save him. Gorski remained unconscious, talked incoherently, and only complained of the pain in his head. He recognised me and I remember his smile with gratitude. I did not leave him; he died on the same day late in the evening, without pain. I felt his loss deeply. He was a true man, with nothing but justice and sincerity in his heart. He had often expressed a desire for a good and short life: his wish was accomplished.

Our three months' leave had now expired, and we returned to St Petersburg. We were sorry to leave our parents and our home, but we were anxious to see Alexander again and resume our relations with him. The letters I had received from him during our stay at Pulawy proved to me, if I had had any doubt on the subject, that he had not changed. We found him the same as before, both as regards his feelings and his opinions.

Towards the end of the year 1797, the follies and eccentricities which had agitated the Court of the Emperor Paul were succeeded by a period of comparative calm, which looked as if it were likely to last. When he was Grand-Duke he had, during his stay at Pavlovsk and Gatchina, conceived a passion for Mdlle. Nelidoff, maid-of-honour to his wife. This sentiment, which was entirely platonic, had continued to exist since his accession. Mdlle. Nelidoff had remarkable qualities of heart and mind, and had captivated the affection and confidence of the Empress. The latter thought she had nothing to fear from her rivalry, as she was tall, fair and handsome, while Mdlle. Nelidoff's figure, complexion, and features were in no way attractive ; her only charms were her sparkling smile and her animated conversation. The two women had a perfect understanding with each other, and the result was that the Emperor's conduct, his selection of high officials, and even his policy, became less changeable and confused, and more consequent, than they had been before. Unfortunately this salutary influence did not last long. On the return of the Court from the coronation, it went to Gatchina, where Paul liked to pass the autumn. His presence added to the naturally depressing effect produced by this season of the year in Russia, as it is foggy and rainy, and the cold, though less intense, is more disagreeable than in winter. The friendship and the extreme confidence shown to us by Alexander, and the familiarity which he and his brother allowed us to use in our relations with them, amply compensated, however, for the tediousness and melancholy of the Court, and we did not complain. I recollect having had some very warm disputes with the Grand-Duke Constantine, in which I did not give way to him either in words or in gestures, and one day I had a struggle with him in which we both fell to the ground. I think it was the recollection of these familiarities of our youth that impelled Constantine to treat me with consideration even at times when he was all-powerful in Poland, and deeply irritated at my opposition. He attempted to cultivate similar relations with my brother to those which existed between Alexander and myself; but his intolerable temper made his company much less agreeable than that of Alexander, though it had the advantage of keeping my brother and myself together. While we were at Gatchina we made the acquaintance of Baron Wintzingerode, a young officer of much nobility of character, a protégé of the princes of Saxe-Coburg, whom Constantine had made his aide-de-camp. Our friendship with him never varied, and lasted until his death.

At the end of the autumn, the Court returned to St Petersburg for the winter. (I may mention here that during the years I passed in Russia the only interesting events that I witnessed happened in Court circles, and I am therefore obliged to be always speaking of the Court). Our King Stanislas Augustus was, I believe, located with his suite at the house known as the Marble Palace, and lived magnificently at the expense of the Government. His niece, the Countess Mniszek, was attached to his suite with her

husband. He also had a certain number of chamberlains, among whom was Trembecki the poet. We
often went to present our respects to his Majesty, who
received us with pleasure at all times. I have often
seen him in the morning in his dressing gown, writing
what I was afterwards told were his memoirs. I
never could learn what had become of this work, which
must have been very voluminous. All I could
recover was the first volume, which only contained an
account of his embassy to Russia at the time of
Augustus III ; the other volumes, which must have
been much more interesting, were either destroyed or
so well concealed, that so far as I know no trace of
them has been found.*

This unfortunate prince seemed to me to accept
his position too patiently. He strove to make himself
agreeable to his masters who had dispossessed him,
and to indulge the capricious fancies of the Emperor,
who pretty frequently came with the Imperial family
to dine with him. His dinners were exquisite and
served to perfection, thanks to the skill of his famous
*maître d' hôtel*, Fremeau, who alone reminded him of
his past existence. The King and his suite, in order
to vary the entertainments he was able to offer to the
Emperor and Empress, were preparing a soirée with
private theatricals, when he was struck down by an
attack of apoplexy on the 2nd of February, 1793.
The news at once spread through the town, and we
hastened to the palace. Dr Bekler had bled the
patient and employed all the resources of his art, but

* They have since been published at Posen (in 1862) under the title 'Mémoires
de Stanislas Auguste Poniatowski et sa correspondance avec Catherine II.'

in vain. The King lay on his bed unconscious, the persons of his suite stood round him in tears, and Trembecki, who had come to have a last look at his sovereign, fled into his room with a gesture of despair. The Emperor also came with the Imperial family. Baciarelli has painted this sad scene in a picture in which he has represented with remarkable talent the likenesses of all those who were present. The King was buried with suitable pomp in the Roman Catholic Church of the Dominicans at St Petersburg.

Stanislas Augustus was only mourned by those whose existence depended on his own; and he had no cause to regret life so far as his happiness was concerned. His conduct as a King had been such that no one looked upon him as a representative of Poland, and his end made no change either in her destinies or her hopes.* There were some people who, in view of the great expense which he had caused to the Imperial Treasury, thought his death had been accelerated for reasons of State. This no doubt is possible, but none of the circumstances of his illness seem to confirm such a suspicion, which, unhappily for Russia, always arises at the death of any illustrious personage in that country.

---

* Stanislas Augustus Poniatowski, the son of the famous statesman and soldier who twice saved the life of Charles XII and with the two Czartoryskis governed Poland during the reign of Augustus III, went with the English Minister Sir Hanbury Williams to St Petersburg in 1755 and there became the favourite of the Empress Catherine, then Grand-Duchess of Russia. Through the influence of the Russian Government, which had concluded a secret alliance with Prussia (21st April 1764) pledging the two powers to prevent 'by force of arms, if necessary,' the establishment of hereditary monarchy in Poland, Stanislas Augustus was, on the death of Augustus III, elected King (7th September 1764). Although at first he endeavoured to act independently of Russia, he was easily outwitted by the superior abilities and greater force of character of the Muscovite diplomatists, and after Poland had been thrice partitioned, he was held in confinement by the Russians at Grodno, and afterwards at St Petersburg, where he died as above described (see Chapter I.)

Things now seemed to be settling down: the Emperor's manias had diminished under the combined influence of the Empress and her friend, and the public also had become accustomed to Paul's way of acting by fits and starts. The life we led at Gatchina or at St Petersburg would have been well adapted for study, if we had known how to profit by it. Our time was regulated, and there was only one indispensable occupation during the day—the military parade; after passing an hour or two in this duty every morning, we had the whole day at our disposal except Sundays and holidays, when certain Court functions had to be performed. These were regarded as so important, that they liberated us from all social conventions and duties, so that there was plenty of time for other occupations, but unfortunately I did not avail myself of the leisure thus afforded me. Being attached to Alexander's person as aide-de-camp, my service obliged me to attend him at military parades, and I used to go to his apartments every afternoon to take his orders; this was our time for intimate conversation. It is also from that period that dates my acquaintance with Prince Peter Volkonski, adjutant of the Semenofsky regiment of the Guards, of which Alexander was colonel. His position placed Prince Peter on a footing of familiarity with Alexander, and he afterwards became his aide-de-camp, then major-general, and finally grand chamberlain, which post he continued to occupy under the Emperor Nicholas. Without possessing brilliant or very superior faculties, Volkonski was very systematic and persistent in his duties, and fulfilled them to the Emperor's entire satisfaction; he also acquired information indispensable to an officer of high military rank. He was good-tempered, his advice was always sensible, and he did not hesitate to give it even when it caused displeasure; moreover, he was always ready and willing to do a service. We passed much time together, and I constantly received from him proofs of good-will to which I gladly bear testimony after an interval of more than half-a-century, when our relations have been interrupted by forty years of separation and by revolutions and other events.

His wife, the Princess Sophia, who belonged to another branch of the Volkonski family that had been more favoured by fortune, had a quicker temper and a more generous heart, and she often showed herself a true friend to me, even since my total withdrawal from the Russian service—for which I am sincerely grateful to her. She never pardoned the Emperor Nicholas for having kept her brother for thirty years in the mines of Siberia; he became old there, and was not restored to his sister and his family until the coronation of Alexander II. Her sorrow had separated the Princess Sophia from the Russian Court during the whole of Nicholas's reign.

Among the young men of the Court there was only one who was received into Alexander's intimacy: this was Prince Alexander Galitzin, one of the Gentlemen of the Chamber. He was called 'Little Galitzin' on account of his short stature, and pleased Alexander by his amusing gossip and his wonderful powers of mimicry, which enabled him closely to

imitate the appearance and the voice of every member
of the Court.    When we were alone without
Alexander, he used to imitate the Emperor Paul
with such accuracy that we feared lest he should be
arrested and punished.    He had been a passionate
admirer of the Empress Catherine, and notwithstanding her advanced age he would have gladly become
one of her favourites.    When I knew him he was a
thorough epicurean, devoting much calculation and
reflection to all possible enjoyments of every kind;
but after Alexander's accession he determined to
enter on a more serious mode of life, and, encouraged
by the Emperor, became Procurator to the Senate.
Afterwards, probably under the inspiration of Alexander's piety, he became very devout, saw visions
with M. de Kocheleff, and was finally appointed
Minister of Public Instruction, a post which I should
never have thought him qualified to fill.    His appointment did not take place, I think, until the year 1822,
when I was still Curator of the University of Wilna.
Remembering 'Little Galitzin' as I had known him,
I could not picture him to myself as a Minister
directing the public instruction of the Empire, as he
did not seem to possess any talent but that of amusing
people and making them laugh.    He was totally
without personal animosity—which did not, however,
prevent crying abuses from occurring at Wilna while
he was Minister, the result of which was that I was
obliged to resign my post of Curator.

There were sometimes select balls at Court, at
which the etiquette was not so strict as usual.    The
Emperor appeared at one of these balls in a dresscoat,

which he never wore on other occasions; it was of dark red velvet and of an old-fashioned shape. He danced that evening with Mdlle. Nelidoff. It was a curious sight, which stills dwells in my memory. The Emperor Paul, short, with very large shoes, placed himself in the third position, rounded his arms, and bent his body in the manner then taught by dancing masters, while opposite him was a lady of equally short stature, who thought it her duty to respond to the would-be graceful airs and harmonious movements of her partner.

In May, 1798, the Court proceeded to Pavlovsk, the property and creation of the Empress Maria, which, considering the general appearance of the environs of St Petersburg, was a pleasant and gay place. The buildings and gardens had been enlarged under the superintendence of the Empress. She attempted to entertain her guests by assembling them after dinner to listen to a reading of a French translation of Thomson's 'Seasons.' The Emperor did not assist at these readings, and the idea was not a success; everyone tried to escape what was generally voted to be a dull and somniferous entertainment.

The Emperor Paul wished this year to make a progress through part of his Empire. The Grand-Dukes took part in the journey, and my brother and myself accompanied them. The Emperor visited the Canal which joins the Volga to the Neva, thereby establishing a communication between the Caspian Sea and the Baltic. This work of Peter the Great, which does great credit to his genius and activity, passes in a diagonal line through the whole of the interior of Russia. Paul went to see the fleet of boats

on the canal, some of which started for St Petersburg
and others for Astrakhan.   M. de Sivers, notorious for
the odious manner in which he carried out the second
partition of Poland, was charged with the Works Department.   Being on a so-called tour of inspection, he
went to meet the Emperor.   He looked old, thin, pale,
and depressed, without any energy or distinction.   The
very cold reception accorded to him by the Emperor
showed him that he would not long remain at his post.

We passed by Tver on our way out, and on our
return by Yaroslav and Vladimir.   These provinces
are rich and populous, with an air of abundance and
prosperity which strikes all who travel through them.
It is in the interior of Russia that her true strength
lies; if it were well administered by a government
concentrated within reasonable limits, this region
should by its resources and prosperity disgust the
Russians with the task of being the tormentors and
gaolers of neighbouring countries.

At Moscow, which was the first place to which
the Emperor went, there was a considerable assem-
blage of troops, which he reviewed and ordered to
perform some manœuvres.   They were regiments of
the line which had not been trained like the Guards,
and had not had time to obtain instruction in the new
system.   The infantry was divided into two lines
which marched in two columns, at the head of each of
which was placed one of the Grand-Dukes.   They
were to deploy at a given signal, and I remember with
pleasure the activity with which we executed this
movement, which was successful beyond our hopes,
without any crowding or spreading out of the lines,

each of which was composed of from twelve to fifteen battalions. The Emperor was highly satisfied at the order in which the troops marched, and liberally distributed rewards among the officers.

From Moscow we went by way of Nijni Novgorod to Kazan. The country between these places is fine, and might be rich through the fertility of its soil and the navigable streams which cross it in all directions, but it is little inhabited. Some of the inhabitants are still half-savage tribes, apparently of the Finnish race—Tchouvasches and Tcheremisses who have preserved their odd national costumes. I made sketches of them, which I gave to my old friend M. Wiesiolowski. At Kazan there are still many Tartars who have also preserved their ancient dress and customs, but I do not think they have any strong national spirit, any more than our Tartars of Lithuania. It is only further east, among the Nogaïs and the populations adjoining the steppes of Great Tartary or the slopes of the Caucasus, that this spirit shows itself and is accompanied by a warlike disposition.

The journey was performed with a rapidity which deprived it of the practical advantage that might have been gained if the Emperor had seen with his own eyes what was going on in the country. We returned without passing through Moscow, and our last stage was Schlusselburg, the fortress which was rendered famous by the catastrophe of the unhappy Ivan.* Paul embarked on the Lake of Ladoga, and while we were on the boat he called my brother and myself

* Ivan VI, killed in 1764 in attempting to escape from the fortress of Schlusselburg, where he had been confined since 1741.

and decorated us with the Order of St Anne of the second class as a reward for our services during the journey. This was the only honourable distinction I ever received in Russia.

We passed the remainder of the summer at Pavlovsk, and then moved to Gatchína for the autumn. This palace, which had recently been enlarged, looked like a prison ; it is built on a perfectly level plain, without trees or fields. The park had a sombre and melancholy air ; the sun seldom shines there, and it was so cold and rainy that we had no temptation to walk. Military parades or manœuvres in the morning, and the French or Italian theatre in the evening, did but little to relieve the prevailing dulness. This latter part of the year 1798, and the beginning of 1799, brought much trouble and unexpected change into the situation of the persons who composed the Russian Court.

At the time of the capture of Kutaysk and the massacre of its inhabitants, a Turkish child, afterwards named Kutayschoff, who had escaped with his life, was adopted by Paul, who had him educated, and then made him first his barber, and afterwards his principal valet. At the beginning of Paul's reign I saw Kutayschoff bring some broth to his master at the training school, where the infantry and cavalry drilled during the winter. He was in his barber's dress, of middle size, a little stout, but alert and quick in his movements, very dark, always smiling, with Eastern eyes and a countenance displaying a sensual joviality. In this costume he looked a sort of Figaro ; but he was already the object of obsequious salutations and hand-shakings on the part of most of the generals and other persons who took part in the drill. Soon his influence with his master made him a dignitary of the Empire and an all-powerful favourite. This metamorphosis was accomplished by the autocratic wand of Czarism. In less than a year he rose from a barber and a valet to be Grand-Equerry, and astonished the Russians by appearing successively with the Orders of St Anne, St Alexander, and St Andrew, accompanied by extensive grants of land and money. He was not, however, promoted to these honours all at once, and he would not have got them so rapidly if the Empress and Mdlle. de Nelidoff had continued to retain their influence over the Emperor's mind. It was difficult, sometimes impossible, for aspiring officials to get what they wanted so long as the influence of the Empress and her friend was preponderant, and this was the principal cause of their defeat. Ambitious people now made overtures to the favourite valet in order to advise him and take advantage of the almost magnetic power which he was able to exercise over his master. The instigator and prime mover of this plot was Count Rostopchin. He had been removed from the post of Minister for War, succeeded by M. Nelidoff, the nephew of the *demoiselle à portrait*,* and even banished to Moscow, for Paul always acted in extremes both with regard to people whom he liked and those who no longer enjoyed his favour. Rostopchin was not the man to forgive such a slight, and, determined to have his revenge upon those who

* See page 132.

had caused his fall, allied himself with Kutayschoff.
In order to divert Paul from his attachment to
Mdlle. Nelidoff, and to make him quarrel with
his wife, it was insinuated that he was in leading-
strings, and that all Russia was convinced that the
two women reigned in his name. The plotters
brought him a younger and prettier woman than
Mdlle. Nelidoff, without her decided character.
She was the daughter of Lapoukin, who had been
Director of Police at Moscow under Catherine ; Paul
made her his mistress, and rewarded her father for
his complaisance by making him a Prince and giving
him the blue ribbon. Rostopchin was then appointed
Minister of Foreign Affairs, and all the high functionaries who belonged to the Empress's party—the
Princes Kourakin and their relatives, the chief of
whom was the old Prince Repnin—lost their places
and were banished to Moscow. The break-up of the
party was complete ; it was enough for any one to be
suspected by the Emperor of having been protected
or liked by the Empress to ensure his dismissal and
banishment from the Court.

Paul now became more suspicious than ever. He
thought his sons were not sufficiently devoted to his
interests, and that his wife wanted to reign in his
place. All who approached the Court were in constant
fear and uncertainty, being exposed at any moment to
be addressed in the presence of the whole Court by
the Court-Marshal with some insulting message from
the Emperor, and then to be sent into exile. It was
like the Reign of Terror. The balls and Court festivals
were arenas where each man risked his position and

his liberty. The Emperor constantly fancied that sufficient respect was not shown to some person who was the object of his favour, or to the relations of that person, and that this neglect was inspired by the Empress, and in such cases he at once ordered the supposed culprit to be dismissed from the Court. His fancies and his decisions were equally sudden, and were at once carried out.

Other sovereigns, after a fit of anger or extreme rigour, sometimes become calm and strive to soften the effects of their first decisions. This was not the case with the Emperor Paul. Usually, after giving a severe order with regard to a man who had displeased him, the punishment did not, after reflection, seem to him sufficient, and he often augmented it. All who belonged to the Court or came before the Emperor were thus in a state of continual fear. No one was sure that he would remain in his place at the end of the day, and in going to bed it was quite uncertain whether during the night or in the early morning some policeman would not come with a *kibitka* to drive you off at once to Siberia. This state of affairs began with the disgrace of Mdlle. Nelidoff, and continued with increasing aggravation during the remainder of Paul's reign. Mdlle. Nelidoff behaved with much pride and dignity. She left the Court, showed no desire to remain there, and did not attempt to return. She said with marked disdain to all who would listen to her, that nothing was more tedious than a Court life, and that she was glad at last to have left it.

Paul had a new hobby which sometimes diverted him from his fanciful suspicions and the rigours which

followed them.   He wanted to become Grand Master
of Malta.*   Political considerations had probably contributed to this wish, as of all the Powers that might
have protected or possessed Malta, England, who had
taken it, was the one that Europe liked least.   Paul
was at that time in intimate relations with the British
Cabinet, which attached great importance to the
active co-operation of Russia against France, and he
may have thought that under these circumstances
England would perhaps not refuse to cede to him a
territory which she had only provisionally occupied
with the express promise to return it to the Order of
St John, to whom it belonged, and to place it under
the protection of a power which should be designated
by Europe.   Paul was full of the idea of himself
becoming Grand Master of Malta, and of uniting in
his person both a title so famous in history and the
power necessary for the protection of the independence
of so important a station in the Mediterranean.   Political considerations were less concerned in this idea than
the vanity of posing as a hero of chivalry before the
Princess Lapoukin.   Being the supreme chief and
defender of the Russian Church, he saw no difficulty in
placing himself at the head of the principal Order of
the Roman Catholic Church.   The combined Cabinets,
with the exception of England, carefully abstained

* The Order of St John, which had obtained possession of Malta in 1530 from
the Emperor Charles V, was divided into eight 'languages,' each of which had its
prior.   The first Russian Knight of Malta was Sheremetieff, who was sent to the
island in 1698 by Peter the Great to learn naval warfare, and diplomatic relations
were then opened by the Order with the Court of St Petersburg.   In 1774, a new
priory of the Order was established in Poland, with six commanderships, each of
which was to be held by a Pole.   The property of the Order in Poland was transferred to Russia at the second partition, and this led to the selection by the Grand
Master, Rohan, of M. de Litta as plenipotentiary to arrange with the Russian
Government as to the disposal of this property.

from contradicting him. Count Litta and his brother, the Papal Nuncio at St Petersburg, who afterwards became a Cardinal, readily fell in with the Emperor's plan and encouraged him in it. In Poland there were still some commanderships of the Order, notwithstanding the bad repute into which it had fallen among us by Prince Poninski having trafficked in its property and been condemned by the Diet after the first partition; and Paul created other commanderships in Russia without troubling himself about differences of creed  Count Litta framed, in accordance with the ancient rite, the ceremonial of a Grand Chapter of the Order, in which the new Grand Master was to enter on his dignities. · The Emperor appeared several times on his throne in the costume of Grand Master, with the cross of the Order, which had been sent him from Rome. Paul was passionately fond of ceremonies; he wished that people taking part in them should preserve an imperturbable gravity and should attach great importance to them. My brother and myself were appointed Commanders of the Order, and had to put on the ancient costume, consisting of long cloaks of black velvet, with belts and embroidered crosses. There had been some rehearsals of the ceremony of offering the Grand Mastership to the Emperor, and the whole business had an appearance of theatrical masquerading which made the spectators and even the performers smile, with the single exception of the Emperor, who was thoroughly identified with his part. The secretary to the Chapter was an old acquaintance of ours, M. de Maisonneuve, a Frenchman who when young had sought his fortune in

Poland, had had some success with the ladies, and had obtained through them rank in the army and the Cross of Malta. He came to Russia in his old age to restore his fortune, which he had squandered twice over. Count Litta appointed him his secretary, and in this capacity M. de Maisonneuve gave entire satisfaction, as he wrote fluently and was well acquainted with legal and diplomatic phraseology.

This hobby of the Emperor's produced a quarrel with England, who, without giving any definitive reply, refused under various pretexts to give up Malta. The only result of his assuming the rank of Grand Master was the marriage of Count Litta, who was relieved from his vow of chastity by the Pope, and became the husband of the Countess Skovronsky, the favourite niece of Prince Potemkin, still a handsome woman, though not in her first youth, who when Alexander became Emperor procured for her husband a large fortune and the important position of Grand Chamberlain, which he held until his death. Her daughter-in-law was the Princess Bagration, whose estates Count Litta administered with much regularity and zeal.

During these continual changes shameful and petty intrigues were as usual mixed up with the events of the day. While the Emperor believed himself to have broken the chains which he fancied had bound him, Kutayschoff entered into relations with Madame Chevalier, a handsome woman and a charming actress engaged at the Court Theatre, who was the object of the assiduous attentions of M. Bignon, the French Minister at Cassel, but had abandoned him on receiving more sumptuous offers from Paul's valet. These amorous intrigues led to mutual confidences which added piquancy to the moments which the Emperor passed with his servant, and augmented the latter's influence.

Paul's nervous excitement was increased by political events. Austria obtained the alliance and help of Russia, and Count Rostopchin, since his recall to the Court, had infused a spirit of firmness into the Foreign Office, which he directed with much activity and an ability all his own. The whole credit of the new coalition * and of its first successes was attributed to him, and his friends used to say with complacency that the two great men of the age were Pitt and Rostopchin. Marshal Souvaroff also was recalled; he had been since Paul's accession in exile on his estates and under close surveillance as a partisan of Catherine. Very censorious remarks of his were quoted about the Government of the Emperor Paul, and he made some rather unseemly jokes on the new organisation and uniforms of the army. But as soon as the Emperor wanted him he loaded him with honours and compliments. Souvaroff took the command of the army, and had some astonishing successes over the French, who were no longer led by Buonaparte. During the year 1796 and the following years we had rejoiced at Buonaparte's extraordinary victories, hoping that they might lead to the reconstruction of Poland. We used to call him 'the friend' in order not to compromise ourselves by mentioning his name; and now every victory gained over the French seemed to us a stab in the body of our country.

* Russia, Turkey, England, Austria, and Naples were then allied against France.

When Souvaroff's first successes became known, the Court was at Pavlovsk. The old Cossack General Denisoff was also there; he had been beaten by Kosciuszko at Raclavice. He took a malicious pleasure in examining our faces each time that the news of a victory was brought from Italy. He used to say to us : 'I told you the French would be beaten; it could not be otherwise. Russia will beat her enemies always and everywhere. She is invincible.' *Te Deums* were continually sung in the churches, while the Emperor still mingled thoughts of his mistress with those of politics, war, and piety, and placed at her feet the trophies of the victories gained by his armies. One day she praised an undecided tint known as chamois, and he at once ordered everything to be coloured with this tint. He ordered chivalrous plays to be performed in which he imagined himself to be the hero ; sometimes he was a Bayard, at others a Nemours. He also published in the papers a challenge to any sovereign who differed from him to settle the difference by single-handed combat. This was addressed especially to the King of Prussia, who had refused to join the coalition. Paul would have been in a great difficulty if the challenge had been accepted, as he had not much personal courage, and was very timid on horseback, so much so that when he was in front of cavalry he never would allow them to charge.

My brother and I suffered with the rest from the Emperor's abrupt changes of temper. The fact that we were Poles, and the antecedents of our family— perhaps also charges made against us or casual remarks uttered with or without intention—had led Paul to suppose that we were liberals, or even Jacobins in disguise. Yet he had treated us with some kindness on various occasions at Court assemblages where we were near him. He especially seemed to like my brother, and he sometimes joked with him. When he was in a good humour Paul was continually saying and doing things which he thought witty. Once he told my brother to make a coarse and insulting remark to one of the persons present. My brother objected, but the Emperor repeated his order with such a menacing air that he had no alternative but to obey. On another occasion when Paul met my brother he put out his tongue at him; and during our stay at Peterhoff, seeing my brother in one of the alleys of the garden leading to the rooms of the Countess Schouvaloff, who had a very pretty chambermaid, Paul took him by the shoulders and told him to go away, adding 'That bird is not for you.' He also asked him to tell him his adventures, and promised not to betray his secrets to any one. The Grand-Duke Constantine was Governor of Peterhoff, and was responsible for the military service of the palace. One day the Bavarian Minister passed out of the gates, and the officer in command of the guard having omitted to report the circumstance, Paul sent him through my brother the usual message that he was a fool. The Grand-Duke was much disturbed at this incident, but the officer simply replied that the message did not produce the slightest effect upon him, as it came from a madman. This shows the impression which was already generally

produced by the Emperor's conduct; and although
he had been kind to us, he gradually became irritated
at seeing us on such intimate terms with his sons.
Prince Bezborodko, who afterwards died suddenly—
which perhaps saved him from a disgrace which he
would certainly have experienced sooner or later, as
Paul looked upon him as a censor and an inconvenient
obstacle to his caprices—had advised Paul to send us
to the Austrian army with letters, but nothing came
of this proposal. The Emperor still suspected us,
and expressed his suspicions to General Levaschoff.
This old general had in his youth been a gambler and
a creature of Potemkin's, but he was very jovial and
good-natured, and liked to render people a service.
He hardly knew us, but he spoke in our favour.
Suddenly the Emperor turned upon him and said:
' Will you answer for them ?'—' Yes, Sire,' was the
reply.   ' With your head?  Mind what you say.'
The General stopped for a moment; but to hesitate
was to ruin us.   He then said deliberately: ' Yes, I
will answer for them with my head.'   This reassured
the Emperor for some time.   I had the story from
Levaschoff himself.   Our turn for promotion by
seniority to the rank of Lieutenant-General having
arrived, and this rank being incompatible with the
appointment of aide-de-camp to the Grand-Dukes,
the Emperor decided to make me Court-Marshal to
the Grand-Duchess Helena, who shortly after married
the Grand-Duke of Mecklenburg, and my brother
Equerry to the Grand-Duchess Maria, who was
betrothed to the hereditary Prince of Weimar.   These
places gave us the effective rank of Lieutenant-

General, but I was sorry not to be officially attached
any longer to the Grand-Duke Alexander nor to be
able to accompany him in his military duties. The
change, however, did not in any way alter our
relations.

Soon after I had to separate from my brother.
Our parents had settled in Galicia, and wanted one of
us to go to them and become an Austrian subject.
The family decided that this should be my brother.
He addressed a very respectful letter to the Emperor,
in which he explained that in order to satisfy the
requirements of the Austrian Government and the
demand of his parents, he found it necessary to ask
permission to join them in Galicia. Paul was
indignant at this very natural step, which was amply
justified, and his irritation was perhaps the greater as
he had shown some special kindness to my brother.
He was so angry that his first impulse was to send
him to Siberia. Fortunately Kutayschoff, who liked
my brother, and who had been spoken to on the
subject by the Grand-Duke Alexander, succeeded in
calming the Emperor's anger. My brother not only
got permission to go, but was decorated with the
order of St Anne of the first class. After he had left
I felt very solitary, and gave myself up to sad reflections. About this time a messenger came from the
army who was asked how the French officers dressed.
He said among other things that they wore large
whiskers. When the Emperor heard this, he at once
ordered every man at the Court to shave off his
whiskers, and the order was executed an hour afterwards. At the ball in the evening there were a

number of, so to say, new faces, with blank spaces on
their cheeks, showing where they had shaved.    People
laughed as they met each other.    The order was conveyed by the Court-Marshal, Naryshkin, who himself
saw that it was at once carried out.

After dinner there were cavalcades at Pavlovsk in
which the Grand-Duchesses managed their horses
with much grace and dexterity.    The Empress, who
was ordered to ride by her physicians, sat astride on
her horse like a man, and only went at a foot pace.
The summer was finer than usual.    I was quartered
in a solitary house at the entrance to a wood at the
end of the Park.    Here I was more isolated, and
could fill up my day with some useful occupation.
One morning I suddenly received a letter from Count
Rostopchin, informing me that I had been appointed
Russian Minister to the Court of Sardinia, that I
must at once go to St Petersburg to get my instructions, and that then I should have to leave in eight
days for Italy.    This was a disgrace in the guise of a
favour.'    The order saddened and displeased me; it
was painful to me to leave the Grand-Duke Alexander, to whom I was sincerely attached, and several
other friends who by their affection had mitigated the
disagreeables of my stay in Russia.    I left Pavlovsk
next day, and Alexander expressed to me his sorrow
at my departure.    On recalling his words to me on
that occasion, it seems to me that he was no longer
the same as when I left him after the coronation of
his father at Moscow.    He had already looked more
closely into the realities of things, and they had
produced their effect.    Some of his dreams—those

especially which related to himself personally, and of which we had not again spoken for a long time—had vanished. Moreover, Alexander had not been able to resist entirely the temptation to do as the people round him did, and he had sought to divert his thoughts by paying court to the most celebrated beauties of the capital. He heartily bade me farewell, and promised to write to me as soon as he could. I asked the Minister to allow me to stop a few days with my parents on my road to Italy. He refused; but as my road passed in the vicinity of Pulawy, I hoped to see them, if only for a few moments.

# CHAPTER X

## 1798-9



I REGRETTED the more my forced departure as I had made arrangements for employing my leisure in literary work, for which purpose the solitary house I occupied at the entrance to the forest of Pavlovsk was eminently suited. This was a pleasant illusion. One fancies that one can create something, but it is only when one sets to work that one becomes convinced that hard labour and more information are necessary to give adequate expression to a favourite idea, and that talent and perseverance are often wanting. On arriving at St Petersburg I proceeded to the Foreign Office as directed, but the documents I found in its archives gave me only a general idea of the duties of my post, and no instructions whatever were furnished me as to the special mission with which I had been entrusted. I passed eight days in preparing for my journey, and then left St Petersburg. At Miendrzyrzec I found my eldest sister, who had come to tell me news of our parents. We passed part of the

night and the following morning in relating our joys
and sorrows. Prudence did not allow me to stop any
longer or to go to see my parents. We parted in
the hope of meeting again at Vienna, where my
young sister Zamoyska was already staying, and
where the eldest also soon arrived.

Four years had elapsed since my brother and I
left Vienna. I was then proceeding to Russia to ask
as a favour that which was only justice—the restitution of our property; while now I came to Vienna as
the representative of the Russian Government. This
change in my situation produced an immense impression on Viennese society, and especially on the
Government functionaries. The few months I passed
here with my sisters were among the happiest of my
life. My aunt, the Princess Lubomirska, also lived at
Vienna in the winter; she had a house on the Bastei
(the old fortifications) and received all the most distinguished people in Viennese society, which was composed of women celebrated for their beauty and wit,
and of foreign travellers, who came there in crowds,
as France and Paris, closed to Europe, were just now
detested by the wealthier classes in all countries.

Vienna was, so to say, the capital of the Continental States which were allied with England
against the horrors of the French revolution. In the
midst of this select society, which was less Austrian
than European, my two sisters had a most amiable
and flattering reception. My younger sister was
then at the climax of her beauty, and my elder sister,
who also was beautiful, was especially distinguished
by the qualities of her mind. An accidental circum-

stance doubled the prestige which they exercised at Vienna. By the order of the Emperor Paul, the Grand-Duke Constantine was to join the army of Souvaroff, which was then pursuing its victories in Italy, and was to stop at Vienna on his way. My sister, the Princess of Würtemberg, who had just been divorced from the Grand-Duke's uncle,* was under these circumstances in a difficult position. She was the intimate friend of the Countess Razumovska, *née* Thun, wife of the Russian Ambassador, and the eldest of three sisters who by their beauty, their grace, their wit, and their noble sentiments, were the ornaments of Viennese society. The youngest, afterwards Lady Guildford, was at one time engaged to Prince Joseph Poniatowski, and always loved him as a brother. The Countess Razumovska, though the wife of the Russian Ambassador, detested the Russians in general as much as her two sisters did. But the Ambassador, not knowing how the Grand-Duke would treat my sister, already began to avoid her company, and though he had professed to be her friend, did not dare to give her any advice. When Constantine arrived, there was a meeting of Russians at the embassy, and as my sister used to go there every day, and she did not want to make any demonstration which might be prejudicial to me, she also was present; but being received with evident embarrassment by the rest of the company, she remained alone in a corner of the room. When, however, Razumovski began to present to Constantine the ladies who had come to meet him, the Grand-Duke

* See page 40.

asked for my sister, went to her, addressed her as his aunt, and conversed with her for some time and with much amiability about her two brothers whom he used to see daily at St Petersburg. When he left, all those who had held aloof from my sister were as eager in their protestations of friendship as they had been distant before. Next day Constantine came to her house, having announced his visit beforehand. Prince Esterhazy and several Austrian generals had to wait in the ante-room, and my sister, who was much vexed at this, begged him to allow them to come in; but he took a pleasure in tormenting them for more than an hour, talking and laughing without intermission. It amused him to keep them waiting; this, indeed, was his usual custom both in Austria and elsewhere. He always treated in this way strangers who wished to do him honour.

It was during my stay at Vienna this year that I made the acquaintance of M. Pozzo di Borgo, and he owed to our meeting the high position and immense fortune which he afterwards obtained. Pozzo was at that time a young man who rightly or wrongly imagined himself a martyr to patriotism. General Paoli, who had become celebrated in the seventeenth century for having defended the independence of Corsica against the armies of Louis XV, had been compelled to take refuge in England, where I often met him in 1790 at the house of the beautiful Mrs Cosway, an artist who used to receive the most distinguished people in London. In that year the English seized Corsica, and made Paoli the head of the Government; the latter appointed Pozzo his secretary of state, which shows that he was already known as a man of ability; and although he was at first a zealous advocate of the French Revolution, in Corsica he belonged to the opposite party. The influence of England in Corsica did not, however, last long. After the capture of Toulon, the French republican and revolutionary party gained the upper hand, turned out the English and their Government, and took possession of the island. Pozzo thus became a refugee; and, passionate and vindictive like a true Corsican, he vowed eternal hatred to France and Buonaparte. He received a pension from England, though he had no employment or mission, and strange to say he never inspired the slightest confidence in the British Government, which, after giving him a pension, took no further notice of him. He now exerted himself to the utmost in all directions to satisfy his ambition. As the protégé of Lord Minto, the British Ambassador, father of the ex-Minister, and known for his diplomatic travels in Italy in 1848, Pozzo was received in the salons of my sisters and of Madame Lanckoronska, a lady who was universally respected, and thus formed part of the Polish coterie, which at that time enjoyed a high reputation in Vienna. This gave him the *entrée* to the best society and the protection of the ladies who were its chiefs. Though still young and generally liked, there was something so underhanded and mysterious in his conduct that he had not a single friend or person who could say he was intimate with him. This at least was the impression he produced upon me when I first made his acquaintance. He had a cultivated mind, and sometimes he seemed inclined to cast a tinge of poetry over his life and to work at history, moral philosophy, and politics; but his face belied his words, and his only thought was how to obtain wealth and a high position. Although circumstances sometimes forced him to enter the sphere of sentiment, he never swerved from this dominant idea. Yet he was regarded at Vienna as an interesting man, as sincere, and as worthy of true friendship. The praises which were generally lavished upon him almost persuaded me that I had formed a mistaken impression of his character.

When I was at Vienna in 1790 Kaunitz was still living. His place was occupied by Thugut, whom I had known at Brussels, and who was now all powerful. He professed to be a friend of my father's, and when he was Ambassador at Warsaw he held his own against adverse pretensions so firmly, that he even offended the King. He was of humble birth, and that he should have been placed at the head of the Government was astonishing in a country like Austria. Thugut was an unshaken partisan of war, and gave up his portfolio after the Battle of Hohenlinden, to the Emperor Francis's great regret, as he possessed his entire confidence. He had extraordinary firmness of character, perseverance, and power of work. While he was Minister he scarcely ever went out, ate no meat, and lived entirely on fish and vegetables. When I afterwards saw him in 1820, his sole occupation was to go every evening to the Kasperle theatre, and his faithful friend, Count Ossolinski, was the only one that did not abandon him.

On my journey to Sardinia I was particularly

struck by the miserable appearance of the villages of Northern Italy as far as Verona. I paid a hurried visit to the principal buildings of Verona, Venice, and Mantua, having but little time to give myself up to the meditations to which those celebrated cities have always given rise in my mind. It is impossible for one who knows something of the arts and literature of antiquity not to feel their influence. In passing by these cities and their fields festooned by vines, my thoughts were full of Virgil and Shakespeare, of Othello and Romeo and Juliet. The country was in a pitiable state; it had been the theatre of war, and had passed from one conqueror to another. Its inhabitants, who were formerly citizens of the Cisalpine Republic, were accustomed to French successes and reckoned upon them; now that the French had been defeated, they were despondent and helpless. It was a melancholy season of the year, and the roads were almost impracticable. At the first stage beyond Mantua my carriage stuck in the mud, and we had to get oxen to extricate us. On arriving at Benedetto, an inhabitant of the place offered me supper, saying that he had shot a bird which was unknown in that country. He at the same time complained of the hardness of the times, watching me, like the rest of his countrymen, as he spoke, to find out what party I belonged to, and what opinions it would be safe for him to express. He gave me some excellent soup, but the bird was thin, black, and with an enormous head and beak; I think it must have been a crow. I passed twenty-four hours under his roof, and this Lombard, who in his heart sympathised with the

French, but feared the Austrians, made a strong impression upon me. The King of Sardinia, who, expelled from the Italian Peninsula by the French, had been forced to take refuge in the Island of Sardinia, had taken advantage of Souvaroff's victories to return and establish himself at Florence; he was encouraged to do this by the Court of St Petersburg, which had taken him under its protection. He could not yet venture as far as Piedmont, where the armies were standing opposite each other. The Battle of Novi had been fought, but Buonaparte was already coming back from Egypt, and Massena had shut himself up in Genoa. The Court of Vienna, too, was doing its utmost to prevent the King of Sardinia from returning to his dominions. At first it feared that his presence might interfere with its military and political plans, and the two Courts had long been estranged. Austria did not care for anybody but herself. Selfishness is no doubt common both among States and individuals, but Austria was more passionately and evidently selfish than any other Power, and this exclusive sentiment prevented her from having any generous impulse, or a friendly and sincere, or even honest policy towards others.

I arrived at Florence in the winter of 1798-9. On the night of my arrival there was a terrible storm, accompanied by thunder and lightning, which reminded me of other similar natural phenomena that preceded some of the gravest events of my life. My diplomatic occupations as the Russian Minister at the Court of King Emmanuel, which consisted only of a few faithful partisans, were not very arduous. My task was to restore courage to this unfortunate prince by assuring him of the friendly sentiments and the protection of the Emperor Paul, and to send to my Cabinet at least once a month a report, which it was difficult to make very interesting, as other Ministers were posted nearer to the places where great events were occurring than I was. I was limited to a certain kind of news, and yet I was expected to invest it with interest. The task was especially difficult to me, as since my arrival in Russia, I had felt nothing but indifference with regard to all I was required to do. This indifference enabled me to bear numerous trials with firmness and equanimity, and it was especially necessary in my new appointment, as I had to regard as a success what I could only consider a calamity. I had to keep up a correspondence with Souvaroff and forget the massacre of Praga,* and I had to write at the end of each of my despatches to the Emperor: 'Your faithful subject and slave (rab),' according to the formula then laid down by him.

The King of Sardinia reminded one a good deal— theological erudition apart—of James I of England as he has been described in history, and especially by Scott. The branch of Savoy, descended from an English princess, the daughter, if I am not mistaken, of James I, was the oldest of the branches of the Hanoverian line. The King did not like business, and though very pious, was fond of telling good stories, for, like his predecessor James, he had a turn for buffoonery. His wife, Queen Clotilda, was one of the sisters of Louis XVI; she used to be

* See page 73.

called at Versailles *le gros Madame*, on account of her enormous size, but when I was presented to her, she was extremely thin. Her eyes were still very beautiful, and her face and the sound of her voice had an expression of sweetness and melancholy.

The diplomatic body of which I formed part was composed of myself and Mr Wyndham, brother to Lord Wyndham, a celebrated member of the House of Lords; he was a stout Englishman who looked more like a brewer or butcher than a diplomatist. We both used to go to the King's residence on every Sunday and holiday. He occupied one of the palaces of the Grand-Duke of Tuscany; it was outside the town, and afterwards became one of his most splendid residences. We were always introduced by Count Chalembert, who was the so-called Minister of Foreign Affairs. The Count presented us to the King and Queen, the conversation usually turned on insignificant subjects, and it did not last longer than twenty minutes. After some jocular remarks the King would dismiss us, sometimes imitating the person of whom he had been speaking, which he did in a very comic way. The Queen used to bow to us with a melancholy smile. There was also a hungry subordinate diplomatist who did not go to Court; his name was Winterhalter, and he was Chargé d'Affaires of Prussia. This poor wretch was so badly paid that he hardly had enough for his living; but though his clothes were threadbare, he was constantly moving about and insinuating himself everywhere. He chatted incessantly, and in order not to lose his wretched pay he doubtless filled his daily report with endless gossip.

Though almost destitute, he had a big stomach and a face like a full moon, and he was not devoid of political ability.

Only a few Piedmontese families had followed their sovereign ; they lived in complete isolation and did not see or receive anybody.  M. Bailly de Saint-Germain, formerly tutor to the King, was supposed to be the Court Chamberlain, but no one ever saw him or did business with him.  He once gave a dinner, and this was the only official function he performed. M. Dunoyer, Count Chalembert's right hand ; M. de Lamarmora (uncle, I believe, of the General of that name) ; M. de la Tour, Governor of Piedmont at the time of the Austrian occupation ; and a noble-man from Sardinia, completed the number of the re-presentatives of Piedmont.  Among the Florentines only the Marquis Corsi used to visit the Piedmontese, and he also called upon me.  Another house which was an exception to the general rule was that of Madame d'Albany, who had been divorced from the Pretender, and was now the wife of Alfieri.  She often gave dinners to which strangers were invited. The painter Fabre was frequently at her house ; I knew him long after at Montpellier, his native town, where he had established a museum of pictures and curiosities collected by Alfieri and left by the latter to the Countess of Albany, who gave them to Fabre and, if I am not mistaken, married him.

While I was staying at Florence Alfieri enjoyed robust health, and occupied the greater part of his time in long walks.  While he was walking he used to declaim aloud verses from his tragedies without paying the slightest attention to passers-by or to the objects which surrounded him. In the evening he looked tired and exhausted, and directly he returned from his rambles he used to sit down to a game of chess. His youth had been, as he himself says in his memoirs, a very stormy one. It was Madame d'Albany, to whom he was warmly attached, who had advised him to write the tragedies and other works which even during his lifetime had gained him a great reputation. Some years before I had met him in Paris. At first he was an ardent admirer of the principles of the French Revolution, but afterwards, disgusted by its excesses, he looked upon France with horror, and devoted all his zeal to the cause of King Emmanuel, strongly blaming himself for not having been constantly faithful to it. When some years later a sudden illness had deprived him of the means of continuing his usual walks, he concluded that he would soon die, and he passed away in a few days. He was a man of great merit, and looked upon events from a truly elevated point of view ; but he was the slave of an exalted imagination, and was subject to illusions.

The inertia into which the Sardinian Court and the society of Florence were plunged, was too monotonous to be interesting ; the days followed each other without bringing anything new. Under these circumstances I decided to go to Pisa to see M. Francis Rzewuski, formerly Marshal of the Polish Court. He was a friend of my parents, and I and my mother had lived in his house during our stay in Paris. He received me with great cordiality, though he was in pain; he had already been attacked by the malady which ended in his death. He was very impatient as regards suffering, and always relieved it by taking opium. He did this with the approval of a physician who was a professor in the university of Pisa; but there is no doubt that by taking so much opium he hastened his end, and that it did not prevent him from suffering horribly. We had known and loved M. Rzewuski since we were children. He always had some sweets for us, and we used often to go from Powonski to his house at Marimont, which he had fitted up with much luxury and taste. He was a man full of good qualities—amiable, beneficent, scrupulously honest, but too fond of ease; he was generous and a great nobleman in the true sense of the word, of a race which is now extinct. Sometimes he would not show himself to his guests, though he treated them with munificent hospitality. When he was in good health he liked to come down to his meals, and was very fond of conversation, which he made very interesting by relating a number of anecdotes. One of these referred to his stay at St Petersburg. He had been sent there by the King after his accession, and was on very friendly terms with Count Panin, Chancellor of the Empire, and tutor to the Grand-Duke Paul. Being one day at the Count's house he took the young prince on his knees, when the latter had a fit. 'I was never so frightened in my life,' he said, 'and I took good care not to play again with this sickly child, who might have died in my arms.' He knew all the scandalous gossip of Warsaw and St Petersburg by heart, and was much attached to the

King, though after being for a long time his Minister he at once abandoned the Court when he perceived that the King was not faithful to his engagements.

I profited by my leisure at Florence in visiting the masterpieces of art in the galleries, and in studying the Italian language. I read Dante with a priest who was remarkable for his extreme cowardice, and was constantly repeating the expression 'ho paura,' which at that time people were not ashamed to use. The Italians have greatly changed since then.

This tranquil and monotonous existence lasted all the winter; in the spring people's faces began to lengthen, they talked in whispers, and signs of great anxiety followed the placid security of the previous months. At length we all had the news of the crossing of the Alps by Buonaparte and of the battle of Marengo and its results. Sommariva disappeared with his troops, and the King of Sardinia with all his Court, myself included, hastily packed our things to go to Rome.

The impression produced by the sight of Rome, when one comes there for the first time, is indefinable. One gathers together all one's recollections, one strives to remember all one has learnt, read, and heard of this ancient capital of the world, and to combine all these echoes of the soul to make them more sonorous. It is difficult to realise the idea that you are really at the spot where such great events have occurred, that you tread the soil trodden by such great men. At the age especially when one has just completed the study of the classic writers who tell you what has passed and give you the names of those who have lived at Rome, the very name of the Holy City raises up a multitude of thoughts. You do not see things as they really are, but by a magical effect of imagination you see them as they were formerly; the present puts on the pomp and the colours of the past. Directly I had alighted from my carriage I hurried to the Capitol and the Palatine Hill. I could not subdue my impatience—I could not sufficiently occupy my eyes and my imagination with the sight of the places which had witnessed such great actions. 'Is it possible,' I said to myself, 'that it was here that lived the Scipios, the Catos, the Gracchi, the Cæsars, that it was here that Cicero thundered and that Horace sang?' and I recalled to my memory all that had since my infancy been the object of my admiration and my sympathies, all that history and the poets had taught me. I regret much that at the time of which I am speaking the Christian antiquities of Rome did not interest me as greatly as they do now; all my dreams were only of heroic but pagan Rome.

Penetrated with these grandeurs of the past, I thought of nothing else during my stay in the Holy City. I determined to visit every trace of its antiquity, and by examining the ruins and studying all that had been written on the streets and buildings of ancient Rome, to construct the plan of the city as it appeared at different epochs. My idea was to make not only general plans, but a series of drawings of portions of Rome, such as the Tiber, the seven hills, and the edifices built upon them, so far as imagination can picture them—beginning with the first foundation of Rome on the Palatine hill and the Capitol, then showing her as she was under the Kings and in the various phases of the Republic, when she was still built of brick, and finally under Augustus, when she became a city of marble. Each of these drawings was to represent something characteristic of the epoch. The above plan, which to me was new, had been conceived by others, but it has never been thoroughly executed. The drawings representing the open spaces, the temples, and the forts of the city divided into seventeen districts (*regioni*) occupied me during the whole period of my stay. I wished my work to be exact and conscientious, and to make it so required much time, expense, and research. It was necessary to consult a multitude of authors, to check their statements, to employ antiquaries, architects and draughtsmen. I did not finish the work; all I could do was to begin it. I had a very good plan and two water-colour drawings made of the city. One represented the Forum as it was at the time of the Republic, with a crowd of people opposite the Palatine hill, as was usual in stormy times; an orator above the rostra; and the *via sacra* with the edifice where the voting was to take place. The other drawing, which was of large size, also represented the Forum, but on the side opposite the Capitol. The subject was the triumph of Germanicus. All the temples on the slope of the Capitoline hill were there, and Tiberius, his face distorted with hatred and rage, was represented as coming out of one of them accompanied by the members of the Senate. A third drawing, which I ordered to be made during my absence, was to represent the grottoes on the Tiber near the Palatine hill during the first period after the foundation of Rome; but it did not in any way carry out my idea.

My enforced absence from my country, my family, and my friends, and the fact that my position was uncongenial and without aim, plunged me into a sort of lethargy similar to that which had oppressed me on my first arrival at St Petersburg, and the gravest and most unexpected events could not rouse me. During the whole of my life the sole motive of my actions has always been one exclusive and dominating sentiment—the love of my country. That which did not in some way promote the welfare of my fatherland or of my fellow-countrymen had no value in my eyes, while the most futile matters relating to Poland interested me. Thus at Warsaw there was a good French theatre and a very indifferent Polish one; yet I went to the latter much oftener than to the former.

The period of my stay in Rome was, however, by no means barren of events. Pius VI, who had been elected Pope at Venice, entered the Holy City while it was still suffering from the excesses committed by the French troops. I recollect that at a reception of Romans and foreigners at the house of Monsignor Consalvi, who had just been promoted cardinal, the Russian Consul, wishing to pay him a compliment, awkwardly predicted that he would become Pope, and that Consalvi very sincerely protested against the idea. I may say in passing that in my official reports I did not hesitate to censure the French for their conduct. This seemed greatly to astonish M. Karpoff, the first secretary of the legation, an old Russian official who had probably been instructed to

watch my movements. Knowing the sympathy
generally felt by the Poles for France, he almost
reproached me for my severity ; but I replied that if
the French behaved badly I could not speak well of
them. All men, whether French or not, lose on a
nearer view much of the prestige and enthusiasm
which they inspire at a distance.

The friendly relations which had existed between
the Emperor Paul and Austria began about this time
to grow cool. There were various reasons for this ;
I will give some which are not generally known.
The Grand-Duchess Alexandra, the eldest of Paul's
daughters, who, as I stated in a previous chapter, was
intended by Catherine to marry the King of Sweden,
became the wife of the Archduke Joseph, Prince
Palatine of Hungary. This union was contracted at
a period when the Courts of St Petersburg and
Vienna were on the best terms with each other,
and at the time when Souvaroff had gained his victories in Italy. The Archduchess was of uncommon
beauty; her features resembled those of her brother
Alexander, she was most graceful, and she possessed
all the moral qualities which are the highest ornaments of her sex. When she came to Vienna, she
inspired universal admiration, respect, and enthusiasm,
without in any way seeking it. Her popularity extended from the highest classes of the capital to the
most populous districts of Vienna. This displeased
the Neapolitan wife of the Emperor Francis II, a
woman of jealous and eccentric character and of extraordinary habits. She loved monsters, and filled
her gardens with burlesque statues. There was

something underhand and cunning in her manner, and she never looked one straight in the face. The only persons with whom she was intimate were her servants, who never ventured to rival her in beauty or wit; she gave them *bizarre* banquets and private theatricals in which she played herself, and her husband, whose mind was also not very brilliant or suited to a more distinguished society, used to take part in these entertainments, of which singular stories were related at Vienna. The Archduke Joseph's beautiful and amiable wife was regarded by the Austrian Empress as a rival, and she rendered the Archduchess's life so intolerable that the latter had to withdraw with her husband to Ofen. She was Paul's favourite child, and when he learnt how she had been treated he flew into a rage, demanded that she should be sent back to St Petersburg, and even threatened war. Her death, which happened almost simultaneously with that of her father, rendered any further action useless, but it plunged the whole of St Petersburg in deep mourning, while Austria, having re-established herself in Italy, had begun to treat the Russian Cabinet with less deference. The Austrians had sent away Souvaroff with little ceremony, and thinking themselves already masters of the country, they were glad to rid themselves of an inconvenient and haughty ally. Then came the defeats of the Russians in Holland and Switzerland, which contributed still further to estrange Paul from Austria. Buonaparte, taking advantage of this change, hastened to send back to Paul all the Russian prisoners, clothed

in new uniforms and well provided in every respect.
This friendly step on the part of the First Consul gained
the Emperor's heart, and he declared to his Ministers
and the people with whom he was intimate that
Russia had been too lavish of her blood and money
for Austria, who only repaid her by ingratitude.
He enlarged on Buonaparte's 'noble conduct,' and
interpreted it as a sign that he sincerely wished for
the alliance of Russia ; he had, Paul said, suppressed
anarchy and the demagogues, and there was no good
reason why Russia should not come to an understanding with him. Paul accordingly sent General
Levaschoff to Naples to mediate between the French
Government and that of the two Sicilies. In passing
through Rome the General gave me a letter from
Count Rostopchin, the Foreign Minister—the first I
had received from him—introducing General Levaschoff to me and instructing me to give him my
services. I did this readily, for the General was not
only a good companion, but was very friendly. Soon
after I received a second missive from Count Rostopchin informing me that the Emperor, not being
satisfied with the conduct of the Sardinian Court,
wished me to leave it under the pretext of visiting
Naples.

I was delighted at this order, and left for Naples
at once. The Court was not there ; its only representative was the Chevalier Acton, an all-powerful
Minister, who had left Sicily to govern the kingdom.
Though Naples, thanks to its brilliant sun and its
unequalled position, cannot be otherwise than beautiful, it had at that time a very melancholy appearance.

M. Italinsky, afterwards envoy at Constantinople
and then at Rome, a Ruthenian and formerly a
surgeon, had for some years been at Naples on a
diplomatic mission.  He was, or at least he tried to
be, a learned man.  He studied archæology and
physics, and knowing how to do his own business
people concluded that he would also know how to do
that of others.  In ordinary matters he certainly
acquitted himself very well, but he was never very
successful, either from want of capacity or of good
fortune, in dealing with affairs of greater importance.
He owed his favour with Catherine to some letters
on the eruptions of Mount Vesuvius, and he always
stated at the end of his despatches that he had blotted
them with some of the volcanic ash that had fallen
upon Pompeii eighteen centuries before.  He was
also helped in his career by his ill-health.  He suffered
from a sort of aneurism which obliged him to lead a
very regular life, but it lasted many years.

The Court of Naples sought to take advantage
of the friendly relations which had been established
between Paul and Buonaparte.  It solicited the
Emperor's intervention against the advance of the
French, which people thought would, after Marengo,
be continued to the most southerly point of the
peninsula.  Italinsky proceeded, at the instigation
of the Chevalier Acton, to Florence, where Murat
then was, to obtain some favourable conditions for
Naples; but his efforts produced no result.  He
started before my departure from Rome, and M.
Karpoff, my first secretary, being jealous of Italinsky,
and wishing to revenge himself for his sarcasms,

called this fruitless journey 'The Italinsky Pilgrimage.'

On my arrival at Naples I requested Italinsky to present me to the Chevalier Acton. We found him at a table covered with papers. He was a thin, sickly-looking man, with a gaunt and sallow countenance and black eyes. His demeanour showed at every movement the ravages of time; he walked with a stoop, and constantly groaned under the weight of his labours and misfortunes. Yet he was said to be the favourite lover of the Queen Caroline, who was the absolute mistress of her husband and the kingdom. Nothing was done except by her will, and even official letters bore her signature by the side of the King's, to show that they governed together. She had all the activity of her brother, the Emperor Joseph; this was sufficiently proved by her sparkling glance, her quick movements, and her shrill voice. I saw her at Leghorn when she was disembarking with her daughters, one of whom, the Princess Amélie, afterwards married Louis-Philippe. Maria Theresa had fashioned her daughter's mind to domination long before she was married to King Ferdinand. This habit of governing afterwards became her passion. She also had a succession of favourites; her fiery temperament was stimulated by the Neapolitan climate, and it would have been difficult to believe her boast that she had never had a child of whom Ferdinand was not the father, if there were not an unfortunate likeness between them and Ferdinand— not only as regards personal appearance, which, in his case, was anything but attractive, but also as to character and mind. Queen Amélie was the only exception to this; her rare moral qualities were in strong contrast to the characteristics of Caroline's other children.

The Russian army corps which then occupied Naples was under the command of General Borozdin, the eldest of three brothers. There was at one time some idea of pushing on the combined forces as far as Rome in order to check the French advance, and the General had himself gone to Rome with this object. But he could not come to an understanding with General Roger de Damas, the commander of the Neapolitan troops, as to who was to have the general command, and the plan was dropped, fortunately for the two generals, who would otherwise have inevitably been defeated. General Borozdin was a dandy of the time of Catherine; he was very amiable in society, but his military talents were doubtful. Being in the most voluptuous of climates and furnished with ample means by the Neapolitan Government, which reckoned on the Russian troops more than on its own, Borozdin had all a Russian can desire—display and enjoyment. To complete his pleasures, fortune had also placed in his hands a conquest which he valued more highly than any other. A British Consul who had married a young and charming lady had thought fit to escape from Naples directly he heard of the defeat of the Austrians at Marengo and the victorious march of the French towards Florence and the south. In order not to expose his young wife to the dangers of a precipitous journey, he determined to place her in the charge of General Borozdin, with whom he was on intimate terms.  The worthy Englishman doubtless thought he had deposited his treasure in safe hands, but the temptation was too strong.  The lady was like a rosebud, and Borozdin had with the husband's permission located her in the house where he himself lived, on the plea that he would thereby be able to take better care of her.  The result may be imagined.  When the panic of a French invasion was over, the Consul returned, took back his wife, and could not sufficiently express his gratitude to his friend for the service he had rendered him.  Shortly after, when I left Naples to go back to Rome, the General accompanied me.  He was in very good spirits, and did not speak any more about the Consul's wife, whom he had doubtless soon forgotten.

# CHAPTER XI

## 1801



ASSASSINATION OF THE EMPEROR PAUL.

THE news of the death of the Emperor Paul suddenly fell upon us like a clap of thunder in a summer sky. The first result of the unexpected news was astonishment accompanied by a sort of fear, but these sentiments were soon followed by others of joy and relief. Paul had never been loved even by those whom he had benefited. He was too fantastic and capricious; no one could ever rely upon him. The messenger who brought the news to the legation looked as if he were deaf and dumb; he did not answer any questions, and merely uttered unintelligible sounds. He was terrified, and had been ordered to keep silence. All he did was to convey to me a few words from the Emperor Alexander, who asked me to come to St Petersburg at once.

[The following is a translation of Alexander's letter :—

*March* 17*th* 1801.

You have already heard, dear friend, that owing to the death of my father, I am at the head of affairs.

I do not mention any details, as I wish to give them to you by word of mouth. I write to ask you at once to hand over all the affairs of your mission to the next senior member of it, and to proceed to St Petersburg. I need not tell you with what impatience I am waiting for you. I hope heaven will watch over you during your journey and bring you here safe. Adieu, dear friend, I cannot say more. I enclose a passport for you to show at the frontier.

ALEXANDER.]

This order gave me immense pleasure. Italy is undoubtedly a delicious country, full of interest, especially for those who have leisure to study it. The wars which had ravaged it had at this period deprived it of some of its charms, though the ravages were in themselves not without interest. But I was far from my country, my family, and all I loved; I was sad and solitary; I was never quick to make acquaintances; much time and peculiar circumstances were necessary to break the ice which separated me even from people whom I saw often. My old friendships, though not numerous, are dear to me, and I do not feel inclined to contract new ones. It was with inexpressible pleasure, therefore, that I made my preparations for departure; but I could not leave Naples without visiting Vesuvius, Herculaneum, Pompeii and Portici. As I was ascending Mount Vesuvius, I stumbled and began to slip down towards the crater, when the guide ran up, gave me his hand, plunged his iron-shod staff into the moving débris, and thus saved my life. The idea of death was at that moment very painful to me; I was about to return to my people, and to exchange a passive for an active existence. I felt that I was more attached to life than ever, as radiant visions of hope, not yet dispelled by experience, were floating before my eyes.

On the day following that on which the news of the death of the Emperor Paul was communicated to us, the messenger sent from St Petersburg by the Neapolitan Ambassador brought us a circumstantial account of the catastrophe. It did not astonish me, as I saw before my departure that the whole of the Court was planning a conspiracy against the Emperor. At Naples the general impression was one of joy almost exceeding the bounds of decency. On the second day after the messenger's arrival, General Borozdin gave a ball to which he invited the best society of the town. The dancing was kept up all night, and the General encouraged by his example public demonstrations of a gaiety which, to say the least, was ill-timed. The wife of the British Consul was conspicuous at this fête in a pink dress.

My companion on the journey from Rome to Florence was General Levaschoff; he was very amiable and full of anecdote. He had been sent to Naples with the secret intention of negotiating an armistice between the belligerents. The Emperor Paul, who had withdrawn from the coalition, wished by this means to avoid all reproach; and General Levaschoff had been despatched immediately after the defeats in Holland and Switzerland on the pretext of visiting Italy for his pleasure. His instructions were drawn up by Count Rostopchin, then Foreign

Minister, who was shortly after deprived of his portfolio and retired to Moscow, upon which Paul broke off his relations with Austria, declared war against England, and prepared to enter into a cordial alliance with Buonaparte. All this happened during my absence, and although I was on good terms with Kutayschoff,* I never could learn the exact details either of Levaschoff's mission or of Rostopchin's dismissal. Levaschoff's negotiations, which he was authorised by the Cabinet to continue after Paul's death, were not successful. The French negotiators at once suspected that Alexander would not be so easy to manage as Paul had been. This was doubtless also Murat's opinion, for, without waiting for instructions from Paris, he occupied the whole of Tuscany, and continued his advance. The more he suspected, however, the more loudly he proclaimed his belief in the maintenance of a friendly understanding between France and Russia. He occupied the palace of the Duke of Tuscany, where he gave me and General Levaschoff a splendid dinner to which all the generals and the principal people of Florence, comprising some sixty persons, were invited. We sat on each side of Madame Murat, who was very slim and pretty. Murat, who sat opposite, paid us constant attention, and was more amiable than his wife. He proposed the health of the Emperor of Russia, and afterwards drank the health of both of us. When the General went to see him in his box at the play he observed that above his head were the Russian and French flags crossing each other.

* The Emperor's barber. See page 184.

Before leaving Italy I went to Leghorn to bid farewell to Marshal Rzewuski, whom I found very ill. I met at his house several of my countrymen; among them was Sokolnicki, a very active officer of engineers whom I had known in Lithuania during our campaign of 1792,* and Rozniecki, who was with me in the camp of Golomb and in the skirmish at Granno. Both heartily shook me by the hand, recalling with emotion the events we had witnessed together. Rozniecki told me that he had introduced into the Polish legions the system of drill practised at Golomb, which made the Polish cavalry of the republican army superior in rapidity of movement to the French cavalry. I left Rzewuski with a heavy heart, and this illustrious man, proved friend, and worthy citizen passed away soon afterwards. He is buried in the Campo Santo at Pisa. His family intended to erect a monument to his memory, but I believe they did not carry out their intention.

After staying two days at Vienna, I went on to Pulawy, where I found the whole of my family; but much as they wished me to stay, they felt that it was necessary I should go on at once. I travelled day and night until I reached St Petersburg, where my brother joined me soon after.

I approached the Russian capital with mixed feelings of joyful impatience to see the persons to whom I was attached, and of uncertainty as to the changes which time and new circumstances might have produced in them. A messenger met me at Riga with a friendly note from the Emperor and a

---

* See page 53.

written order for post-horses to accelerate my journey.
The note was addressed to me in the Emperor's own
hand, and gave me the title of Privy Councillor,
which gives the rank of General. I was surprised at
this rapid promotion, which I decided not to accept.
When I arrived at St Petersburg I showed Alexander the envelope, and he admitted that he had
given me the title in a moment of forgetfulness, but I
could have taken advantage of the mistake had I
wished to do so. I never received any rank or
honorary distinction in Russia than that which had
been conferred upon me by the Emperor Paul.

The first impression produced upon me by the
Emperor Alexander confirmed my presentiments.
He had just come back from parade, and was pale
and tired. He received me cordially, but with a sad
and depressed air, as if he were under a feeling of
constraint. Now he was the master, I thought I
observed in him—perhaps wrongly—a tinge of reserve and embarrassment which pained me. He took
me into his room. 'You have done well to come,'
he said; 'our people expect you with impatience'—
alluding to some persons who he thought were more
enlightened and liberal than the rest, whom he regarded as his particular friends, and in whom he
placed entire confidence. 'If you had been here,'
he added, 'things would not have turned out as they
did; I should never have been led away if I had
had you by my side.' Then he spoke to me of his
father's death with inexpressible grief and remorse.
We often returned to this subject, and Alexander
gave me full details of it which I shall repeat below,

together with information communicated to me by
other actors in the tragedy. As regards the matters
which had formerly absorbed our attention, and as
to which I wished to ascertain how far his feelings
had been changed by his sudden elevation to the
throne, I found him much as I expected ; not quite
aroused from his past dreams, to which he still always
returned, but already in the iron hands of reality ;
yielding to force, and not yet knowing the extent of
his power or how to use it.

Alexander told me that the first man who spoke
to him about the plans of the conspirators was Count
Panin, and he never forgave him. This personage
seemed destined more than anyone else to play an
important part in the affairs of the Empire, and he
had all that was wanted for such an undertaking ;
a celebrated name, uncommon talents, and much
ambition. While still young he had made a brilliant
career. He was appointed Russian Minister at
Berlin, from which post he was recalled by the
Emperor Paul to be a member of the Council of
Foreign Affairs under the orders of Prince Alexander
Kourakin, his maternal uncle and Paul's faithful
friend, the companion of his infancy and youth, who
alone of the leading men at the Imperial Court had
escaped the Emperor's caprices and remained steadily
in favour. Besides his relationship to Prince
Kourakin, Count Panin was the son of the eminent
General of that name, and the nephew of the Minister
who had been the Grand-Duke Paul's tutor. These
antecedents gave Count Panin a certain assurance
and air of importance. He was a tall, reserved-looking

man, and wrote in excellent French; his despatches were perfect in every respect both as regards matter and style. He had the reputation of being a man of great talent, energy, and good sense, but of dry and imperious character. After remaining for some months in the Foreign Office, he displeased the Emperor, who deprived him of his appointment and sent him back to Moscow. As will be seen further on, Panin was one of the chief leaders of the conspiracy which brought about Paul's death, though he did not actually take part in it. During my previous stay in the Russian capital I had never met him, for having entered the diplomatic career at an early age, he scarcely ever came there. His wife, a Countess Orloff, did not follow him abroad; she was good and amiable, and had been very kind to me. When I returned to St Petersburg she insisted on bringing me and her husband together, and did everything in her power to make us friends, but without success. Apart from other reasons, the Count's exterior would, I think, almost have alone been sufficient to make this impossible. I have often been struck by his icy expression; his impassive countenance, on a body as straight as a spike, did not induce one to address him. I saw him but little, however, and my judgment of his character might have been erroneous and even unjust.

The two Counts Panin and Pahlen were at that time the strongest heads of the Empire. They saw further and more clearly than the other members of Paul's Council, to which both of them belonged; and they agreed to initiate Alexander into their plans.

It would not have been prudent to attempt anything without being assured of the consent of the heir to the crown. Devoted fanatics or enthusiasts might no doubt have acted otherwise. By not implicating the son in the dethronement of his father, by exposing themselves to a certain death, they would have better served both Russia and the prince who was to be called upon to govern her ; but such a course would have been almost impracticable, and it would have demanded an audacity and antique virtue which in these days very few men possess. Pahlen, as Governor of St Petersburg, had easy means of access to the Grand-Duke, and obtained from him a secret audience for Panin ; their first interview took place in a bath. Panin represented to Alexander the evils from which Russia was suffering and would continue to suffer if Paul continued to reign. He said that Alexander's most sacred duty was to his country, and that he must not sacrifice millions of people to the extravagant caprices and follies of a single man, even if that man was his father; that the life, or at least the liberty, of his mother, of himself, and of the whole of the Imperial family was threatened by Paul's inconceivable aversion for his wife, from whom he was entirely separated ; that this aversion increased from day to day, and might prompt him to the most outrageous acts ; and that it was therefore necessary to save Russia, whose fate was in Alexander's hands, by deposing Paul, which would be the only means of preventing him from inflicting greater calamities on his country and his family, and securing to him a quieter and more happy life. This speech produced a great impression on Alexander, but it did not con-: vince him. It required more than six months to enable his tempters to obtain his consent to their plans. Pahlen had at first left all the speaking to Panin, who was an adept at specious arguments; but when the latter was sent to Moscow, Pahlen completed the work of his colleague by hints and allusions, intelligible only to Alexander himself, which were so skilfully introduced, with a military frankness which he made almost as effective as eloquence, that Alexander became more and more persuaded that the aims of the conspiracy were just and good.*

It was a thousand pities that a prince so anxious and so well qualified to be a benefactor to his country did not hold entirely aloof from a conspiracy which resulted almost inevitably in his father's assassination. Russia certainly suffered much under the almost maniacal Government of Paul, and there are no means in that country of restraining or confining a mad sovereign; but Alexander felt and exaggerated in his own mind all his life the sombre reflection of the crime committed on his father, which had fallen on himself, and which he thought he could never wipe out. This ineffaceable stain, although it was brought about solely by his inexperience and his total and innocent ignorance of Russian affairs and the Russian people, settled like a vulture on his conscience, paralysed his best faculties at the commencement of

---

* Pahlen had the reputation of being one of the most astute men in Russia. There was no one like him to get out of a difficulty, and to advance his interests in spite of all obstacles. He fell, however, just at the moment when he seemed to have nothing to fear. He came from Livonia, where they used to say of him : ' Er hat die Fiffologie studiert ' (he was a student of Fiffology—from the German word, *fiffig* cunning).

his reign, and plunged him into a mysticism sometimes degenerating into superstition at its close.

At the same time it must be admitted that the
Emperor Paul was precipitating his country into
incalculable disasters and into a complete disorganisation and deterioration of the Government machine.
Paul governed intermittently, without troubling himself about the consequences, like a man who acts
without reflection according to the impulse of the
moment.  The higher classes, the principal officials,
the generals and other officers of rank—all, in a
word, who thought and acted in Russia—were more
or less convinced that the Emperor had fits of
mental alienation.  His reign became a rule of terror.
He was hated even for his good qualities, for at
bottom he desired justice, and this impulse sometimes
led him to do a just thing in his outburst of rage;
but his feeling of justice was blind, and struck
at all without discrimination of circumstances; always
passionate, often capricious and cruel, his decrees
were constantly suspended over the heads of the
military and civil officers, and made them detest the
man who thus filled their lives with uncertainty and
terror.  The conspiracy had the sympathy of all, for
it promised to put an end to a régime which had
become intolerable.  A sovereign may commit grave
mistakes, bring evils on his country, cause its wealth
or its power to decline, without exposing himself to
death as a punishment for his misdeeds.  But when
the sovereign authority weighs at every moment on
each individual in the State, and continually disturbs
like a fever the peace of families in the ordinary

relations of life, passions are excited which are much more formidable than those produced by evils which, though affecting the entire community, are little felt by individuals. This was the real motive of Paul's assassination. I utterly disbelieve the story that English money contributed to this event. For even supposing—and I am sincerely convinced there is no foundation for such a belief—that the English Government of that day was devoid of all feelings of morality, such an expenditure would have been totally unnecessary. The deposition, if not the murder, of Paul had become inevitable in the natural course of events. Even before my departure from St Petersburg it was the fashion among the young men of the Court to talk freely on this subject, to make satirical epigrams on Paul's eccentricities, and to suggest all kinds of absurd plans for getting rid of him. The universal aversion to his rule was shown, often without any attempt at concealment, on every possible occasion ; it was a State secret which was confided to all, and which no one betrayed, though the people lived under the most redoubted and the most suspicious of sovereigns, who encouraged espionage, and spared no means of obtaining exact information not only of the actions, but of the thoughts and intentions of his subjects. The wish to get rid of the Emperor Paul showed itself more strongly the nearer one approached the Court and the capital, but it did not really become active until almost at the moment of its execution. Notwithstanding the extreme favour with which the conspiracy was regarded in the most distinguished society of the Empire, it could not have attained its objects, and would probably have been discovered, if the appointment of Governor-General of St Petersburg, which placed at his disposal the garrison and the police, had not been in the hands of the chief promoter of the enterprise.

One day the Emperor said, with a scrutinizing glance at Pahlen: 'I hear a conspiracy is being formed against me.' 'Such a thing is impossible, Sire,' replied the General with his frank and good-natured smile; 'it cannot be formed unless I belong to it.' This reassured Paul, though it is said that his suspicions were aroused by anonymous letters, and that on the eve of his death he had sent for General Araktcheyeff to give him the place of Governor-General of St Petersburg, after dismissing Pahlen. If Araktcheyeff had come in time St Petersburg would have been the scene of many tragic events; he was a man imbued with a strong sentiment of order and with an energy which sometimes grew into ferocity. His return would probably have been followed by that of Count Rostopchin, and Paul might then have been saved. He had dismissed so many of his Ministers that he was surrounded by incapable men to whom he had given the highest offices of State. Prince Kourakin continued to direct Foreign Affairs with much kindness of heart and little wisdom, while an insignificant man named Obalianinoff held the important post of Procurator-General, involving the direction of the police and the whole administration of the Empire, solely because he had formerly been steward of the Gatchina estate. Kutayschoff was still the man in whom Paul most trusted. When he was arrested on the day after his master's death, letters were found in his pocket revealing the objects of the conspiracy, the time when it was to be executed, and the names of the conspirators. But he never opened his letters directly he received them. His favourite saying was 'business to-morrow,' and he put these important letters in his pocket in order not to interrupt his pleasures that evening.

Paul had just finished the construction at immense expense of the palace of St Michael.*  This building was erected after his own designs, and was a sort of fortified castle where the Emperor thought his life would be safe.  'I never felt happier or more at ease,' he said when he took up his residence in this palace, and he became more self-indulgent and ·autocratic than ever.

Although everybody sympathised with the conspiracy, nothing was done until Alexander had given his consent to his father's deposition.  The men who undertook to carry out the plan were Pahlen and the two Zuboffs, whom Paul had recalled from exile and loaded with favours, thinking he had nothing to fear from them now he was in his new castle.  Their first step was to induce a number of Generals and other officers of rank who were their friends to come under various pretexts to St Petersburg ; and this was rendered more easy by the fact that Paul himself had invited many high functionaries and Generals to be

---

* The swindling which took place at the erection of this building is almost incredible.  The chief architect, B . . ., was an Italian foreman, whom Count Stanislas Potocki had brought from Italy, and who passed from Warsaw to the service of the Grand-Duke Paul at Gatchina.  B . . . 's commissions on the work he performed were enormous, and he left a large fortune to his daughter's husband and their children, who became Russian diplomatists.

present at the fêtes he was about to give on the marriage of one of his daughters. Pahlen and the Zuboffs took steps to enlist the services of some of the more eminent of the Generals, without stating positively what they intended to do. But it was necessary to act at once, for the slightest imprudence or revelation might place the Emperor in possession of their secret, and he was already so suspicious that he might at any moment take some step which would be their ruin. It was not known whether he had already sent for Araktcheyeff and Rostopchin. The former lived at twenty-four hours' journey from St Petersburg and might come at any moment. Doubtless he and Rostopchin would endeavour to moderate the Emperor's excesses, but their influence would probably not be sufficient to put a stop to the severities he wished to exercise with regard to several members of the Imperial family. It was evident that any further delay or vacillation would be most dangerous, and might be the cause of incalculable calamities; and the conspirators accordingly decided to strike the blow on the 3rd of March, 1801.

On that evening Plato Zuboff gave a grand supper, to which were invited all the Generals and other officers of rank who were supposed to approve of the objects of the conspiracy. These were only now clearly explained to them, as the only way to secure the enterprise against accidents was for two or three leaders to prepare it, and not to announce it to the others who were to take part in it until the moment for its execution should arrive.

Zuboff represented to his guests the deplorable condition in which Russia was placed by the insanity of her sovereign, the dangers to which both the State and each individual citizen were exposed, and the probability that new and more outrageous excesses might at any moment be expected. He pointed out that the insane act of a rupture with England was contrary to the essential interests of the Russian nation, dried up the sources of its wealth, and exposed the Baltic ports, and the capital itself, to the gravest disasters; and that none of those whom he addressed could be sure of their fate on the morrow. He enlarged on the virtues of the Grand-Duke Alexander, and on the brilliant destinies of Russia under the sceptre of a young Prince of such promise, whom the Empress Catherine, of glorious memory, had regarded as her successor, and had intended, if she had not been prevented by her death, to place on the throne. He concluded by declaring that Alexander, rendered desperate by the misfortunes of his country, had decided to save it, and that all that was now necessary was to depose the Emperor Paul, to oblige him to sign a deed of abdication, and, by proclaiming Alexander Emperor, to prevent his father from ruining both himself and his Empire. Pahlen and both the Zuboffs repeated to the assembled guests the assurance that the Grand-Duke Alexander approved of their plan. They were careful not to say how much time it took them to persuade him, and with what extreme difficulty and with how many restrictions and modifications his consent was finally obtained. The last point was left vague, and every-one probably explained it after his own fashion.

When the company had been made to understand that Alexander's consent had been given, there was no further hesitation. Meanwhile champagne was drunk freely and there was general excitement. Pahlen, who had gone away for a short time on business connected with his functions as Governor-General, came back from the Court and announced that the Emperor did not seem to suspect anything, and had said good-night to the Empress and the Grand-Dukes as usual. Those who had been at supper in the palace afterwards said they recollected that Alexander, when he took leave of his father, did not change countenance or show that he was conscious of the scene which was preparing. Probably they did not look at him, for he has often told me how agitated he was, and certainly the risks he ran not only for himself, but for his mother, his family, and many others were enough to make him sad and anxious. The Grand-Dukes were always obliged to maintain an attitude of strict reserve before their father, and this constant habit of concealing their emotions and thoughts may explain why at this grave and supreme moment no one perceived in Alexander's countenance what was passing in his mind.

At the Zuboffs' house the guests had become so convivial that time went fast. At midnight the conspirators set out for the Emperor's palace. The leaders had drunk but moderately, wishing to keep their heads clear, but the majority of those who followed them were more or less intoxicated; some could even hardly keep their legs. They were divided

into two bands, each composed of some sixty Generals
and other officers. The two Zuboffs and General
Bennigsen were at the head of the first band,
which was to go to the palace direct; the second
was to enter through the garden, and was under
the command of Pahlen. The aide-de-camp in waiting,
who knew all the doors and passages of the palace,
as he was daily on duty there, guided the first band
with a dark lantern to the entrance of the Emperor's
dressing-room, which adjoined his bedroom. A
young valet who was on duty stopped the conspirators and cried out that rebels were coming to
murder the Emperor. He was wounded in the
struggle which ensued, and rendered incapable of
further resistance. His cries waked the Emperor,
who got out of bed and ran to a door which communicated with the Empress's apartments and was hidden
by a large curtain. Unfortunately, in one of his fits
of dislike for his wife, he had ordered the door to be
locked; and the key was not in the lock, either because
Paul had ordered it to be taken away or because his
favourites, who were opposed to the Empress, had
done so, fearing lest he should some day have a fancy
to return to her. Meanwhile the conspirators were
confused and terrified at the cries of Paul's faithful
defender, the only one he had at a moment of supreme
danger when he believed in his omnipotence more
than ever and was surrounded by a triple line of walls
and guards. Zuboff, the chief of the band, lost heart
and proposed to retire at once, but General Bennigsen
(from whom I obtained some of these details) seized
him by the arm and protested against such a dangerous

step. 'What?' he said, 'You have brought us so far, and now you want to withdraw? We are too far advanced to follow your advice, which would ruin us all. The wine is drawn, it must be drunk. Let us march on.'

It was this Hanoverian that decided the Emperor's fate; he was one of those who had only that evening been informed of the conspiracy. He placed himself at the head of the band, and those who had most courage, or most hatred for Paul, were the first to follow him. They entered the Emperor's bedroom, went straight to his bed, and were much alarmed at not finding him there. They searched the room with a light, and at last discovered the unfortunate Paul hiding behind the folds of the curtain. They dragged him out in his shirt more dead than alive; the terror he had inspired was now repaid to him with usury. Fear had paralysed his senses and had deprived him of speech; his whole body shivered. He was placed on a chair before a desk. The long, thin, pale, and angular form of General Bennigsen, with his hat on his head and a drawn sword in his hand, must have seemed to him a terrible spectre. 'Sire,' said the General, 'you are my prisoner, and have ceased to reign; you will now at once write and sign a deed of abdication in favour of the Grand-Duke Alexander.' Paul was still unable to speak, and a pen was put in his hand. Trembling and almost unconscious, he was about to obey, when more cries were heard. General Bennigsen then left the room, as he has often assured me, to ascertain what these cries meant, and to take steps for securing the safety of the palace and of the Imperial family. He had only just gone out at the door when a terrible scene began. The unfortunate Paul remained alone with men who were maddened by a furious hatred of him, owing to the numerous acts of persecution and injustice they had suffered at his hands, and it appears that several of them had decided to assassinate him, perhaps without the knowledge of the leaders or at least without their formal consent. The catastrophe, which in such a case was, in a country like Russia, almost inevitable, was doubtless hastened by the cries above referred to, which alarmed the conspirators for their own safety. Count Nicholas Zuboff, a man of herculean proportions, was said to be the first that placed his hand on his sovereign, and thereby broke the spell of imperial authority which still surrounded him. The others now saw in Paul nothing but a monster, a tyrant, an implacable enemy—and his abject submission, instead of disarming them, rendered him despicable and ridiculous as well as odious in their eyes.

One of the conspirators took off his official scarf and tied it round the Emperor's throat. Paul struggled, the approach of death restoring him to strength and speech. He set free one of his hands and thrust it between the scarf and his throat, crying out for air. Just then he perceived a red uniform, which was at that time worn by the officers of the cavalry guard, and thinking that one of the assassins was his son Constantine, who was a colonel of that regiment, he exclaimed : ' Mercy, your Highness, mercy ! Some air, for God's sake ! ' But the conspirators seized the hand with which he was striving to prolong his life, and furiously tugged at both ends of the scarf. The unhappy Emperor had already breathed his last, and yet they tightened the knot and dragged along the dead body, striking it with their hands and feet. The cowards who until then had held aloof, surpassed in atrocity those who had done the deed. Just at that time General Bennigsen returned. I do not know whether he was sincerely grieved at what had happened in his absence; all he did was to stop the further desecration of the Emperor's body.

Meanwhile the cry ' Paul is dead!' was heard by the other conspirators, and filled them with a joy that deprived them of all sentiment of decency and dignity. They wandered tumultuously about the corridors and rooms of the palace, boasting to each other of their prowess; many of them found means of adding to the intoxication of the supper by breaking into the wine cellars and drinking to the Emperor's death.

Pahlen, who seems to have lost his way in the garden, came to the palace with his band immediately after the deed had been consummated. It is said that he had delayed his arrival on purpose, so as to be able to profess to have come to the Emperor's assistance in case his colleagues should have failed. Be this as it may, he was extremely active directly he arrived, giving the necessary orders during the rest of the night, and omitting nothing which could give him a claim to reward as the prime mover and commander of the enterprise.

It will be seen from the above narrative how easy
it would have been for the undertaking to have been
foiled by an accident, notwithstanding the precautions
which had been taken to ensure its success. The
conspiracy had the sympathies of the higher classes
and most of the officers; but not of the lower ranks
of the army. The persons who suffered from Paul's
insane fits of rage and severity were usually the
higher military and civil officials; his caprices very
seldom affected men of the lower ranks, who, moreover, were continually receiving extra pay and rations
of bread, wine, and brandy when they were on drill
or on a parade. The punishments to which the
officers were exposed did not therefore produce any
unpleasant impression on the common soldier; on the
contrary, they were a sort of satisfaction to him for
the blows and ill-treatment he constantly had to
endure. Moreover, his pride was flattered by the
great importance attached to his calling, for to Paul
nothing could be more important than a foot raised
too soon on the march, or a coat badly buttoned on
parade. It amused and pleased the soldiers to see
their Emperor dispensing endless punishments and
severities among the officers, while he took every
opportunity to afford to the men ample compensation
for the work and trouble that was required of them.
The soldiers of the Guard, many of whom were
married, lived with their families almost in opulence,
and both they and those of the other regiments
were satisfied with and attached to their Emperor.
General Talyzin, one of the principal conspirators,
who was very popular among the soldiers, had under-

taken to bring to the palace one of the battalions of the first regiment of the Guard which was under his command. He assembled the men after leaving Zuboff's supper, and began to tell them that their fatigues were about to cease, and that they would now have an indulgent and kind sovereign who would not impose upon them the rigorous duties they had hitherto had to perform. He soon perceived, however, that his words were not listened to with favour; the soldiers preserved a gloomy silence, their faces had a sombre expression, and some murmurs were heard. The General cut short his speech, uttered in a sharp tone of command the words ' Right wheel—march,' and the battalion, which had now again become a machine, marched to the palace, all the outlets from which it occupied.

Count Valerian Zuboff, having lost a leg in the Polish War, could not belong to either of the bands of the conspirators. He entered the palace soon after the death of the Emperor became known, and then went to the guard-room to sound the opinions of the soldiers. He congratulated them on having a new and a young Emperor; but this compliment was ill received, and he was obliged to leave the room hastily to avoid disagreeable manifestations. All this shows how easy it would have been for Paul to crush the conspirators if he had been able to escape them for a moment and to show himself to the guards in the courtyard. It also shows how illusory and impracticable was Alexander's plan of keeping his father in confinement. If Paul's life had been saved, blood would have flowed on the scaffold, Siberia would have been crowded with exiles, and his vengeance would probably have extended to his sons.

I will now, describe what happened during this terrible night in the part of the palace which was inhabited by the Imperial family. The Grand-Duke Alexander knew that his father would in a few hours be called upon to abdicate, and without undressing he threw himself on his bed full of anxiety and doubt. About one o'clock he heard a knock at his door, and saw Count Nicholas Zuboff, his dress in disorder, and his face flushed with wine and the excitement of the murder which had just been committed. He came up to Alexander, who was sitting on his bed, and said in a hoarse voice: 'All is over.' 'What is over?' asked Alexander in consternation. He was somewhat deaf, and perhaps he feared to misunderstand what was being said to him, while Zuboff on his side feared to state exactly what had been done. This somewhat prolonged the conversation; Alexander had not the least idea that his father was dead, and did not therefore admit the possibility of such a thing. At length he perceived that Zuboff, without clearly explaining himself, repeatedly addressed him as 'Sire' and 'Your Majesty,' while Alexander thought he was merely Regent. This led to further questioning, and he then learnt the truth. Alexander was prostrated with grief and despair. This was not surprising, for even ambitious men cannot commit a crime or believe themselves the cause of one without repulsion, while Alexander was not at all ambitious. The idea of having caused the death of his father filled him with horror, and he felt that his reputation had received a stain which could never be effaced. As for the Empress, directly the news reached her she dressed hastily and rushed out of her apartments with cries of despair and rage. Perceiving some grenadiers, she said to them repeatedly : ' As your Emperor has died a victim to treason, I am your Empress, I alone am your legitimate sovereign ; follow me and protect me.' General Bennigsen and Count Pahlen, who had just brought a detachment of men whom they could trust to the palace to restore order, strove to calm her and forced her with difficulty to return to her room. She had scarcely entered it, however, than she wished to go out again, although guards had been placed at her door. At first she seemed determined at all risks to seize the reins of government and avenge her husband's murder. But though she was generally respected, she was not capable of inspiring those feelings of enthusiastic devotion which cause men to act impulsively and without weighing the consequences. Her appeals to the soldiers (which were perhaps rendered somewhat ridiculous by her German accent) produced no effect, and she retired in confusion, vexed at having uselessly disclosed her ambitious views.

I never heard any details of the first interview between the Empress and her son after Paul's assassination. Subsequently they came to an understanding with each other ; but during the first terrible moments Alexander was so absorbed by his remorse that he seemed incapable of saying a word or thinking of anybody. His mother, on the other hand, was in a passion of grief and animosity ; the only member of the Imperial family that retained her presence of mind was the young Empress. She did her utmost to console Alexander and give him courage and self-reliance. She did not leave him during the whole of the night, except when she went for a few moments to calm her mother-in-law and persuade her to stop in her room and not expose herself to the fury of the conspirators. While in this night of trouble and horror some were intoxicated with triumph and others plunged in grief and despair, the Empress Elizabeth alone exercised a mediatory influence between her husband, her mother-in-law, and the conspirators.

During the first years of his reign, Alexander's position with regard to his father's murderers was an extremely difficult and painful one. For a few months he believed himself to be at their mercy, but it was chiefly his conscience and a feeling of natural equity which prevented him from giving up to justice the most guilty of the conspirators. He knew that there was a general sympathy for the objects of the conspiracy, and that those who had personally taken part in their realisation had only decided to do so when they were assured of his consent. It would have been difficult under these circumstances to distinguish between degrees of guilt; every member of the society of St Petersburg was more or less an accomplice in the fatal deed, for those who wished Paul to be deposed must have known that his deposition, if resisted, might have involved his death. If the assassins alone had been brought to trial, they would certainly have accused the other conspirators and have referred to Alexander's consent in justification of their action, though the crime had been committed against his express wish. Moreover, he did not for many years know who they were, as all the conspirators were interested in keeping the secret. The assassins all perished miserably, including Count Nicholas Zuboff, who, not daring to show himself at Court, died in retirement, consumed by illness, by remorse, and by disappointed ambition.

Although Alexander's mother continually urged him to proceed against his father's murderers, it was not possible for him to do so by the ordinary and public legal means. He looked with horror upon those who had led him to give his consent to the conspiracy, and he used every other means in his power to discover and punish the assassins. General Bennigsen was removed from his post of Governor-General of Lithuania, which was given to General Kutuzoff, and it was not until the year 1806 that Bennigsen's military reputation compelled Alexander to place him at the head of the army which fought at Eylau and Friedland. Prince Plato Zuboff, the ostensible chief of the conspiracy, failed, notwithstanding all his efforts, to obtain any appointment, and feeling that his presence was disagreeable to the Emperor, he retired to his estates, married a handsome Polish woman, and then went abroad. His bad reputation, however, everywhere preceded him, and he died obscure and unregretted.

As for General Pahlen, he at first thought himself strong enough to maintain his position without support. It was he who took the external and internal measures which had become urgently necessary by the probability of the British fleet entering the waters of Riga, Revel, and Cronstadt, after the battle of Copenhagen. Nelson had won this battle shortly after the Emperor Paul was assassinated.* The news did not become public for some days, and in the trouble and confusion which followed, Pahlen took into his own hands the reins of State, wishing to add to his important functions as Governor-General of St Petersburg the still more important ones of Secretary of State for Foreign Affairs. The proclamations issued at that time were all signed by him; nothing could be done except through him and with his consent; he affected to protect the young Emperor, and scolded him when he did not do what he wished, or rather ordered. Alexander, overcome with sadness and despair, seemed to be in the power of the conspirators; he thought it necessary to treat them with consideration and bend his will to theirs.

Just at this time the important post of Procurator-General, which combined the direction of all the administrative departments of the Empire, became vacant by the dismissal of one of Paul's favourites who had occupied it. Alexander had the happy idea of selecting for this place General Beklescheff, who had been summoned by Paul to St Petersburg perhaps with the same object. He was a Russian of the old school, with coarse and abrupt manners, ignorant of the French language or barely under-

---

* Paul was assassinated on the night of the 23rd of March 1801; the battle of Copenhagen was fought on the 2nd of April, 1801.

standing it, but firm, straightforward, and compassion-
ate for other people's misfortunes.   His reputation as
a man of high character was generally established,
and he had even preserved it while he was Governor-
General of the Polish provinces of the South, where
he showed himself just to the people he governed and
severe to his subordinates.   He had done his best to
prevent robbery and falsehood, and did not permit the
officials to sell justice by auction as other Russian
governors did.   When he left he was followed by the
gratitude of the people whom he had ruled.   No more
difficult task can be given to a high Russian official,
and not many have acquitted themselves so well.   He
knew nothing of what was going on beyond the
frontier, but he was thoroughly acquainted with the
ukases and the routine of·Russian administration ; he
executed them with rigour, but with all the justice of
which they were capable.   He had been a complete
stranger to the conspiracy, and Alexander complained
to him of Pahlen's dictatorial ways.   Beklescheff,
with his usual abruptness, expressed surprise at a
Russian autocrat complaining that he did not do as
he pleased.   'When flies annoy me,' he said, 'I
drive them away.'   The Emperor took the hint, and
signed an order directing Pahlen at once to leave St
Petersburg and proceed to his country house.
Beklescheff, who was an old friend of Pahlen's, undertook as Procurator-General to take this order to him
and make him leave within twenty-four hours.   He
came to Pahlen early on the following morning, and
the latter at once obeyed the Emperor's decree.   This
event made much noise at St Petersburg, and Alex-

ander was accused of duplicity because on the day before Pahlen was banished he had behaved to him as usual when he received his daily report. He could, however, hardly have done otherwise, and the fact is that this act of absolute sovereignty on the part of the young Emperor displeased and alarmed the leaders of the conspiracy.

The views of the Zuboffs as to the conspiracy were communicated to me by Count Valerian Zuboff a few days after my return to St Petersburg. He complained that the Emperor did not declare himself for his true friends, who had placed him on the throne and had not feared any danger they had incurred in his service. The Empress Catherine had acted otherwise; she had always supported those who had helped her, and had not hesitated to maintain them in power. By this wise and sagacious conduct, said Zuboff, she had been able always to reckon on their devotion. No one hesitated to make a sacrifice for her, as such sacrifices were always rewarded; but Alexander was exposing himself by his vacillating conduct to the most serious consequences, and was discouraging his best friends. Zuboff added that the Empress Catherine had expressly enjoined him and his brother to look upon Alexander as their only legitimate sovereign, and to serve him alone with unshaken zeal and fidelity. This they had done, and what was their reward? He said this to exculpate his brother and himself in the eyes of the young Emperor with regard to the assassination of his father, and to prove to him that their conduct was the .necessary result of the engagements Catherine had demanded of them as to her grandson. But they did not know that Alexander, and even his brother Constantine, by no means regarded their grandmother's memory with veneration or attachment. During this conversation, which lasted more than an hour, I several times interrupted the Count to explain the young Emperor's conduct. It was evident that the Zuboffs wished me to communicate their views to the Emperor, and though I did not promise, I considered it my duty to do so. Their statements produced but little impression on Alexander, but they showed that the conspirators were still very proud of their achievement, and that they felt convinced they had done a great service to Russia, had a right to Alexander's gratitude and confidence, and were necessary to the security and prosperity of the new reign. They even hinted that their discontent might be dangerous to him. Alexander, however, was deaf both to their arguments and their threats. He could not look with favour on his father's murderers, or give himself up into their hands. Moreover, he had already dismissed Pahlen, who was perhaps the only one of the conspirators who by his ability, his connections, his boldness, and his ambition, could inspire serious fear or become really dangerous. Alexander also dismissed other leaders of the conspiracy who were not dangerous, but the sight of whom was odious and disagreeable to him. The only leader who remained at St Petersburg was Count Valerian Zuboff, who was a member of the Imperial Council. His amiability and frankness pleased Alexander and inspired him with confidence; and this feeling was confirmed by the attachment which the Count professed (I think sincerely) to have for the Emperor personally, and also by his indolence, his unwillingness to take appointments to which onerous duties were attached, and especially by his amours, which occupied nearly the whole of his time.

The punishment of Pahlen and the other leaders of the conspiracy was the most painful that could have been inflicted on them, and Alexander punished himself with more severity than the others. His grief and the remorse which he was continually reviving in his heart were inexpressibly deep and touching. In the midst of the pomp and the festivals of the coronation, the young Emperor was reminded of the similar ceremonies which had been passed through by his father, and he saw in imagination Paul's mutilated and blood-stained body on the steps of the throne which he was now himself to ascend. This brilliant display of supreme power, instead of rousing his ambition or flattering his vanity, increased his mental tortures, and he was never, I think, more unhappy. He remained alone for hours, sitting in silence with fixed and haggard looks.

With me, as the confidant of his secret thoughts and troubles, he was most at his ease, and I sometimes entered his room when he had been too long under the painful influence of these fits of despair and remorse. I tried to recall him to his duties; he acknowledged that a painful task was before him, but the severity of his condemnation of his own conduct deprived him of all energy. He replied to all my exhortations and words of encouragement and hope: 'No, it is impossible, there is no remedy. I must suffer. How can I cease to suffer? This cannot change.'

Those who approached him often feared that his mind would be affected, and as I was then the only person who could speak to him freely I was constantly urged to do so. I think I was of some use in preventing Alexander from succumbing under the weight of the terrible thought that pursued him. Some years later, the great events in which he took a leading and glorious part gave him some consolation and for a time, perhaps, absorbed all his faculties; but I am certain that towards the end of his life it was the same terrible thought that so depressed him, filling him with a disgust of life and a piety which was perhaps exaggerated, but which is the sole possible and real support in the most poignant grief. When we returned to this sad topic, Alexander often repeated to me the details of the plan he had formed to establish his father in the Palace of St Michael and afterwards to enable him as much as possible to reside in the Imperial Palaces in the country. 'The Palace of St Michael,' he said, 'was his favourite residence, and he would have been happy there. He would have had the whole of the winter garden to walk and ride in.' Alexander intended to attach a riding-school and a theatre to the palace, so as to bring together within its precincts everything that could have amused the Emperor Paul and made his life happy. He judged of his father by himself. There was always in his noble character a feminine element, with its strength and weakness. He often used to make plans which could not be realised, and on this idealistic foundation he raised complete structures which he made as perfect as possible. Nothing was more impracticable—especially in Russia—than the romantic means which Alexander had devised of rendering his father happy, while depriving him of his crown and of the possibility of tormenting and ruining the country. Alexander was not only young and inexperienced; he had almost the blind and confiding inexperience of childhood, and this characteristic remained with him for some years until it was destroyed by the realities of life.

I have not concealed anything in regard to the catastrophe which inaugurated his reign, ·for this was the best way of doing him justice. The complete truth, without any restriction, exculpates him up to a certain point from an odious accusation, and explains how he was led into an action which he abhorred and why he seemed not to have punished the assassins with sufficient rigour. I have shown how inexperienced and unambitious he was, and what were the plausible and even honourable motives by which he was actuated. We may pity Alexander, but we must hesitate to condemn him.*

---

* M. de Langeron's account of the assassination of the Emperor Paul is true, but it does not give the whole truth, as it does not explain how Alexander was induced to give his consent to his father's deposition and why he did not bring the conspirators to trial. (*Note by Prince Adam Czartoryski.*)

# CHAPTER XII

## 1801-2



THE opinions and sentiments which had seemed to
me so admirable in Alexander when he was Grand-
Duke did not change when he became Emperor;
they were somewhat modified by the possession of
absolute power, but they remained the foundation
of all his principles and thoughts. They were for
many years like a secret passion which one dares not
acknowledge before a world incapable of compre-
hending it, but which constantly dominates us and
colours our actions whenever its influence can make
itself felt. I shall often have occasion to return to
this important subject in explanation of Alexander's
character, for at other times the Emperor, being
thoroughly aware of his power and the obligations it
imposed upon him, might have been compared to a

man who still likes to amuse himself with the toys of his childhood, and leaves his favourite recreation with regret in order to return to the occupations and duties of real life.

There was no longer any question of the old reveries of extreme liberalism; the Emperor ceased to speak to me of his plan of giving up the throne, or of the document he had made me write. But he was constantly thinking of more practical matters, such as the administration of justice, the emancipation of the masses, equitable reforms, and liberal institutions; this was his diversion when he was alone with me. He understood the often insurmountable obstacles which the most elementary reforms would meet with in Russia; but he wished to prove to those with whom he was intimate that the sentiments he had expressed to them were still the same, notwithstanding the change in his position. It was necessary, however, not to disclose them, and still less to take a pride in them, in the presence of a public which was at that time so little prepared to appreciate them, and would have regarded them with surprise and horror. Meanwhile the government machine continued to work according to the old routine, and the Emperor was obliged to take part in its management. In order to remedy the discrepancy between Alexander's opinions and his acts, he established a Secret Council composed of persons whom he regarded as his friends and believed to be animated by sentiments and opinions in conformity with his own. The first nucleus of this Council was formed by the young

Count Paul Strogonoff, M. de Novosiltzoff, and myself. We had long been in near relations with each other, and these now became more serious. The necessity of rallying round the Emperor and not leaving him alone in his desire of reform drew us more closely together. We were regarded for some years as models of intimate and unshakeable friendship. To be superior to every personal interest, and not to accept either presents or distinctions, was the principle of our alliance. Such a principle could not take root in Russia, but it was in accordance with the ideas of Alexander's youth and inspired him with special esteem for his friends. I was the sole author of the principle, which indeed was specially suited to my peculiar position. It was not always liked by my companions, and the Emperor himself afterwards grew tired of servants who wished to distinguish themselves by refusing to accept rewards which were so eagerly sought by everyone else.

The understanding between us had, as I have shown, begun at the coronation of the Emperor Paul at Moscow, and we had for a long time been on intimate terms, as we met daily at Count Strogonoff's. The fourth member admitted by the Emperor to the Secret Council was Count Kotchoubey. Being the nephew of Count Bezborodko, a Minister who had been held in high esteem by the Empress Catherine, he was sent when still very young to the embassy at Constantinople, and was recalled under the Emperor Paul to give place to M. Tamara. While at Constantinople he conducted himself to the satisfaction of his Government, and was perhaps the only Russian who was well treated in the capital. This was at the time of our grand Diet,* and during the reign of Leopold, when Russians used to be received by ladies in drawing-rooms in a manner anything but flattering. I remember the Countess Caroline, afterwards Lady Guildford, being asked by Count Tchernitcheff to insult him in order to enable him to gain a wager, upon which she said: 'You are a Russian.' But to return to Count Kotchoubey. He had acquired a certain European varnish and grand manners which made him a favourite in society. Vanity, a general defect among men, and especially among Russians and Slavs of all kinds, exposed Kotchoubey to sarcasms from other vain people, but he was too good-natured to resent them. He was also accustomed to business, but he had not much knowledge; his intelligence was clear, but not deep, and he had more good-nature and sincerity than are usually found in Russians. This did not save him from certain weaknesses characteristic of his nation—a great wish for place, for distinction, and especially for a fortune to cover his expenses and those of his family, which had become very numerous. He showed an extreme readiness to adopt any opinion that might be in fashion and to follow any lead imposed upon him by a superior will or by the conventions of society. When he was with us he professed liberalism, though with a certain reserve, as it was not to be reconciled with his real opinions. His vanity was such that it betrayed itself when he strove most to conceal it, which ex-

---

* The Diet which passed the Constitution of the 3rd of May, 1791. It sat for four years, from 1788 to 1792. (See page 52).

posed him to the satire of my two colleagues. I did not join in their jokes, as he had estimable qualities and showed me much friendly feeling, of which I had strong evidence some years later.

We were privileged to dine with the Emperor without a previous invitation, and we used to meet two or three times a week. After coffee and a little conversation, the Emperor used to retire, and while the other guests left the palace, the four members of the Secret Council entered through a corridor into a little dressing-room, which was in direct communication with the private rooms of their Majesties, and there met the Emperor. Various plans of reform were debated; each member brought his ideas, and sometimes his work, and information which he had obtained as to what was passing in the existing administration and the abuses which he had observed. The Emperor freely expressed his thoughts and sentiments, and although the discussions at these meetings for a long time had no practical result, no useful reform was tried or carried out during Alexander's reign which did not originate in them. Meanwhile the Official Council, namely, the Senate and the Ministers, governed the country in the old way. Directly the Emperor left his dressing-room he came under the influence of the old Ministers, and could do nothing of what had been decided upon in the Secret Council; it was like a masonic lodge from which one entered the practical world.

This mysterious Council, which was not long concealed from the suspicions, or ultimately from the knowledge, of the Court, and was designated 'the young men's party,' grew impatient at not obtaining any result whatever from its deliberations; it pressed the Emperor to carry out the views he had expressed to us and the proposals he considered desirable and necessary. Once or twice an attempt was made to induce him to adopt energetic resolutions, to give orders and make himself obeyed, to dismiss certain superannuated officials who were a constant obstacle to every reform and to put young men in their place. But the Emperor's character inclined him to attain his end by compromises and concessions, and moreover he did not yet feel sufficiently master of the position to risk measures which he thought too violent. In our Council Strogonoff was the most ardent, Novosiltzoff the most prudent, Kotchoubey the most time-serving, and I the most disinterested, always striving to curb undue impatience. Those who urged the Emperor to take immediate and severe measures did not know him. Such a proposal always made him draw back, and was of a nature to diminish his confidence. But as he complained of his Ministers and did not like any of them, an attempt was made in the Council, before inducing him to change them, to discuss the matter in a practical spirit, apart from the abstract considerations of reform which had previously occupied us. Strogonoff accepted the post of Procurator of the First Department of the Senate; and Novosiltzoff was appointed one of the Emperor's secretaries, a place which gave him many advantages, as every letter addressed to the Emperor passed through his hands, and he had a right to publish the

Emperor's ukases.  His special department, however, was at first to deal with promoters of public undertakings, who are sometimes men of talent, but more often adventurers of very doubtful honesty who flock to Russia from abroad at the beginning of each new reign.  This was a duty for which he was qualified by his varied knowledge in matters of finance and industry, and it was at the same time a school which did much to form his character. I must not here forget the fifth member of the Secret Council, M. de la Harpe, Alexander's tutor, who had come on a visit to his former pupil.  He did not take part in the after dinner meetings, but he used to have private conversations with the Emperor, and frequently handed to him memoranda reviewing all the branches of the administration.  These memoranda were first read at the secret sittings, and afterwards passed on from one member of the Council to the other to be considered at leisure, as they were interminably long.  M. de la Harpe was at that time about forty-four years of age; he had been a member of the Swiss Directory, and always wore the uniform of that appointment, with a large sword fastened to an embroidered belt outside his coat.  We were all of opinion that he did not merit his high reputation and the esteem in which Alexander held him.  He belonged to the generation of men nourished with the illusions of the last part of the eighteenth century, who thought their doctrine a sort of philosopher's stone, or universal remedy which removed all difficulties to the regeneration of society.  M. de la Harpe had his own particular panacea for Russia, and he explained it in such diffuse papers that Alexander himself had not the courage to read them. One of his favourite phrases was *organisation réglementaire;* an important idea no doubt, but he used to repeat it so often and with such emphasis that it was at last attached to him as a sort of nickname.

The Emperor, perhaps without admitting it to himself, began to think less of the capacity of his former tutor, though he was always seeking reasons for raising him in our esteem; his character he always continued to value highly. He did not like us to cast ridicule on the inanity of M. de la Harpe's papers, and he was always much pleased when we praised any of his former tutor's suggestions. But in truth M. de la Harpe had little or no influence on the reforms which Alexander afterwards introduced. He had the good sense to hold aloof from our meetings, and the Emperor himself preferred this, in order, I suppose, to avoid the scandal which might have been produced by an ex-director of the Swiss Republic and a recognised revolutionist preparing reforms for the Russian Empire. He was, however, recognised as one of our colleagues; there was always a chair ready for him at our meetings, and when he left St Petersburg he assured us that he would still in spirit take part in our deliberations.

Immediately after the Emperor's accession the Margravine of Baden, mother of the Empress Elizabeth, hastened to St Petersburg, being happy and impatient to see again a beloved daughter from whom she had been separated for seven years. She was accompanied by the Margrave of Baden, her husband, son of the reigning Grand-Duke, and the Princess Amelia, the eldest of their children. These visitors represented an influence totally opposed to the principles which were at that moment being advocated by M. de la Harpe at St Petersburg. The Margravine was the sister of the first wife of the Emperor Paul,* who died in Russia while still young and beautiful, and was more regretted by the Empress Catherine, her family, and the whole Court than by her husband, who discovered after her death from some letters which she had imprudently kept that he was not the sole possessor of her heart.†

The Margravine was tall, with a grand air and much dignity in her movements, and it was evident that in her youth she must have been beautiful. She had justly obtained a high reputation for wisdom, prudence, and wit, which placed her far above the generality of German princesses of similar rank. The Empress Dowager, instead of rejoicing at the prospect of the Margravine's influence counteracting that of M. de la Harpe, took umbrage at it; the two princesses were too unlike each other to agree. Moreover, the Margravine had brought about the marriage of her youngest daughter with the King of Sweden, who had refused the Grand-Duchess Alexandra.‡ This marriage, which at that time was

---

* A third sister was married to the Grand-Duke of Saxe-Weimar; she had a daughter who was married to the Duke of Mecklenburg, and became the mother of the Duchess of Orleans. I recollect that when the Duchess of Orleans arrived in Paris I was struck by her likeness to the members of her family whom I had known in Russia. *(Note by Prince Adam Czartoryski.)*

† The gentleman who had attracted the Grand-Duchess's attention was Count Andrew Razumovski, then young and strikingly handsome. He made so many conquests among the ladies of St Petersburg that he was sent as ambassador to Stockholm, and afterwards to Naples, where he gained the favour of the Queen. *(Note by Prince Adam Czartoryski.)*     ‡ See page 135.

regarded as the most brilliant in Europe, was a triumph of which the Margravine was very proud, and did not contribute to reconcile her with the Empress Dowager, especially as the eldest of the daughters of the House of Baden, the twin sister of the Princess Amelia, had married the Elector, who afterwards became King of Bavaria, while none of the Russian Grand-Duchesses had attained so elevated a position. On the other hand, the Margravine was disappointed to see that the Empress Dowager retained all the advantages of a reigning sovereign and had not given up any of them to her daughter-in-law. When Alexander ascended the throne, being desirous above all to appease the continual regrets of his mother since the catastrophe which had made him Emperor, he left her the dower of a million roubles which Paul had assigned to her at the beginning of his reign, and added nothing to the moderate allowance of which his wife was in receipt as a Grand-Duchess. The latter readily and graciously accepted this arrangement, which afterwards placed her in a painful position, and deprived her of the means of responding to the numerous applications for assistance which were addressed to her. The Empress Dowager continued to have the sole direction of various charitable, educational, and even manufacturing, establishments with which she had been charged during the preceding reign, while the Margravine would have liked her daughter to take a more active part in affairs and to be in a position to distribute the largesses and benefits which one has a right to expect from the wife of the sovereign.

I was very amiably received by the Margravine, and afterwards she honoured me for many years with marks of her kindness. She often spoke to me about the Emperor with the most lively interest. She feared that the reforms he was contemplating would prove ill-timed, hurtful, and dangerous, and wished him to be dissuaded from introducing them; she did not approve his tendency to diminish the ceremonial and the splendour of the Court, and she especially objected to his assumed simplicity of manner, which, she said, made those who approached him and whose duty was to obey him too familiar, thereby giving his Court an appearance ill-suited to the greatness of the Empire. She pointed to the example of Buonaparte, who, she said, was better acquainted with mankind and with what was necessary to obtain its respect, its obedience, and its admiration; who surrounded himself by pomp and magnificence, and neglected nothing that could augment the prestige without which supreme authority cannot be maintained. She wished to rouse Alexander's ambition, to make him profit by the lessons which so great a genius was then giving to the world, and to induce him to become Napoleon's rival without being his enemy, so that the acts of his Government, like those of the First Consul, should be continual proofs of greatness, of strength, and of decided will. The Russians, she said, want such a Government quite as much as the French. I communicated these conversations to the Emperor; I thought some of the things said by the Margravine were just and true, and that they might strike him and be of use to him. But they made no impression whatever. He admired Napoleon, but did not think himself capable of imitating him. They were two opposite natures, and their lines of action were different. It was not till many years after that a supreme danger, the boundless ambition of the ruler of France, and his incredible blunders, gave Alexander an opportunity of showing great though always defensive qualities, which enabled him to conquer his rival. After some months' stay, the Baden family left St Petersburg to visit the Queen of Sweden, the youngest sister of the Empress Elizabeth, at Stockholm. During this journey a great misfortune happened: the Margrave died in consequence of a carriage accident. This made it impossible for the Margravine to reign over the Grand-Duchy, and had fatal consequences for her family.

During the summer of 1801 the Secret Council continued to meet. The only measure it decided upon before the coronation was the dismissal of Count Panin, whose participation in the conspiracy which brought about the death of Paul filled Alexander with dislike and suspicion. After much discussion it was resolved that Panin should be succeeded as Minister of Foreign Affairs by Count Kotchoubey, but should be allowed to remain at St Petersburg. The Emperor, wishing to avoid disagreeable scenes, treated Panin as a Minister up to the last moment, and this again was interpreted as a sign of duplicity. The Emperor's will was notified to Panin by letter, and Kotchoubey entered upon his duties to the great satisfaction of Alexander and of our council.

So long as Panin remained at St Petersburg he

was surrounded by spies, and the Emperor every day received reports from the secret police stating in detail all that Panin had done from the morning till the evening, where he had been, whom he had spoken to in the street, how many hours he had passed out of doors, who had visited him, and as far as possible what he had said. These reports were read in the Secret Council, and were drawn up in the mysterious style affected by police agents to give a certain interest to the most insignificant circumstances. They did not really contain anything remarkable, but the Emperor was extremely anxious, and was always suspecting Panin of new plots. He had no peace till Panin had left St Petersburg, which he did soon after, knowing that he was everywhere pursued by spies, and that his presence was disagreeable to the Emperor. He subsequently received orders never to show himself in any town where the Emperor might be staying, and passed the rest of his life in retirement at Moscow or in the country.

In this way three of ' ours,' as the members of the Secret Council were called by the Emperor, were placed in the sphere of practical affairs, and obtained experience of the difficulties and obstacles which are met with directly one becomes a wheel in the government machine. As for me, I had no ambition to serve Russia; I was there merely by accident, like an exotic plant in a foreign land, with sentiments which could not, as regards their full scope, be brought into entire accord even with the intimate opinions of the friends whom accidental and quite ordinary circumstances had given me; and I remained the only

member of the Secret Council that had held aloof
from practical life, and was glad not to enter it. I
was often tired of my position, and yearned after
my country and my parents; I wished for nothing
so much as to go back to them, and the only thing
that retained me was my personal attachment to the
Emperor and the wish to be able to serve my country
through my influence with him. But this hope often
seemed entirely to disappear. The dreams of my
early youth had vanished like the morning mists
before the sun's rays, and whose was the blame?
Could I expect of men more than they can or know
how to give? Those whose pretensions and hopes are
in advance of realities and possibilities in this short
life of ours are doomed to cruel disappointment; but
when one's illusions have gone, one hopes at least not
to be deprived of some prospect of happiness, and this
was in many respects denied me. I accordingly often
thought of leaving St Petersburg. The Emperor
spoke to me of Poland at more and more prolonged
intervals; when he found me anxious and discouraged,
he returned to the subject, but no longer in the same
way. He used to console me vaguely or keep silence
on a matter with which he found it more and more
difficult to deal, though it was the only real bond of
connection between us. At the same time, while
avoiding precise explanations, he wished me always
to believe that on this point as on many others he
had not changed his opinions or his intentions. But
in his position what could he do and what could I
reasonably ask for?

On my return to St Petersburg, I had no longer

found there Buonaparte's aide-de-camp, Duroc, who had come with another officer to compliment Alexander on his accession. Paul's death was a severe blow to the First Consul; he had hoped much from a sovereign who would never admit that what he ordered was impossible. Fortune had favoured Buonaparte in his efforts to gain the good-will of the Emperor Paul. The news of the Russian prisoners who had been clothed and sent back to their country by France, and that of other advances skilfully made to Russia, had arrived at St Petersburg at the moment when Paul was in a violent rage with Austria and England, partly on account of the defeat of the Russian armies in Switzerland and Holland, which Paul attributed to the lukewarmness of the allies, and partly because of the capture of Malta, which Buonaparte had offered Paul, and which the English, now masters of the island, had refused to give up to him, although he had already been appointed Grand-Master of the Order. Under these circumstances, Paul, always passionate and impulsive, took a violent fancy to Napoleon and the French Government, whom he had detested, and an equally violent dislike for the allies, who had been the particular objects of his affection and zealous support. As usual with him, his likes and dislikes became stronger as time went on. After the chivalrous challenge which I have already mentioned,* he concluded a maritime alliance with Denmark and Sweden with the object of closing the Baltic to the English, and maintaining the inviolability of neutral flags. France, Spain, and Holland were to join their

---

* See page 192.

fleets to those of the Northern powers in order to destroy the maritime supremacy of England. Paul had ordered the whole of the Don Cossacks to march at once to India under the command of their attaman Platoff; and although this order had spread consternation among the Cossacks, and their chief did not know how to execute it, he was preparing to obey it.

What would have happened if Paul had continued to reign it is not easy to say. Nelson's expedition to Copenhagen had certainly foiled the plan of a naval combination against England, but its success had been almost entirely due to Nelson's boldness and good fortune. If the Danes had had the courage to persevere, this rash enterprise might have ended very differently. So great, however, was the terror inspired by Paul that the Danes adhered to his alliance in spite of their defeat. He had ordered his coasts and his harbours to be placed in a state of defence, and I doubt whether the British fleet could without considerable reinforcements have attempted an attack upon Cronstadt or Revel; if not, time would have been given for reforming and strengthening the alliance of the naval powers.

Paul's sudden death at once dissipated all the difficulties of the coalition, and created new ones for Napoleon, as it lost him a powerful friend. In his infatuation for the First Consul, Paul had persuaded himself that it did not matter whether the ruler of France were legitimate or not, so long as he could make himself obeyed. He had accordingly expelled Louis XVIII from his dominions,* and encouraged

* Louis returned to Russia after Paul's death.

Napoleon in his ambition to become Emperor of France. His death changed everything. The naval alliance lost its strength and value, there was no further necessity for fortifying the coasts and harbours, and trade, which had been suspended in Russia to the great detriment of the proprietors of mines and land, resumed its ordinary course, while the Don Cossacks, who had already proceeded on a day's march towards the Caucasus, turned their horses' heads homewards and crossed themselves in gratitude for the abandonment of Paul's insane enterprise.

The immediate result of Paul's death, so far as European politics were concerned, was an arrangement between Russia and England. The state of war which Paul had maintained against that power—which had long been Russia's best customer for iron, corn, wood for building, sulphur, and hemp—was one of the principal grievances of the Russian people against their Emperor, and immediately after his death the Government hastened to effect an arrangement with England which showed how eager Russia was to effect a reconciliation at any price. The interests of her maritime allies were not sufficiently considered, and essential points on the question of the neutral flag were either passed over in silence or left in doubt. The cessation of hostilities was the great object aimed at. Alexander had in reality no great sympathy for England. His education had given him ideas and inclinations totally different from those of the policy of Pitt ; and Napoleon's aide-de-camp Duroc was accordingly received by him with a sincere cordiality which was hardly to be expected in a moment of reaction against Paul's infatuation for the First Consul. Duroc's reception was, indeed, the result of Alexander's secret and personal sympathy for the principles of 1789, which had been inspired in him by M. de la Harpe. Alexander was glad to see at last Frenchmen of the famous Revolution, who he supposed were still Republicans; he regarded them with curiosity and interest, having talked and thought so much about them. Both he and the Grand-Duke Constantine took great pleasure in addressing them as 'citizens,' thinking that the title was one they were proud of. This was a great mistake, and Napoleon's envoys had repeatedly to point out that the term had gone out of fashion in France before Alexander and his brother ceased to use it. Napoleon's chief motive in sending his confidential aide-de-camp to St Petersburg was to sound the young Emperor as to his feelings with regard to a French alliance. I was told that Duroc wrote to Napoleon that there was no cause for either hope or fear; this statement was at the time perfectly accurate, and was founded on an exact knowledge of Alexander's character at the beginning of his reign; but later on it was belied by events.

Count Panin, who was then Foreign Minister, had concluded a convention with Duroc which did not mention any of the difficulties that had long sown discord between the two countries, and had prevented them from being at peace with each other. In this convention there was only one remarkable article, and it was directed against Poland and the Poles.

Russia and France engaged reciprocally not to protect political refugees, and not to help them in their efforts against the order of things established in their respective countries. This article was aimed by France against the Legitimists, and by Russia against the Poles. Thus Alexander's first public act was an abandonment of the sentiments which had united us. He did not tell me anything of it, and it was doubtless a very natural arrangement to make between two countries that wished to be on good terms with each other ; it was the necessary consequence of an agreement between Russia and France, which must be always fatal to the Poles. I made this remark with some sadness to the Emperor, who answered with embarrassment that the article had no real significance, that he could not avoid accepting it, as it had been proposed by France and agreed to by Count Panin, that it was a mere formality which ought not to cause me any anxiety, and that the destinies of Poland were as dear to him as ever. The best and most powerful man can do nothing if circumstances do not permit him to act and to keep his promises ; and it may safely be asserted that Alexander was the only sovereign of that time who, without publicly admitting it, still remembered and busied himself about the future of Poland. She had for the moment been forgotten by all Europe, with France at its head. Since the treaty of Lunéville there had not been any Polish troops in France ; the legions were either broken up or sent to St Domingo never to return.*

* The Polish legions were formed in Italy by Dombrovski in 1797, with the object of restoring Poland to her former independence. They rendered great services to France in her Italian campaigns, but were afterwards abandoned by Napoleon, who did not wish to offend the partitioning powers.

Our patriots, having lost all hope for their country, had retired from the French service, and the glorious fall of Kosciuszko and the massacre of Praga had been effaced by the misfortunes we had suffered in other countries. No one thought of us, and it is not surprising that this general oblivion should have had some influence on Alexander's disposition in our behalf.

Not having any wish to take a prominent part in Russian affairs, and often losing the hope which had sustained me of being able to serve my country, I continually had fits of depression and did not conceal my wish to go back to my parents. The Emperor, to fulfil his old promises and prove to me that he had not changed, generously determined of his own initiative to give the inhabitants of the Polish provinces he governed proofs of his good-will. This sometimes raised my spirits and consoled me for the impossibility of realising brighter hopes whose disappointment became the regret and torment of my life. In the two first years of Alexander's reign I had the happiness of rendering services to many of my countrymen who had been sent to Siberia either by Catherine or by Paul, and had been forgotten in their banishment; these were restored by Alexander to their liberty and their families. Their sentences were cancelled, their confiscated estates were given back to them, either in land or in money, and the refugees who had served in France or in the legions were allowed to come back without any difficulty. The Emperor also interfered on behalf of the Poles confined in the fortress of Spielberg and other foreign prisons, and his wishes were zealously carried out by Kotchoubey, Panin's successor at the Russian Foreign Office.   The abbé Kollontay, who was regarded as the most revolutionary of the Poles, was set free and came to live and die in the part of Poland which was under Alexander's rule.   Count Oginski and several others were also invited to return ; they were received with distinction and were given back their fortunes, which were in several cases considerable. The days of persecution, of political trials and enquiries, of suspicious precautions, had gone by, and for some time the Poles were trusted and left at peace by their Russian rulers.

The Emperor also wished to improve the administration and regularise the course of justice in the Polish provinces.   He looked for Poles capable of filling the principal posts, which had previously been occupied by Russians.   Trials were expedited and made more equitable, both on the spot and in the third department of the Senate of St Petersburg, which was the final Court of Appeal charged with cases arising in the Polish provinces.   These acts deserved our gratitude, but could not compensate us for the loss of our national existence, and they were far from realising the hopes expressed in the conversations of our youth.   While consoled from time to time by the advantages which were granted to my countrymen, I could not see what more I could obtain for my country.   My life was one continuous struggle between the consolation of having done some good and the regret—not to say the self-reproach—of never being able to reach the object of my wishes and hopes. When I felt that the realisation of the noble sentiments Alexander had expressed for my country was indefinitely postponed, I was utterly discouraged, and felt invincible disgust for the Court and all its members. Although on intimate terms with my colleagues of the Secret Council, I could not entirely confide in them; their Russian thoughts and feelings, which they often expressed, were too incompatible with my hopes. It was to Alexander only that I could freely disclose my sadness and its cause. Our old intimacy, though it was more restricted, had not ceased, and while my position with regard to current affairs was insignificant, I still possessed the Emperor's confidence more than any one else; when he was with me he was more confiding and more at his ease than with the others; I understood him better, and could more freely tell him the truth about men and things, and even about himself.

Our secret interviews were interrupted by the coronation at Moscow. The recollection of this ceremony, to which I have already alluded, left me a painful impression. I know nothing more disagreeable than these occasions, when everything is thrust out of its accustomed order. Festivals generally give me a feeling of emptiness and melancholy; there is an inflated and exaggerated spirit about them which causes fatigue and is typical of the vanity of human things. The gaiety which would be naturally elicited by the occasion disappears directly it becomes obligatory. One gets tired of the long periods of waiting, during which one has ample time to think of the nullity of such pleasures; and while surfeited with inaction, one is incapable of action. In Russia these festivals are very sumptuous, and comprise innumerable masked balls, banquets, illuminations, fireworks, and popular amusements of all sorts. I have seen so many of them that I look upon them with aversion, and I am truly glad whenever I can avoid them.

The melancholy shed over the beginning of Alexander's reign was in strong contrast to the brilliancy with which it was endeavoured to invest his coronation. The father's tragical death and the son's remorse deprived these fêtes of the vivacity and freshness they should have had, and the joy which was at first felt by the people at their deliverance from the fantastic tyranny of the Emperor Paul was followed by the exhaustion produced by deceived expectations, as often happens at the beginning of a new reign, when all classes imagine their hopes will be realised, and are always disappointed. The young and handsome couple who were to be crowned did not look happy, and could not inspire a joy or satisfaction which they did not appear to feel themselves. Alexander had not the art of influencing and contenting those whom he wished to please ; this faculty, so necessary to a sovereign, was absent in him, especially at the beginning of his reign.

The ceremony of the coronation increased his sadness ; he had never more strongly felt remorse at having contributed, though against his will, to his father's death. I again strove to pacify him by reminding him of the great task he was called upon to perform ; these exhortations were only partially effectual, but they contributed to give him sufficient self-command not to betray his despair in public. The recollection of that time is one of the saddest of my life, and I cannot recall it without painful emotion.

The Court returned to St Petersburg for the winter, and our after-dinner meetings were resumed. They were soon interrupted, however, by the meeting of Alexander and the King of Prussia * at Memel in the spring of 1802.

The Emperor was at that time beginning to pay special attention to foreign affairs. Kotchoubey, the Foreign Minister, had adopted a system which he believed to be in entire conformity with the Emperor's opinions and views, and at the same time with his own. This was to hold Russia aloof from European affairs, and to keep on good terms with all foreign Powers, so as to devote all her time and attention to internal reforms. Such was indeed the Emperor's wish and that of his intimate advisers, but none of them had adopted it with more conviction, or maintained it with more persistence, than Kotchoubey. Russia, he used to say, is great and powerful enough both as regards population and extent of territory, and geographical position ; she has nothing to fear from any one so long as she leaves other Powers in peace ; and she has too often mixed herself up with matters which did not directly affect her. Nothing had happened in Europe but she claimed to have a part in it ; she had made costly and useless wars. The Emperor Alexander was now in such a fortunate position that he could remain at peace with

* Frederick William III.

all the world and devote himself to internal reforms. It was at home, not abroad, that Russia could make immense conquests, by establishing order, economy, and justice in all parts of her vast empire, and by making agriculture, commerce, and industry flourish. European affairs and European wars were of no advantage whatever to the numerous inhabitants of the Russian Empire; they only lost their lives through them or had to furnish new recruits and taxes. What was necessary to their prosperity was a long peace and the incessant care of a wise and pacific administration—a task eminently suited to the Emperor, with his ideas of reform and liberal government.

This system was somewhat similar to that advocated by the English radicals. The idea is plausible and not without a basis of truth, but it has the disadvantage of reducing to insignificance and humiliation the State which follows it too literally, as by so doing it incurs the risk of becoming the vassal and tool of more enterprising and active States. Moreover, a consistent adherence to such a system would require much tact and firmness to avoid damaging compromises, which, in the then existing state of European relations, would have become almost inevitable. This is what happened to the Emperor Alexander in the case of the Memel interview.

The Prussian and Russian sovereigns had both expressed a wish to meet each other. The former thought this would be a means of facilitating to his advantage the question of indemnities in Germany, which at that time was being dealt with under the influence of France, while Alexander's sole object was to become personally acquainted with his neighbour and relative. He had a liking for the Prussians and their King which arose from his military education at Gatchina, and he looked forward to seeing the Prussian troops, of whom he had a great idea; he would, moreover, get an opportunity of augmenting his knowledge of drill, uniform, and parades, to which he attached great importance. He also wished to make the acquaintance of the beautiful Queen of Prussia, and to appear before her and her Court as the Emperor of Russia. For all these reasons he started on his journey with much anticipation of pleasure, and he was accompanied by Kotchoubey as Foreign Minister, Novosiltzoff as Secretary, and Count Tolstoï, who had administered the affairs of his house when he was Grand-Duke, as Marshal. Tolstoï was sincerely attached to the Emperor, and was very zealous in his service; but he possessed little intelligence or instruction, and was often laughed at by Alexander, though he placed implicit trust in his fidelity.

At Memel, where the same sovereigns had afterwards to meet in very different circumstances, there were many parades, reviews, and balls. The Emperor contracted a personal friendship for the King of Prussia to which the latter afterwards owed the preservation of his monarchy, and the King hastened to take advantage of the good impression he had made on Alexander to secure his consent and support for the arrangements which were then preparing between Prussia and France with the object of withdrawing Germany from the influence of the Church. Kotchoubey had been opposed to the interview, whose consequences he foresaw ; he endeavoured to dissuade the Emperor from going to Memel, and went there himself very unwillingly. To interfere in the affair of the indemnities would be contrary to the principle of non-intervention adopted in the Secret Council, and would be playing into Prussia's hands. What especially displeased Kotchoubey in the proposed arrangements, and made him wish not to take part in them, was that the disposal of the indemnities was left entirely to Napoleon's good pleasure, and that the latter might consequently be regarded as the prime mover in the whole business. But the two sovereigns settled the matter personally, without consulting their Ministers—a bad way of dealing with political affairs, as it necessarily makes dupes of those who are straightforward, disinterested, and generous.

It was also at this first interview at Memel that began the Platonic coquetry between the Emperor of Russia and the Queen of Prussia—a sort of connection which was especially pleasing to Alexander and to which he was always ready to sacrifice much time. It very seldom happened that the virtue of the ladies to whom Alexander paid his attentions was really in danger. The Queen was always accompanied by her favourite sister, the Princess of Salm, now Duchess of Cumberland,* about whom there was much scandalous gossip. She relaxed the Court etiquette, made conversation more merry, and introduced more familiarity into intimate society. She was thoroughly informed of her sister's secret thoughts, and would have been of her secret actions if there had been any.

* Afterwards Queen of Hanover.

After one of his interviews the Emperor, who then had transferred his affections to some one else, told me he was seriously alarmed at the distribution of the rooms which communicated with his, and that at night he used carefully to lock his bedroom door to prevent his being surprised and led into dangerous temptations which he wished to avoid. He even said this plainly, with more frankness than gallantry, to the Queen of Prussia and her sister.

On returning from Memel, the Emperor made a tour in Lithuania, and showed that he took an interest in the Poles by distributing some favours and repairing some acts of injustice, and at the same time holding out the prospect of further benefits. All this was very hurriedly done, as is usually the case during the tour of a sovereign in his dominions. When he arrived at St Petersburg, the treaty relative to the indemnities was made public, and it turned out to be a general distribution of ecclesiastical property in which Prussia had the largest share. In Paris the property was sold by auction; the First Consul took the leading part in the arrangements, but Talleyrand was entrusted with the details of the distribution, and as a] rule the highest bidder got the property. Right had little chance unless it had money to back it. Germany was parcelled out for the advantage of Prussia—whose favour the First Consul wished to gain—and of the distributors in Paris. The importance of France was sensibly increased, while that of Russia was greatly diminished; she played a secondary part and was led into giving her assent to an arrangement which was far from honourable in its origin and the results of which she could hardly approve. Kotchoubey was much distressed, and in the salons people talked of the insignificant part Russia had been made to play. France, on the other hand, boasted of her triumph, and the Prussian Ministers were delighted. In order to gild the pill for Russia, Napoleon offered some advantages to the houses of Würtemberg and Baden, which were allied with her; but these States felt that their fate must ultimately depend on the good-will of France, and not on the power of Russia. As for the Duke of Oldenburg, the Empress Dowager's son-in-law, he complained of the prejudicial effect of the treaty upon his estates, but he could not obtain any redress: Napoleon had been offended by his strong German feeling and his stiff manners.

The meetings of the Secret Council were now resumed, and they had become the more important as three of its members—Kotchoubey, Novosiltzoff, and Strogonoff—were now in the service of the State. Novosiltzoff's ante-chamber began to fill; men with new ideas sought and obtained employment. Many matters passed through his hands and were influenced by his liberal leanings. The Emperor found him useful for giving Russian forms to his European aspirations. We were also supported by some of the older and more distinguished functionaries of the Empire. One of these was the father of Count Paul Strogonoff, who had passed the greater part of his life in Paris at the time of Louis XV. He had been in the society of Grimm, d'Holbach, and d'Alembert; he had been a frequent visitor in the salons of celebrated women, where the greatest noblemen used to meet men of letters; his conversation was full of the anecdotes and good sayings of that day, and he had in many things adopted its opinions. He was very impulsive and enthusiastic, but the slightest obstacle sufficed to cool his enthusiasm. He was a singular mixture of the encyclopædist and the old Russian boyard. His mind and his language were French, his manners and customs Russian; he had a great fortune and many debts, a large elegantly furnished house, a good picture gallery, of which he had himself drawn up a catalogue, and an immense number of servants (including some French valets) whom he treated as slaves, though with great kindness. He was surrounded by disorder, and his servants robbed him; but he did not care. He kept open house, and anybody could come to meals on certain days in the week. The society was less mixed, and included more learned men and artists, than at the house of the Grand Equerry Narishkin, and the complete absence of etiquette, together with the Count's extreme amiability, made his house very pleasant. He had taken a great liking to me, and was angry when I did not come to his dinners; he treated me as one of the family.

By natural inclination and by his French training the Count was liberal so far as his words and desires were concerned. He wished to give happiness and liberty to everybody; but at the same time he was a thorough courtier, and the favour and consideration of his sovereign was to him a necessity. He was not ambitious or desirous of place; but a cold reception or

a frown from the Emperor made him unhappy and
deprived him of all energy and rest.  He had been
liked by Catherine, by Paul, and by the Empress
Maria, and he was especially so by Alexander.  The
latter was his son's friend, and was very fond of the
young Countess, who by her amiable character had
obtained a great influence over him.  At the old
Count's he felt in his element, for he used to meet
people who understood and appreciated those modern
and liberal ideas which were at that time Alexander's
secret passion.

The special favour enjoyed by the Strogonoff
family at the beginning of Alexander's reign gave the
old Count more weight than he had ever had before,
and as he was a senator, and his Russian manners had
gained him much popularity among the nobility of the
district of which he was Marshal, his enthusiastic
approval of the new ideas which were supposed to be
entertained by Alexander and the members of the
Secret Council was very valuable to the latter.  An
even more important supporter was Count Alexander
Vorontzoff, who was regarded in Russia as one of her
ablest statesmen.  He and Count Zavadovsky had
been Count Bezborodko's friends ; they used to come
to see him to talk about public affairs, and it is said
that when they left Bezborodko used to have the
doors and windows opened, and to wander about the
rooms panting, fanning himself, and saying, 'Thank
God, the pedagogues have gone,' as they were constantly reproaching him for his indolence and his
yielding temper.  They were, however, true friends.
I do not know what induced Count Vorontzoff to

withdraw from public affairs during the reign of Catherine. He used to have fits of bad temper, and his ambition was not easily satisfied. While Paul was on the throne the Count had the good sense to remain in retirement, although Paul was very well disposed towards the Vorontzoff family on account of the *liaison* of Peter III with one of their sisters. It was only at the time of the new Emperor's accession that Vorontzoff reappeared at St Petersburg, with the reputation he had enjoyed during the reign of Catherine still further increased by his having so long and so wisely remained in retirement. He did not join the old Ministers, most of whom were inferior to him in knowledge and judgment, and whom it would have been necessary to dismiss in order to find a place for him. The position he assumed was a more elevated one; he undertook the task of reconciling the Emperor's ideas with those of the old Russian routine, of moderating the changes which he foresaw might arise from Alexander's inclinations. It was easy to adopt and at the same time to guide them, and thereby to gain favour and power. Vorontzoff accordingly entered the 'young men's party,' feeling that in order to rise it was necessary to free one's self from the old traditions, and that in any new arrangement the first place would be secured to him.

Vorontzoff's brother Simon had also arrived at St Petersburg after a long absence. He had very fixed opinions and sentiments, and was always a blind and passionate partisan of any idea he adopted, or any man he chose as his idol. During the revolution which placed Catherine II on the throne he was a subaltern officer in the grenadiers, and loudly declared himself in favour of the unfortunate Peter III, which did not prevent him from being afterwards employed by Catherine and appointed Ambassador in London. It is known that one of Vorontzoff's sisters was Peter III's mistress, while another was a *confidante* of the Empress Catherine. The zeal he had shown in his youth for Peter III, induced the Emperor Paul to recall him from London to St Petersburg, and offer him the first posts in the Empire, but he refused them all and asked to be left in London. He had acquired friends in England by his noble, frank, and determined character, and had, so to say, taken root in the country. England had quite fascinated him ; he loved her more than the most bigoted of Tories, and he adored Pitt to such an extent that he looked upon the slightest criticism or even doubt as to his policy and doctrines as simple nonsense, and as showing an inexcusable perversion of mind or heart. Besides his worship of England and Pitt, he cultivated another which was more natural and of older date— that of his elder brother. He considered him the ablest and most virtuous man in Russia, and his decisions were to him oracles. His devotion to his brother was indeed touching, for it was quite spontaneous and sincere. The two brothers were so united that they did not even divide the property left them by their father. Alexander, who managed the property, gave his brother his share, and there was never the slightest altercation between them on the subject.

Novosiltzoff, during the years he had passed in England while Paul was on the throne, had been a frequent visitor to Simon Vorontzoff's house, to which he had been introduced by Count Strogonoff; he had gained his intimacy and confidence, and thus became a sort of bond between Alexander Vorontzoff and the 'young men's party.' Simon's arrival at St Petersburg made these relations more intimate and effective. His Tory opinions were regarded in Russia as extremely Liberal, and they had considerable influence on his brother, through whom they were transmitted to the Emperor, who was already elaborating a plan of reform. Alexander Vorontzoff was in no way opposed to certain Liberal ideas; on the contrary, he was inclined to adopt and support them, and this inclination was fostered by the traditions of the old Russian aristocracy which had wished to limit the power of the Empress Anne when she was called to the throne. He once told me that in passing through Warsaw in his youth, during the reign of Augustus III, to make a tour in Europe, he had thought that nothing could have been better or more fortunate for himself and his country than that he should be a great nobleman like those of Poland, with the same rights and privileges. The Russian aristocratic spirit of one of the brothers and the pure Toryism of the other both looked to the Senate for a solution of the problem. The basis and the source of all reforms should, they thought, be found in the Senate; by that body alone could they be carried out without danger. Yet, though various plans were discussed in the Secret Council, nothing was done. This discontented the Vorontzoffs, and they agreed with the 'young men's party' to take a decided step to draw the Emperor out of the timid inertia in which he had entrenched himself.

The country house of Kamienny Ostrog, where the Emperor then lived, was separated from that of Count Strogonoff by the river Neva, over which there was a bridge. The Emperor and Empress went to dine at Count Strogonoff's, and the Vorontzoffs were also there. After we had got up from table, the Emperor walked in the garden and went into one of the pavilions, where he found Novosiltzoff; we all followed him, and entered into conversation. Simon Vorontzoff had been chosen as the speaker on this occasion, as, having only just come from England, and being a stranger to what had passed at St Petersburg, he had a right to be regarded as impartial and to state his views freely. His speech was not as eloquent as we had expected; the Emperor, who was very clever in raising objections and difficulties, repeatedly disconcerted both Simon and his brother. They tried to prove to him that it was necessary to do something, that improvements were expected of a new reign, and that both Russia and Europe generally expected them, especially of him. These were only vague phrases; and when the Emperor asked what line the improvements should take and how he was to proceed, the Vorontzoffs could only answer that if the authority of the Senate were re-established all difficulties would be removed. They held that this body, if restored to its power and dignity, would possess all the safeguards and the means necessary for bringing about the projected improvements. Each sentence in

Simon Vorontzoff's speech began and ended with the Senate, and when he did not know what to say or answer he simply repeated the word. This affectation was somewhat awkward and ridiculous, and was more likely to chill the Emperor than to rouse him. The Senate had certainly much changed since its establishment by Peter I, and it could no longer be said even to have the power it enjoyed in the reigns which immediately succeeded that of the founder of modern Russia. In all difficult questions the Senate was always referred to, but it was nothing but a name; it was composed of men who were for the most part incapable and without energy, selected for their insignificance, and it could not therefore act as a mediator between parties or be of any weight either on one side or the other.

At length the Emperor's vague and floating ideas were consolidated into a practical shape. All the eccentric views which were mere fireworks were abandoned, and Alexander had to restrict his wishes to the realities and possibilities of the moment. He consoled himself by indulging in his hours of leisure, which were daily becoming more rare, in hopes of progress which enabled him not to give up entirely the dreams of his youth. These dreams seemed to me like a tree transplanted into a dry and arid soil and deprived of its exuberant vegetation, whose despoiled trunk puts forth a few weak branches and then perishes. The Emperor's first step was to issue an ukase or manifesto to restore the authority and dignity of the Senate; this was a prudent course, calculated to predispose the public for the changes which

were to follow.  In speaking of the Senate he spoke
a language which the Russians understood and which
flattered the nobility ; it was already the Supreme
Court of Justice and Administration, for although every
order of the Emperor, whether written or spoken,
had the force of law, they had (especially those relating to general administration and the civil and
criminal law) all to be addressed to the Senate, which
was entrusted with the task of publishing them and
seeing to their due execution.  The various departments of the Senate were charged not only with
trying on final appeal the civil and criminal cases of
the empire, but also with punishing contraventions
of the administrative regulations.  It had the right
of issuing ukases of its own founded on those of the
Emperor, and, when necessary, explaining and develop-
ing them ; and it presented him with reports for his
approval.  The governors and financial authorities of
the provinces were under its direct supervision, and it
was their duty to send to the Senate regular and
formal reports upon which the sovereign gave such
orders as he pleased.  It was accordingly called ‘ The
Senate administering the Empire.’  Its vague functions, partly judicial and partly executive, were not
in accordance with modern ideas, being so cumbrous
in form that they retarded and might even em-
barrass the course of government ; but there was no
way of touching this ancient organisation without
exposing internal affairs to even greater confusion, as
the institution of the Senate had become part of the
routine and the habits of the government machine.
The Senate was consequently allowed to retain its

administrative functions, though it was intended to let them fall by degrees into desuetude. All its powers were confirmed in pompous terms of which the author was Vorontzoff, and to them was added the right of making representations on the Emperor's ukases. It was at the same time laid down that all the Ministers should make detailed reports of their functions, which the Emperor would send to the Senate for its opinion.

This, it was hoped, would be a first step in the direction of national and representative government. The idea was to deprive the Senate of its executive powers, to leave it those of a Supreme Court of Justice, and gradually to convert it into a sort of upper chamber to which would afterwards be attached deputies of the nobility who, either as part of the chamber or as a separate body, would, for the Emperor's information, state their views on the management of affairs by the Ministers and on the laws which were in existence or in preparation. This plan was never carried out, and what really happened was very different.

Those who think that the Senate of St Petersburg can ever be of any importance for the destinies of Russia are entirely mistaken, and only show that they do not know Russia. The Russian Senate in its present form is less able than any political body in the world to make itself respected or to act on its own initiative. It can neither give an impulse nor even receive one; it is a marionette which one can move about as one pleases, but which has no motive power of its own.

Those who are tired of official life and wish to retire and live quietly in idleness are the sort of people who seek the appointment of Senator. The Senate thus becomes a receptacle for the indolent and the superannuated; all its work is done by the procurators and the secretaries, who decide questions at their pleasure and then take the decisions to the Senators, who as a rule sign them without reading them. These decrees are drawn up in a more diffuse and tedious style even than the official documents of other countries; the minutes in each case fill an immense volume, and it would require some courage to read them. One or two Senators who do read the decrees that are submitted to them for signature are spoken of with admiration as heroes. It is evident that such a political body is incapable of undertaking or following up any reform.

After laying the first stone of the edifice of a regulated legislative power, and devising a limit to the autocratic power, the Emperor turned his attention to the organisation of his government, so as to make its action more enlightened, more just, and more methodical. The government machine was irregular and intermittent in its action, and the administration was a chaos in which nothing was regulated or clearly defined. The only administrative authorities that were recognised were the Senate and the Committees of War, of the Navy, and of Foreign Affairs. These were not deliberative or consultative bodies; one of the members of each committee, usually the president, brought the reports of the committee to the sovereign and then informed it of his decisions. The Procu-

rator-General united in his person the offices of
Minister of the Interior, of Police, of Finance, and of
Justice ; but sometimes the sovereign created separate
departments, and the Empress Catherine placed the
conquered provinces under the direction of one of her
favourites, such as Potemkin or Zuboff, who were
independent of the Senate and reported direct to the
sovereign.  Moreover, when the reports of the Senate
and the various committees were handed to the
sovereign by the Ministers or other high functionaries of State, they were often put away in a drawer,
and after some time had elapsed a decision totally
opposed to the one suggested was issued.  Thus there
was practically no bar to the caprices of the sovereign.
Paul, who thought he was a great general, and was
especially jealous of any control over the army apart
from his own, appointed one of his aides-de-camp in
whom he had confidence to examine and submit to
him all the proposals of the War Committee, and all
promotions and appointments.  The direction of
Foreign Affairs was nominally entrusted to a committee of three members, each of whom worked with
the sovereign separately, and had the management of
some particular question which was kept a secret from
his colleagues.  This post was much sought after,
and Catherine's favourites obtained some magnificent
presents from foreign powers in employing for a
negotiation with which they had been charged by the
Empress one of the members of the Foreign Affairs
Committee on whose complaisance they could rely.
This was the case with Prince Zuboff and Count

Markoff, who were handsomely rewarded for advoca-
ting the two last partitions of Poland.

In the time of the Emperor Paul foreign affairs
were often directed by his favourite aides-de-camp.
The Vice-Chancellor or the eldest of the members of
the committee only had the direction of the administrative and financial branch, and of the current
correspondence.   This system suited an able sovereign
like the Empress Catherine, who, notwithstanding its
disadvantages and a complete absence of unity, still
ultimately carried out a consistent policy.   Paul, with
his incessant caprices and changes of mind, yet had a
most decided, almost furious, will which all the
wheels of the government machine had at once to
obey.   But with a sovereign of vacillating character
it is evident that the system of administration above
described must lead to serious evils.   The Emperor
was continually exposed to making mistakes, to
seeing only one side of a question; he was liable to
be confused by a mass of opinions from persons many
of whom had an interest in not letting him know the
whole truth ; and he could never advance towards a
definite object.   Russia therefore had reason to be
grateful to the Emperor Alexander and those whose
advice he then followed for having sought to introduce
more order and method in the Imperial administration.

The object of the reform was to establish a system
somewhat similar to those adopted in most other
European States by separating the departments, defin-
ing their limits, assembling in each department matters
of the same kind, centralising their management, and
thereby augmenting the responsibility of the principal

functionaries of State. It was hoped among other things that this would be an efficacious means of checking the numberless abuses and frauds which are the curse of Russia. The Emperor accordingly created for the first time Ministries of the Interior and of Police, of Finance, of Justice, of Public Instruction, of Commerce, of Foreign Affairs, of War, and of the Navy. As to the War Department, Alexander continued the system adopted by his father, insisting that everything relating to the army, down to the smallest appointment, should emanate direct from the sovereign, and that the army should know it. The post of aide-de-camp charged with the management of the *personnel* of the army became gradually converted, in imitation of Napoleon, into that of Major-General, so as to show that Russia always considers herself in a state of war, and wishes to be in a position to make war at any moment. In the manifesto establishing the changes above referred to, it was stated that all the Emperor's ukases were in future to be countersigned by one of the Ministers— an attempt to introduce the principle of responsibility —and the Ministers were directed to meet in a council, in which they were to discuss the most important questions of State. This was a new administrative machine superior to the Senate, which retained all its functions and was invested with new ones ; but those which related to administration properly so called, became in its case almost purely formal. By the creation of the new Ministers the administrative authority of the Government was concentrated, while hitherto it had not had any legal

or definite status except in the person of the sovereign.
The Council of State also was not changed, although
some of its most eminent members became Ministers.
The Emperor continued occasionally to refer to this
Council various disagreeable or complicated questions,
in order to give it something to do, and not let it die
too soon ; but it speedily perished through its insignificance, and Alexander afterwards created another
Imperial Council on quite a different and much more
extensive plan.

These changes, which elsewhere would seem the
very A B C of politics, seemed at that time to the
Russians novel and immense.  The manifesto made
much noise in the whole Empire and especially in the
salons of St Petersburg and Moscow ; each man had
his own opinion of it, and the majority judged it not
by its intrinsic merits or the benefits it might confer
on the State, but by the effect it would be likely to
have on their own advancement.  Those who obtained
places approved it, while those who remained in the
cold criticised the juvenile infatuation that wished to
change the old and venerable institutions under which
Russia had become great.  The personages high in
office who had not been consulted, and did not expect
so considerable a change, were taken by surprise,
finding themselves eclipsed by those who during the
reign of Paul and the beginning of that of Alexander
had held aloof.  They strove to vent their disappointment by smiling with pity at the young men who
were trying to reform the Empire, and at the foolish-
ness of some older men who consented to be the
instruments of a servile and awkward imitation of

foreign institutions. The easy good-nature of the Emperor encouraged these criticisms, so far as they were possible in Russia, and they found a certain amount of support in the Empress Dowager, who was annoyed, without admitting it, at not having been more consulted by her son and at not being able to influence his decisions. She perceived in all these novelties a germ of liberalism whose development she feared, and her salon became a centre of opposition where people came to express their discontent.

The head of the new administration was Count Alexander Vorontzoff, who was made Foreign Minister, and also Chancellor—a title of which he had long been ambitious, and which had not been given to any one for many years. Kotchoubey left the Foreign Office without regret, even with pleasure, as he thought nothing could be done in it under that system of impassiveness which he considered most suitable to Russia and most in conformity with the Emperor's character and his views and wishes; he threw himself with extreme ardour into the new sphere of action opened to him by his appointment as Minister of the Interior. The important branches of police and general administration of which this department was composed had until then been buried in the mass of the functions attributed to the Senate, to the Procurator-General, and occasionally to some of the sovereign's secretaries. Kotchoubey had entirely to reorganise an administration which had been long neglected, and which in the more distant provinces was without any direction or supervision, and given up to all the abuses arising from the ignorance and cupidity of subordinate officials. It was a noble and arduous task, and if he did not succeed as well as he had wished, it was not for want of zeal or good-will. He began by organising his office, dividing it into several sections, each of which had to deal with a distinct branch of the vast department. He invited the assistance of all the able and experienced officials he could find, and endeavoured to raise in general estimation the post of Governor of a province by appointing in that capacity men whose character and position afforded guarantees of integrity, and who, though inexperienced in official work, were likely soon to obtain the necessary knowledge. It seemed as if order was going to break through the chaos, and the immediate effects of the change were soon felt by the people. One of the reforms he introduced was in the supply of salt, which in Russia is a matter of great importance. This was not nominally a Government monopoly, but the Government alone was able to supply salt to all parts of the Empire by obtaining it from the salt marshes or distilling it from sea-water. Kotchoubey took steps to reduce the cost of production and of conveyance to the lowest possible point, so as to enable the people to buy salt more cheaply, and the Government to be repaid its expenses.

The new Finance Minister was Count Vasilieff, a capable and honest official who had in financial matters been the right hand of Prince Viaziemskoy, the only Procurator-General who had been mentioned with praise at the time of the Empress Catherine.

In the various changes which had taken place since the Prince's death in 1794, M. Vasilieff, as treasurer of the Empire, had been indispensable; he was a steady worker, appreciated new ideas, and adopted them when he thought they were opportune. All the branches of the public revenue, the brandy traffic, the Imperial Bank, etc., were comprised in this department, to which was added the mines department, which had been reorganised on a larger scale.

The functions of Minister of Justice were united to those of Procurator-General of the Senate. General Beklescheff did not wish to stop in this department, as it had been deprived of the greater part of its functions by the creation of the Ministers of the Interior and of Finance; and he was succeeded by the Senator Dzierzanin. He was the personal choice of the Emperor, without communication with the Secret Council. A worthy man, and the writer of some much admired lyrics which were full of swing and passion, he was imperfectly educated and knew no language but Russian. The Emperor had been attracted to him by his ardent sentiments and poetic dreams, not being able to resist fine phrases; the vaguer they were the better they pleased him, as he could then easily assimilate them to his hopes, which also were not very clear. He liked expressions of energetic liberalism, and was especially attracted by admiration of himself when it was couched in the language of devotion to the cause of humanity.

The Emperor had direct and special relations with certain persons whom he himself introduced at our meetings; he liked to patronise them and defend

them against objections raised sometimes by people
who knew them more intimately. It gave him
pleasure to have these relations without the knowledge of his friends, who already at that time had
begun to displease him because they were so united
among themselves. Yet it was absolutely necessary
to introduce members of 'the young men's party'
into the administration, for all Alexander's hopes
rested upon them for the zealous continuation and
accomplishment of the reforms he had at heart.
Kotchoubey was provided for, but what was to be
done with the others? It would be too much to
make them Ministers, and it was accordingly decided
that assistants to the Ministers should be appointed;
in this way the Emperor's friends would be able
to direct their chiefs in accordance with the Emperor's
views, and to keep him fully acquainted with what
was going on.

Count Paul Strogonoff was at his request appointed assistant to the Minister of the Interior, and
Novosiltzoff obtained the post of assistant to the
Minister of Justice, retaining his former appointment
of Secretary to the Emperor. This gave Novosiltzoff
the most important place in the administration, as it
was through him that the Emperor was to begin the
work of reforming jurisprudence and the existing
laws. He was well qualified for the task, as he had
studied jurisprudence and political economy in England, and had made good use of the opportunities
thereby afforded him of becoming conversant with
those subjects. No one in Russia was at that time
his superior in that administrative knowledge which

was then only to be obtained by reading French and
English works. His practical mind rejected all vain
theories ; he possessed skill and tact in dealing not
only with individuals, but with the Russian public,
which he knew thoroughly. He had bad qualities
also ; but these had not yet developed themselves.
One of his greatest merits was that he seconded
Alexander's wishes as to the improvement of the
condition of the peasants, and he drew up the
first ukase on this subject. He also reconstituted
the commission for the revision of the law. This commission had been formed by the Empress Catherine,
who thereby gained the flattering appreciation of
Voltaire and the Diderots ; but the only result was
the publication of the philanthropic and philosophical
instructions addressed by Catherine to the commission.
It was dissolved soon after, and its proceedings were
never made public. The new commission was organ-
ised by Novosiltzoff with the assistance of a German
jurist, Baron Rosenkampf, on a vast and well-con-
ceived plan. It was directed to codify all the existing Russian laws, which were very numerous and
often contradicted each other, classifying them according to subjects, omitting such as were obsolete, and
adding new ones when necessary, but taking care to retain in the new codes all that had entered for many
years into the life of the Russian people, even if not
quite reconcilable with the ideas of modern jurisprudence. The system adopted was somewhat similar to
that of Justinian ; but the task of the Russian codifiers
was far more difficult than that of the Roman ones.
The latter merely had to select and classify out of a

somewhat confused mass of laws, most of which were admirable examples of wisdom and legislative science, while in Russia the laws were not only confused, but in many respects defective and insufficient. For such a work not only jurists, but real legislators were wanted. A similar code was to be prepared for the outlying provinces of the Empire, such as Livonia, Esthonia, Courland, and the Polish provinces of Little Russia, each of which had its own particular language, laws, and customs.

This great undertaking was begun methodically and pursued for some time with activity; Novosiltzoff was allowed by the Minister of Justice to make it his exclusive occupation. The classifications were prepared by Baron Rosenkampf, and so long as they were adhered to the work progressed; but it did not produce the results which were expected of it. This, is usually the case in Russia; if there is no immediate result, the persons entrusted with the execution of the work are changed, and it has to be begun over again.

I was the only member of the Secret Council who remained without employment. Alexander offered me, with Count Vorontzoff's concurrence, the post of assistant to the Minister of Foreign Affairs, and all my friends, the Emperor especially, pressed me to accept the offer. I hesitated for a long time, feeling how much surprise and dissatisfaction such an appointment would cause in Russia. The Emperor observed that during my mission to the King of Sardinia I had made myself favourably known by my despatches, and that my nomination to the Foreign Office ought not therefore to be a matter of astonishment, besides which Count Vorontzoff, who alone had a right to be consulted on the subject, had consented to my becoming his assistant. I replied that he (the Emperor) knew more than anyone my feelings with regard to my country; that they could never change, and that I had some reason to fear that they might be incompatible with the duties of the appointment he wished to give me; the safest and most proper course, therefore, would be for me not to accept it. To this Alexander rejoined that he did not at present anticipate any such contradiction as that which I feared; that I should always be at liberty to give up my post if such a contradiction were to arise; and that, on the contrary, he thought that events would occur which would be favourable to my views. He added some very flattering expressions with regard to my qualifications for the post. It is every man's duty, he said, to pay his debt to humanity; when one has talents one must not refuse to employ them in the most useful way. I still declined, but Alexander was bent on my taking the appointment; this was one of his irresistible fancies which nothing could induce him to abandon until they were satisfied. His persistence and kindness to me were such that at length I yielded, on the express condition that I should be allowed to resign the appointment directly its functions should become incompatible with my feelings as a Pole. My chief object in this was, by spending some years in the Emperor's service, to prove to him my sincere attachment and my gratitude for his friendship and confidence. I accepted with some sadness, as by so doing I was entering on a new career full of pitfalls which would retain me at St Petersburg, where I was always like an exotic plant which could not take root; I felt I could not enjoy life unless I were with my own people.

I will not pretend that I had more foresight and prudence than was really the case. In accepting the post which was offered me, I was determined not to do anything which might exercise an injurious influence on the destinies of my country; but I had no clear or decided idea as to the nature of the services I might be called upon to render to Poland in my new position. In this respect, a substantial bait was offered me as a reward for having at length yielded to the Emperor's wishes. He entrusted to me the direction of the schools in the eight Polish provinces, which at that time constituted the whole of that portion of Poland which belonged to his dominions.

The creation of a Ministry of Public Instruction was a remarkable innovation in Russia which was fruitful of great and salutary results, and posterity will owe gratitude both to Alexander and to the young men, then so much criticised, who supported him in his plans and gave them practical shape by dividing into special branches the confused organisation which was then in existence. Nothing could be more wretched or insufficient than public instruction in Russia up to the reign of Alexander. There was an Academy of Sciences at St Petersburg which owed its only celebrity to the presence of some learned men whom the Government had brought to the Russian capital from abroad. Euler came when he was already an old man, and died there soon after. The transactions of this Academy were for the most part written in the French and German languages; it had no relations whatever with the country, and exercised no influence on its progress. At Moscow there was a university which was equally isolated, and was attended by not more than a hundred students maintained at the expense of the Government. The only other educational establishments in Russia proper were the so-called 'National Schools.' The teaching in these schools was bad and extremely meagre; the teachers were poor wretches whom idleness and *ennui* had rendered drunkards, and no respectable person sent his children to them. The establishment of the Ministry of Public Instruction completely changed all this. The existing universities of Moscow, Wilna, and Dorpat were better endowed, and three new ones were created—those of St Petersburg, Kharkoff, and Kazan,—each forming an educational centre for a prescribed district, in which it directed all the educational arrangements. The University of Wilna was exclusively Polish, and during the next few years the whole of Russian Poland was covered with schools in which Polish feeling freely developed itself. This University, to which I appointed the most distinguished literary and scientific men of the country, and some eminent professors from abroad, directed the movement with admirable zeal and intelligence, and its consequences, which the Russians afterwards deeply regretted, seemed at that time to flow naturally from the Emperor's generous intentions with regard to the Poles. The University of Kazan was to look after the instruction of the Tartars and of Siberia generally. Each university had its curator, and the curators formed a council of public instruction, the President of which was the Minister. The persons appointed to these posts by the Emperor were such as to give a hope that the work of public instruction would be pushed forward with zeal and success. General Klinger, commandant of one of the cadet corps, was appointed curator of Dorpat. He was a distinguished German author, with liberal opinions which might almost be called utopian, although he had been in the service of the greatest despots; his intentions, however, were good, and he was full of zeal for the advancement of science and instruction. His eccentric and dreamy views were expressed with a German bluntness which gave him an appearance of frankness and energy, and all this had gained him Alexander's favour. Count Severin Potocki was appointed Curator of the University of Kharkoff, which was the centre of a district the inhabitants of which were strongly desirous of obtaining the means of instruction. Count Severin, as a Pole, had been treated with great consideration by Alexander when he was Grand-Duke; he had been admitted, like my brother and myself, into his familiar circle, and was one of his most enthusiastic admirers. The Emperor appointed him not only curator of Kharkoff, but also senator of the third department of the Senate, which issued decisions on appeals against measures taken by the administrations of the Polish provinces. Count Severin obtained some celebrity in Russia as a senator, and in his capacity of curator he showed zeal and perseverance.

The universities which were most progressive were Wilna, Dorpat, and Kharkoff. The nobility of Livonia, Esthonia, and Courland did not look with favour upon the University of Dorpat, which had declared itself the protector of the peasants and the bourgeoisie. One of the professors of this university was named Parot; he was a worthy man who expressed boundless attachment to the Emperor Alexander, and was very anxious about his health. Once Madame Parot sent a waistcoat, woven by herself, which she said would preserve the Emperor's life. Parot begged him to wear it, and by such manifestations of affection he gained Alexander's favour, and had private conferences with him during his frequent journeys to St Petersburg. The Curator of Moscow was M. de Mouravieff, one of the gentlemen formerly attached to Alexander's service when he was Grand-Duke, and also his former secretary. He was a worthy man, but excessively timid and quite devoid of energy. The Emperor appointed him assistant to the Minister of Instruction in order that it should not be said that young men only performed the duties of assistant, and that these posts were created only for the members of the Secret Council. Novosiltzoff was appointed Curator of St Petersburg. As there was already in that capital a faculty of medicine dependent on the Ministry of the Interior, and a faculty of law could not be established before the commission for the revision of the laws had terminated its labours, Novosiltzoff for the present

confined himself to establishing a faculty of philosophy, with the special object of training professors of
the exact sciences, of administration, and of literature,
This faculty began brilliantly by turning out some
distinguished pupils, but they did not afterwards
realise the hopes that had been formed of them, and
the institution perished without leaving any durable
results.  A university with privileges and endow-
ments would have better maintained itself, as was
shown by the universities of Moscow and Kharkoff,
which, though they declined, were still active in the
midst of the indifference and oblivion by which they
were long surrounded.

Count Zavadovsky was appointed Minister of
Public Instruction.  He had been secretary to Count
Romantzoff at the same time as Prince Bezborodko,
and they had remained friends ever since.  Count
Romantzoff had presented them both as secretaries
to the Empress Catherine, and this was the origin of
their brilliant fortunes.  Bezborodko, to whom I have
already referred, soon rose by his great capacity for
work; he enjoyed the confidence of his sovereign and
attained to the highest dignities.  Zavadovsky's
success was obtained by other means.  The Empress
made him her favourite; he became attached to her
and was very unhappy when after six months had
elapsed he was dismissed.  His friends Bezborodko
and Vorontzoff endeavoured to console him, and the
presents which Catherine always lavished on a dismissed favourite were in his case richer than usual,
as she recognised in him other merits than those
which had merely attracted her fancy.  He after-

wards married, and continued to be well received at Court. His friendship with Vorontzoff, and the reputation for writing pure Russian which he had gained by certain manifestoes that he had written for the Empress Catherine, obtained him the post of Minister of Instruction. He was a man of just and benevolent character, but of somewhat stolid mind. He was not quick of intelligence, and did not perceive shades of meaning, while at the same time he wished to understand new ideas, and not to be reckoned among those who could neither learn nor forget anything. Yet he possessed in a high degree one of the most marked traits of a Russian administrator— profound submission to everything that comes from superior authority. He was enthusiastic in his admiration of classic writers and was fond of quoting the passages he remembered. The literature of his own country also greatly interested him. By a singular accident he had learnt Latin in one of the Polish schools managed by the Jesuits; he had not forgotten his Polish, and he prided himself on his knowledge of that language, speaking with much admiration of our ancient poet John Kochanowski,* some fragments of whose poems he knew by heart. All this gave him a certain predilection for Poland and the Poles; as was shown even at his dinners, which always consisted of Polish dishes.

While the other curators were often overruled in their projects by the Minister, who was not always disposed to yield to ideas of reform and progress, I never had to complain on this score. Vorontzoff

* Born 1530. Died 1584.

always trusted me implicitly, and he was always most kind in supporting every proposal I made. I owe him much gratitude for the condescension, the frankness, and the friendly feeling with which he always treated me.

# CHAPTER XIII

## 1803-4



DIRECTLY after my appointment I was admitted to all
the Chancellor's Conferences with the Foreign Ministers, and I drew up the protocols which he took to
the Emperor. I did this work with much care, and
to his satisfaction. A well-written protocol often
gives precision and clearness to a desultory conversation. Vorontzoff was satisfied with what I made him
say, as it expressed what he thought, though in a more
complete manner than he had himself done ; I had
guessed his intentions, and this greatly pleased him.
The practice I thus gained was very useful to me, and
the conferences at which I was present enabled me to
be fully informed of the relations of Russia with
Foreign Governments. It was also my duty to draw
up the despatches which resulted from these conferences, and the Emperor's rescripts to his Ministers

abroad. Having accepted these functions, I threw myself heartily into the work. I sometimes wrote incessantly for eight or nine hours at a time. This produced a sort of nervous disorder which Dr Rogerson said might have serious consequences; but I was young, and did not pay any attention to his counsels. Later on I had reason to regret that I did not do so.

The policy of Russia was in essence the same under Vorontzoff as it had been under Kotchoubey; but it became stronger and more dignified in form. Its leading principle, which was well adapted to Alexander's character and projects, was to be on good terms with all the world, and not to interfere in European affairs, in order to avoid being carried too far; in a word, carefully to avoid difficulties without appearing to fear them. The principle was not changed; it was only the way of carrying it out that was different. The Russian Cabinet assumed a tone of hauteur which deceived people as to its true policy, and somewhat reminded one of the spirit of Catherine's diplomacy. The Chancellor was very careful to avoid any quarrel, or even slight estrangement, with any of the great Powers; but he was not sorry when an opportunity presented itself to frighten the weak ones and crush them under the weight of Russian power. This is what happened with Sweden. The two Governments had a difference as to the possession of a wretched little island in a river which at that time separated Finland proper from the Russian province of that name. The point at issue was on which branch of the river was to be the bridge constituting the frontier. This question had been pending for some time, and the Chancellor resolved to cut the knot. He addressed Sweden in a dry and imperious tone, and I was very glad that I was not asked to write the despatches on this matter, which were in Russian; my abstinence afterwards obtained for me proofs of confidence on the part of the King of Sweden and his Government. At the same time Russia seemed to prepare for a rupture, and Russian generals were sent to inspect the Swedish frontier. The Emperor himself went there, and I accompanied him with Strogonoff and Novosiltzoff.

We passed along the greater part of the frontier on horseback. The soil mostly consists of a slight layer of earth on a substratum of granite, and there is some extraordinary scenery, with magnificent water-falls, but the country was not populous, and we often had to sleep in thinly scattered villages, at the houses of the clergy, some of whom knew no other language than the Finnish. The villages and parsonages were surrounded by meadows, but the general appearance of the country was melancholy and arid. I refer here only to the portion of Finland which at that time belonged to Russia, as other portions are rich and abound in corn. Beyond the town of Abo the country looked more cultivated, and the people seemed more prosperous. We visited the disputed island, and the fortress and harbour in its vicinity, which in case of war were to form the basis of our operations. General Suchtelen, then commander of the engineers, and afterwards Russian Minister in Sweden, was having some works constructed in this fortress according to a new system of his own invention; it was more simple, he said, than those of Vauban and Coëhorn, which it combined and made more effective.

The King of Sweden was very obstinate in his resistance to the demands we had made in so imperious a tone. Count Stedingk, the Swedish Ambassador at St Petersburg, often expressed to me his astonishment on this subject, and shrugged his shoulders in speaking of the offensive way in which Russia dealt with a matter which in reality was quite unimportant. Sweden resisted for a long time, and we continued preparations for war. She had to give way at last, but the conditions imposed upon her were insignificant, and Sweden could not be mad enough to make war on account of them. The Chancellor was very proud of his victory, but it might easily have been obtained without humiliating Sweden—which I think would have been preferable. The conduct of Russia left a bitter feeling in the mind of a neighbour which had already been often ill-treated, and which, notwithstanding its relative weakness, might on occasion do much harm. But Vorontzoff knew Russia, or at least those who spoke in her name. He knew that every demonstration of power, even if unjust, pleases the Russians; that to domineer, to command, to crush is a necessity of their national pride. Not being able to overcome the strong, the Chancellor attacked the weak, hoping thereby to bring into prominence the young Emperor's government. I am convinced that this was one of the motives which induced him loudly to proclaim his pretended victory over Sweden; but the Russian public was not deceived.   There was at that time in the two capitals among the civil officials and in the army—the class which afterwards formed the elements of public opinion—a vague desire of improvement, or rather of events which should be more interesting, more profitable, and especially more flattering to their vanity. It must be admitted that the Emperor Alexander did not at that time have public opinion on his side, and this was indeed but seldom the case during the whole of his reign.   At that period especially his conduct was too natural, his views too pure and too much in conformity with the welfare of the great majority of his subjects, to be appreciated by a country whose upper classes had tasted of a corrupt civilisation and had been excessively indulged in their avidity and vanity.   The goodness, the kindness, and the pure intentions of Alexander as he then was did not suffice to make him popular.   Notwithstanding all the Chancellor's efforts, no great satisfaction was expressed at the advantage gained by him over an adversary of such little importance as Sweden ; on the contrary, the old Minister was reproached for attempting to throw dust in the eyes of the public and take advantage of its vanity.

Count Sauvan was then the Austrian Ambassador ; he used always to come to the Chancellor in full dress, and conferred with him in a very solemn manner. The policy of Austria was at that time lachrymose and sentimental.   The peace of Lunéville had only lately been signed,* and the Vienna Cabinet sought for consolation.   Russia did not reject its mournful

* On the 29th of February, 1801.

representations, but only replied by assurances of interest and good-will which meant nothing. Prussia was represented by Count Goltz; the only qualities which had obtained him advancement were a good memory, a knowledge of routine, and a kind heart, and he was completely under the domination of his wife, remarkable for a somewhat noisy and brusque vivacity. When Prussia, perfidiously violating the treaties of the past ten years, took her share of the plunder of Poland, he succeeded M. Lucchesini as Ambassador at Vienna. He treated me with a deference which betrayed a feeling of regret, almost of shame, at the conduct of his Government towards my country. His predecessor at St Petersburg was M. Tauentzien, afterwards known as one of the ablest of the Prussian generals. While my mother was at Berlin on the occasion of my sister's marriage with the Prince of Würtemberg, he was an officer of the Guards, and often came to her house, where he was deeply smitten by Mdlle. Constance Narbutt (afterwards Madame Denbowska). She refused his offer of marriage, but the only result was that during his stay at St Petersburg he often asked me and my brother to dinner. The relations of Russia with Prussia were purely personal between the two sovereigns, as there was no sympathy between the Cabinets, the armies, or the people of the two States. Prussia's equivocal conduct, her base submission to France, and the acquisitions which she obtained by it, were much disapproved by the Russians, who did not spare their sarcasms on the subject. The Emperor, however, remained faithful to his friendship with the King, and to the high opinion he had formed of the Prussian army. This perseverance, which was often blamed at St Petersburg, was nevertheless of great advantage to Russia, as she managed thereby to attract Prussia to her side and make her a sort of satellite.

England had just concluded the peace of Amiens. Her ambassador at St Petersburg was Sir John Warren, an excellent admiral, but an indifferent diplomatist. He was a perfect representative of the nullity and incapacity of the Addington Ministry which had appointed him. In those days the English Government was seldom happy in its choice of ambassadors. The diplomatic service, though much sought after, contained few able men; the most important posts were given by favour or through party arrangements, either to satisfy some supporter of the Ministry or to obtain a few more votes in the House of Commons. Other promotions were entirely by seniority; want of knowledge or of intelligence was no disqualification. It was generally remarked at that time that there was neither ability nor zeal among the great majority of English diplomatists. All this is entirely changed; the English diplomatists are now among the ablest in Europe.

General Hédouville represented France. He had obtained a reputation as a General by his pacification of La Vendée, but he did not seem very likely to sustain the reputation of French diplomacy, whose cleverness and general ability seemed even to increase under the Consulate and the Ministry of Talleyrand. In selecting a Minister so benevolent and quiet, not to say tedious, in manner and conversation, the French

Government probably intended to reassure and tranquillise those whose friendship it wished to gain.  He represented one of those dead calms which in diplomacy follow or precede a storm.

There was nothing important or even interesting in the relations of Russia with the other great Powers; they reduced themselves, so far as I remember, to an exchange of rounded phrases the drift of which was: 'Let us be quiet and avoid all embarrassments and conflicts.'  This feeling was shared even by the Governments which had suffered from the peace; they would have been glad to strike another blow in the hope of regaining what they had lost, but they did not dare to confess it.  Even England did not expect a speedy rupture.  Austria groaned only in secret, and when she thought she could complain without compromising herself; while Prussia congratulated herself on her constant neutrality and looked upon it as a source of prosperity and progress. France, too, seemed to have turned all her attention to internal affairs.  The First Consul was organising the administration and the laws of the country ; but all eyes were still turned to this vigorous sap which could not long be satisfied with the immense territories it had already fertilised.  All continental Europe feared France, while Russia, although she was both pacific and inoffensive, assumed a tone which denoted a consciousness of equal power and a feeling of independence.  The relations of the Chancellor with General Hédouville showed a friendliness based on mutual consideration.  A convention of no great significance was concluded, and the Chancellor took the opportunity of offering to the French Minister the usual present of 4000 ducats and a gold snuff box adorned with diamonds and the Emperor's portrait. The Chancellor was ill, and received the Ambassador in bed while the ratifications were being exchanged. The presents were laid out on the bed, and I never saw a face so beam with pleasure as did the General's when he saw the bags of ducats. Forgetting all decorum and the little speech he should have delivered on the Emperor's portrait, his eyes were fixed on the money-bags, and he carried them away with an expression of delight which was quite comic. He was a very worthy man, however, and everyone would have been glad to see him so happy if he had been a little more dignified in showing his joy.

Among the members of the diplomatic body the most remarkable was Baron Stedingk, the Swedish Ambassador. He was distinguished both by his wisdom and by his noble sentiments; with a simple exterior, his conduct also was marked by simplicity, by tact, and by perfect loyalty, and was strictly honourable in the highest sense of the word. He had that rare perspicacity which always appreciates both men and events at their true value. In his youth he had served with distinction against the English in the American war, and had been decorated with the cross of St Louis, which, being a Protestant, he wore with a blue ribbon. Afterwards, being honoured with the confidence of Gustavus III, he distinguished himself at the head of the army corps which fought the Russians in 1789 and 1790. When peace was signed he was appointed Ambassador at the Court of St Petersburg, where he was already known by his military successes.   He remained at this post during three consecutive reigns, serving his country in the most difficult emergencies, without ever losing any of the high consideration he had acquired.   Of all the men I ever met he seemed to me one of the best and the most worthy of confidence ; he was a man whom one could not help liking, and whom one would wish always to have for a friend.   I think he was mine, so far as he could be in view of our different positions, which afterwards entirely separated us.   As second in the Ministry, I was not obliged to take an active part in the difficulty which had arisen between Russia and Sweden, and the Chancellor wished to conduct the matter himself in order to gain the merit of having brought it to a triumphant conclusion.   His insulting affectation of superiority, and the way in which he deprived a weaker power of a worthless island which was only taken to humiliate her, inspired me with profound repugnance, and, as I have already remarked, this gained for me marks of gratitude and confidence from the Swedes.

The progress of internal reform in Russia was abruptly stopped by an unexpected incident.   Count Severin Potocki, who, as I said above, was a great admirer of the Emperor, often addressed memoranda to him on various subjects.   The Senate had received from the Emperor, among other important prerogatives, the right of making representations to him, but it had hitherto not made any use of this right.   Count Severin naturally thought the Emperor was sincere in his liberal opinions; the Emperor himself thought so; and the Count therefore imagined it would be a good thing, and would please his Imperial master, if the Senate were prompted to exercise its prerogatives. For this an opportunity soon presented itself. Although almost every noble in Russia entered the army, he was not obliged to do so, and could leave it when he thought proper. This double privilege was granted by Peter III in an ukase for which many blessed his memory. Alexander, however, restricted the privilege to nobles who held the rank of officer; those below that rank were obliged to serve for twelve years. This was looked upon as an attack on the guaranteed rights of the nobility, and produced a deep and painful sensation. The Minister of War, an old military bureaucrat of low origin, was said to be the author of the new ukase, and Count Severin Potocki proposed to the Senate that it should address representations to the Emperor on this violation of the nobles' charter. His proposal was read to the general assembly of all the departments, and the senators, seeing that one of the confidential advisers of the Court was taking the initiative in the matter, and that his opinion was warmly supported by Count Strogonoff, thought they could safely vote in its favour. They gladly did this, under the impression that by so doing they could without danger assume an air of independence in a matter to which it was believed the Emperor did not attach any serious importance. Count Severin's proposal was adopted, notwithstanding the opposition of the Procurator-General (Minister of Justice), which was supposed to be feigned in order

to give more appearance of reality to the little scene
which it was believed had been got up for the occasion.
Count Strogonoff, who was deputed with two other
senators to take the representations of the Senate to
the Emperor, readily set out on his mission; but the
deputation was received by Alexander very coldly,
and Strogonoff, disconcerted and not knowing what
to say, withdrew.   The Emperor sharply reprimanded
the Senate, ordered it not to meddle with things
which did not concern it, and directed it by a new
decree to carry out the very ukase against which it
had appealed.   To my great astonishment it was
Novosiltzoff who was the agent of the Emperor's
unjust anger in this matter.   This failure of the first
move of the Senate in the direction of liberalism
sufficed to discourage people whose generous aspirations were not, it must be admitted, very strong.
The Senate did not again attempt any independent
action, and its rights became a dead letter.   At my
first interview with the Emperor after this incident, I
could not help smiling at his extreme alarm in
presence of the new attitude of the Senate.   My
jocular remarks on this point were ill received by
Alexander, and I believe they left in his mind a
certain anxiety as to my liberal tendencies which
afterwards came back to him.   This was an indication
of Alexander's true character, which then appeared to
me in a novel and unfortunately too real light.   Grand
ideas of the general good, generous sentiments, and
the desire to sacrifice to them part of the Imperial
authority, and resign an immense and arbitrary power
in order the better to secure the future happiness of

the people, had really occupied the Emperor's mind and did so still, but they were rather a young man's fancies than a grown man's decided will. The Emperor liked forms of liberty as he liked the theatre; it gave him pleasure and flattered his vanity to see the appearances of free government in his Empire; but all he wanted in this respect was forms and appearances; he did not expect them to become realities. In a word, he would willingly have agreed that every man should be free, on the condition that he should voluntarily do only what the Emperor wished.

Alexander never forgot Count Severin's indiscretion; he was still received at Court on the same footing as heretofore, but he no longer shared the confidence and favour of his sovereign. The incident gained him great credit at Moscow and in the ancient provinces of the Empire, where he was regarded as a true Russian patriot and a generous defender of the immunities of the nobility. This wave of popularity had so much charm for the Count that it made him forget his old Polish sentiments. In his youth, at the diet of the 3rd of May, he had been an ardent Polish patriot; in his old age he forgot his country, thought only of augmenting his fortune and living pleasantly, and amused himself by opposing the Russian Government. He got into the habit of travelling continually between his estates and the Senate, reading much on the journey, and preparing the speeches which he made every year either at Moscow or at St Petersburg. His mind tended rather towards doubt than action; he seldom expressed any positive opinion, and sentiment did not in any way affect his decisions, which were invariably prompted by considerations of personal interest. His self-love was greater than his fear, which could not indeed be very great, as Alexander, at that time especially, never persecuted anybody, and his displeasure could be incurred without danger. Count Severin retained as long as he liked his appointments of senator and curator, which gave him a circle of activity that pleased him. He was able and well informed, but made light of everything except what touched his material interests, and had no religious sentiments whatever. Such a man was destined to end his days without friends or sympathy. I did not see him again. Alexander had given him the use of a considerable estate for fifty years; I had done my best to arrange the matter, and later on I did some service to his son Leo. All this established a reciprocity of good feeling between us which lastèd as long as I was in Russia, and afterwards gradually died out.

If it had been in the nature of man to be satisfied with what is practicable, Alexander ought to have satisfied the Russians, for he gave them a tranquillity, a prosperity, and even a degree of liberty which were unknown before his reign. But the Russians wanted something else. Like the gambler who seeks violent emotions, they were tired of the monotony of their prosperity. They did not like their young Emperor: he was too simple in his manners, too averse to pomp, too disdainful of etiquette. The Russians regretted the brilliant Court of Catherine and its abuses, the opening which it gave to so many passions, struggles,

intrigues and successes. They regretted the days of
the Imperial favourites, and the possibility of gaining
colossal positions and fortunes like those of Orloff and
Potemkin. The courtiers had no ante-chambers to go
to, and sought in vain for an idol before which they could
burn their incense ; their platitude was condemned
to inaction, and there was no one to whom they could
cringe and bow. The grumblers at Moscow, too, did
not like the Court because it no longer afforded food
for their censure, while it did not offer them any of
the advantages which they valued. Their liberalism,
moreover, was very different from that of the Emperor
Alexander; he inclined rather to the democratic and
levelling ideas of the Emperor Joseph of Austria,
though in a milder form.

Only the Empress Dowager attempted to maintain the customs and the brilliancy of the old Court.
Alexander's Court was of an exaggerated simplicity,
totally devoid of etiquette, and he met his courtiers only
on intimate and familiar terms. The Emperor and his
family only appeared in full dress on Sundays and
holidays, when they went to church. Dinners and
soirées were mostly given in the private apartments,
and were quite different from what they had been in the
preceding reigns. Later on, Alexander became more
sumptuous in his receptions, but at the beginning of
his reign he was not sufficiently so. While Napoleon
surrounded himself with a pomp and ceremonial revived from the times of the monarchy, Alexander
liked to eclipse himself and to behave like an ordinary
citizen. His friends found fault with him for this—
especially the Margravine of Baden, his mother-in-

law, who wanted to give the young Emperor every possible quality and success. She endeavoured to stimulate him by the example of Napoleon, but in vain. The two Emperors went in opposite directions in everything; one demolished, while the other restored, old ideas; and the comparison made between them was not to Alexander's advantage in the eyes of the very Russians for whom he was working. He was, in fact, not at all popular during the first few years of his reign, although he was never more devoted than he was then to the good of his country. But men want to be dominated and fooled, and this necessity is nowhere so much felt as in Russia. At the beginning of his reign, Alexander did not know how to do this; he learnt it later, but even then, and notwithstanding his great success, he never attained the popularity and the moral power of his grandmother, who could have said of the Russians, as Buonaparte said of the French, that they were in her pocket.

The Emperor had made it a maxim to respect other people's opinions, and not to punish anybody for expressing them, so that no great courage was required to criticise the sovereign and tell him unpleasant truths. Full advantage was taken of this privilege, especially in the salons of the two capitals. Everything that the Government did was found fault with, and these criticisms, growing like the waves of a heavy sea, used in the same way to subside and grow again at the least breath of wind. Such was the constant state of opinion in Russia during the first year of Alexander's reign. The old courtiers used to say, in order to calm the anxiety of the young ones, that all new reigns began in the same way, and that the first years of the reign of Catherine were marked by the same pre-occupations. What people most objected to, however, in the case of Alexander, was my presence at his Court, and my appointment as assistant to the Minister of Foreign Affairs. ·A merely honorary title would not have shocked the Russians, but they could not accustom themselves to see me at the head of the department: a Pole enjoying the confidence of the Emperor, and initiated into all the secrets of State, was to them an intolerable innovation.*

This was a fertile subject of suspicion and calumny in the Russian salons. My parents had always been averse to Russian influence, and their fortune had been confiscated on account of their participation in Polish revolutions. That their son, who had never concealed his enthusiastic devotion to his country's cause, who had often loudly proclaimed it, and proved it by the national spirit in which he promoted public instruction in the Polish provinces, should be the intimate and confidential adviser of the sovereign, was naturally the subject of much comment. It was easy to imagine that I betrayed the interests of Russia, and that I would at any moment prove false to my duties as a Minister and a friend in order to advance the cause of Poland. All the ambitious men who thought themselves more worthy of the Emperor's confidence than a stranger—all the young men of

* 'Prince Czartoryski,' says Lord Whitworth in a despatch to Lord Hawkesbury (in the Record Office), dated January 4, 1803, 'for some years past the intimate and most confidential friend of the present Emperor of Russia, . . . is now second in point of precedency, but perhaps first in point of influence, in the Foreign Department.'

Alexander's Court—were agreed on this point. But their suspicions were unfounded. I do not think I have ever been more zealous and devoted than I was in the Emperor's service. He knew better than anyone my attachment to my country, and it was this knowledge which was the first basis of our intimate relations and the source of the esteem and friendship with which he honoured me. He did not at that time think that the welfare of Russia was really incompatible with that of Poland. Perhaps he did not have a very clear idea of that grave question, and as its solution appeared distant, he did not think it necessary to go very deeply into it. Meanwhile he accepted the services which I cordially rendered him, and he thought it just and proper to reward them by giving me a certain liberty of action in regard to the Polish provinces under his rule. I of course availed myself of this concession; I reorganised public instruction in Poland on a larger and more national basis, and made it more conformable with modern ideas. The Russians could not understand my relations with Alexander, and indeed they were only to be explained by the fact that we were both very young and had become friends at an age when generous impulses are stronger than reflection. The Russians, however, attributed our connection to personal ambition and dissimulation on my part and silly good-nature on that of Alexander. They imagined that I secretly favoured France, and that I wished to bring Alexander under the fascination of Buonaparte's genius. It was to my influence that they ascribed the somewhat colourless policy adopted by the Emperor in

European politics, which they thought arose from my connivance with France. This was also the Empress Dowager's opinion, and she propagated it among the young officers of the army.

My position was not an easy one. The part played by Russia was certainly not so brilliant or preponderant as might have been desirable, and was not at all in accordance with Russian vanity or Russian pretensions. Alexander was eclipsed by Napoleon, who, at the pinnacle of military glory, introduced into diplomacy, hitherto so discreet, that bluntness and rapidity of decision which were the secrets of his success on the battlefield. He took the initiative in every European question, and daily gained ground, increased his preponderance, and showed that he intended to become the arbiter of Europe. I constantly heard Russians complain of the weakness and want of dignity of their Cabinet ; and if I had ascribed these faults to Alexander's character and opinions, I would have cast the whole blame upon him. Among the most active and ambitious of the malcontents was the young Prince Dolgorouky. He was the prime mover of the Russian party, and his passionate vexation at seeing a stranger occupy a post which he considered should have been given to him made him witty, much to the surprise of his friends. Being one of the Emperor's aides-de-camp, he was continually at Court, and I often met him, on which occasions he used to pursue me with reproaches and sarcasms on the indolence of the Russian Foreign Office. He provoked me so far that I once told him he should address his remarks to the Chancellor,

who was the head of the department.   He replied
that he knew well there was an understanding
between the Chancellor and myself to refer matters
from one to the other in order to avoid the difficulty of a precise answer.   The discussion almost
became a quarrel, and the Emperor had to interfere
to put a stop to Dolgorouky's remarks.   We no
longer spoke to each other, but he continued his intrigues with more animosity than ever.   Under the
reign of Paul we had been on very good terms, and
he had shown me much confidence in an affair of
honour which he had with M. de Wintzingerode, a
worthy German, very stiff and punctilious.   Having
quarrelled with Dolgorouky, he challenged him, and
both agreed to take me as the only witness of the
duel.   The scene of the encounter was a garden, and
I loaded the pistols and placed the adversaries in
such a way as to make it exceedingly difficult for
them to hit each other.   The result was that both
missed, and the incident was closed by a complete
reconciliation.

The Chancellor's health now began to break down.
He was several times seriously ill, and he often
thought of temporarily retiring to his estates near
Moscow, though he had no wish to withdraw from
political life altogether.   One day when he was ill
I was seated by his bed; he was in a high fever, and
speaking with much animation, though somewhat
delirious, he said several times: 'These young men
wish to govern everything, but I will not allow it; I
alone will remain at the head of affairs.'   I thought it
probable that some one had led him to suspect those

who were called the Emperor's friends; perhaps these suspicions had spontaneously arisen in his mind. I am convinced, however, that he never distrusted me, or listened to the insinuations which people made against me. The extreme and entire confidence which he showed me lasted to the end of his life, which is surprising, as so many people had an interest in making us quarrel. He gave his confidence and friendship to very few people; his sentiments were delicate and noble, and although they were not based on strict principle, they showed that he was kind-hearted and sensitive. Always inclined to render a service, he judged others with great indulgence, and even at times when he spoke his mind most freely, I have never detected in him any feeling of hatred or desire for revenge. The Emperor, however, had an invincible dislike for him, which increased every day. His somewhat old-fashioned manners, his voice, his deliberate way of speaking, even his gestures, were antipathetic to him. During his frequent attacks of illness, the Chancellor used to send me with his papers to the Emperor, and the latter expressed his joy at not being obliged to see him. In spite of all I said in his behalf, he used to ridicule the old Minister, and often told me he would like to be rid of him. I was at this time in high favour with the Emperor, and he spoke with marked approval of my drafts of despatches and rescripts. He in no way opposed the Chancellor's wish for rest; on the contrary, he encouraged it in every way.

The friendly relations which had hitherto existed between Russia and France began about this time to be disturbed.  Count Markoff, supposed to be the ablest man in Russia, and the prototype and almost the last living representative of the diplomacy of Catherine, had been sent as Ambassador to Paris. When Paul became Emperor Markoff fell into disgrace, and was banished to Podolia, on one of my father's confiscated estates.  After Alexander's accession he hastened back to the capital, and Count Panin, who was then Foreign Minister, fearing in him a dangerous rival, decided to send him on a mission abroad.  The most important task in foreign affairs was at that time the renewal of friendly relations with France, and for this it was necessary to send Napoleon an Ambassador capable of controlling and restraining his policy, and sustaining the dignity of Russia.  Markoff, who was selected for this post, accepted it with eagerness, for he knew Alexander did not like him, and he was pleased at the idea of playing an important part in a capital where Napoleon and other personages already celebrated were influencing the destinies of the world.  He did not, however, justify his reputation,* which had already been impaired by his extraordinary want of tact in the affair of the proposed marriage of the King of Sweden with the Grand Duchess Alexandra, which was the cause of Catherine's death.  Notwithstanding his aversion for Napoleon and his Ministers, Markoff did not succeed in preventing the dismemberment of Germany to compensate the princes who had lost part of their

---

* Lord Whitworth, then English Ambassador in Paris, says of him : 'He has not the talent of inspiring confidence, and indeed his conduct here is such as to render any confidential intercourse with him extremely dangerous.' (Despatch to Lord Hawkesbury of November 16, 1802, in the Record office).

dominions, and to indulge the avidity of Prussia. The Convention was sent to the Emperor for his approval after it had been concluded, and when it was too late to make any change in it. A more favourable result would no doubt have been difficult to obtain, but Markoff did not even attempt to do so; he did not give the Cabinet of St Petersburg the necessary time to state and defend its opinions, and compelled it to accept the Convention like a child forced to obey orders. He was a creature of the Zuboffs, and he had voted with them for the partition of Poland; he was the incarnation of an unscrupulous State policy and a diplomacy without justice or pity; very extravagant, he was inflexible in money affairs, and though fond of presents, he would not take them if by so doing his pride would suffer. His face, seamed with the smallpox, constantly expressed irony and scorn; his round eyes and his mouth, depressed at the corners, resembled those of a tiger. Though he had adopted the language and the grand airs of the Court of Versailles, his manners were haughty and rude. He spoke, excellent French, but what he said was generally harsh, trenchant, disagreeable, and totally devoid of feeling.

Such was the pearl of Russian diplomatists sent to Napoleon by Russia in evidence of her desire to be on good terms with him. He was at first received with much distinction, and he satisfied the First Consul by his complaisance in the matter of the indemnities; but after a time his scornful manner and his sarcasms irritated Napoleon and gave rise to violent scenes. One evening the latter looked about for a Pole to give him an opportunity of venting his bile on the Russian Ambassador, thinking this would be the best way of mortally offending him. Seeing M. Z. . ., a stupid and insignificant personage who happened to be present, he took him by the button of his coat, moved him forward into the middle of the room, and after asking him whether he was a Pole, violently condemned the partition of Poland and the Powers which had committed and allowed it, after which he left without taking any notice of Markoff Shortly after, the French Government sent a despatch to St Petersburg complaining of Markoff's conduct but the Chancellor, feeling the necessity of demonstratively asserting the dignity of Russia, proposed to the Emperor that Markoff should be invested with the ribbon of St Andrew, which he had long desired The Emperor entirely approved of this proposal, and Markoff appeared at his next audience of Napoleo decorated with the order, and looking more proud and satisfied than ever. This time the First Consul had not the laugh on his side; but Markoff did not think it right to remain in Paris after his triumph, and he was recalled at his own request.

**END OF VOL. I**